She looked at him in the dim light, trying to remember what she'd felt the first time she saw him.

"Kent, if we'd never met that afternoon in front of Cox-Rushing-Greer…or at the Roof Garden…if the war hadn't happened…do you think we'd have been attracted to each other?"

He grinned. "Not if we'd never met."

"It was a silly question."

"I think meeting each other was meant to be. You thought so, too, at least you used to."

"I think you were right, that night when you said I'm still a little girl. My head's still too full of dreams."

"Dreams are all right."

"Nobody's perfect, Kent, not you, not me, not anybody."

"At least you know that."

"If I was really mature, what Claudia said wouldn't have made any difference."

"I wish it hadn't."

"I wish it, too. I'm trying, Kent. I want to grow up and look at things the right way."

"I don't mind waiting." He stretched his hand across the table.

She touched it quickly, then pulled back. "Will you wait for me on the corner?"

"I'll wait for you forever, Velvet."

Praise for Judy Nickles

"In *THE SHOWBOAT AFFAIR* Gwyneth Greer spins a delightful story full of family, deceit, romance, mystery, rebuilding relationships, and hope for the future….The Showboat Affair is a delightful page turner; a heartwarming tale of starting over."

~*Valerie, Romancing the Book*

"*THE SHOWBOAT AFFAIR* is a heart-warming love story with a splash of intrigue and mystery…Cleverly written, I couldn't put this book down!"

~*Wendy L. Hines, The Minding Spot*

THE SHOWBOAT AFFAIR: "Fast-paced storyline that draws you in--deeply, emotionally…This is one you'll enjoy from Chapter One to The End."

~*Vonnie Davis, TWRP author*

~*~

Judy Nickles/Gwyneth Greer also has short stories published online at *A Long Story Short* and *Literary Magic*, in print anthologies *'Tis the Season* (Editor's Choice Award), *My First Year in the Classroom*, *The Heart and the Harsh—Patriots Dream*, in print magazine *The Storyteller*, with an Honorable Mention in "Write to Win" in *Writer's Journal*.

Dancing with Velvet

by

Judy Nickles

This is a work of fiction. Names, characters, places, and incidents are either the product of the author's imagination or are used fictitiously, and any resemblance to actual persons living or dead, business establishments, events, or locales, is entirely coincidental.

Dancing with Velvet

COPYRIGHT © 2012 by Judy Nickles

All rights reserved. No part of this book may be used or reproduced in any manner whatsoever without written permission of the author or The Wild Rose Press except in the case of brief quotations embodied in critical articles or reviews.
Contact Information: info@thewildrosepress.com

Cover Art by *Tina Lynn Stout*

The Wild Rose Press, Inc.
PO Box 708
Adams Basin, NY 14410-0708
Visit us at www.thewildrosepress.com

Publishing History
First Vintage Rose Edition, 2012
Print ISBN 978-1-61217-199-9
Digital ISBN 978-1-61217-200-2

Published in the United States of America

Dedication

To my parents, Charles and Wilma Moore,
who spoke of the Roof Garden often
and smiled.

Acknowledgments

Special thanks to Rick Smith, columnist for the *San Angelo Standard Times,* who wrote four columns in response to my query about information on the St. Angelus Hotel and Roof Garden.

~*~

Thanks also to the following people who contacted Rick and shared their memories:
- Bill Wynne
- Florence McClellan
- Bill Kershaw
- Linney Peeples
- Ross McSwain
- Wyvon McCrohan
- Melba Carmichael
- Hazel Dooley
- Ron Perry
- Jim McCoy
- Adela Jeschke
- Bill Edgar
- Benny and Mary Stuard

~*~

Suzanne Campbell, Director of the West Texas Collection, and her wonderful staff helped me with long-distance research, and also made available the picture of the St. Angelus for use on the book's cover.

Chapter One

The blue velvet curtain billowing in an unseen wind revealed the man she hardly dared think of, though no matter how many times she saw him, she could never describe him to anyone. But she knew him…loved him…longed for him to take her in his arms as the music swelled beyond the velvet portiere. His fingers on her cheek electrified her. Then he smoothed her hair away from her face, and let his hand skim her shoulder and drift down her arm until he enveloped her hand in his. Leaning toward her, he brushed her lips, then her throat. An unbearable ache possessed her body.

Smiling in silent invitation, he stepped away from her, moving inexorably toward the shimmering midnight blue drape until it parted. Though he stood there waiting, his hand extended, beckoning her beyond the confines of her sheltered life, she couldn't move, couldn't even lift her arm. His smile faded, and the curtain billowed outward, this time with the roar of the ocean, and swept him away before falling limp and still. She thought she heard him calling her, but her lips wouldn't part in response. When she woke, her pillow was wet with tears.

****

"Come on, Cece, it's the weekend. Put away that dreary paper bag and come with us to Concho Drug for lunch."

Celeste shook her head, wishing her straight shoulder-length hair, the color of her paper lunch sack, didn't fall over her face every time she moved, and continued to spread her lunch on the desk.

"Thanks, Marilyn, but I'm going to eat here. Saves money."

"Isn't that what we work for? Money to do something fun with?"

"Sure, I guess, but I've got a Christmas layaway at Cox-Rushing-Greer, and I need every penny."

"Then be that way. I'll think of you and that boring apple when I'm eating my yummy grilled cheese." With a toss of her head and a friendly wink, the other girl swept out of the upstairs office at Woolworth.

Celeste's mouth twisted with regret as she refastened the tortoiseshell barrette that was supposed to keep her shiny hair in place. It might have been nice to go out to lunch with Marilyn and the others for a change, but it was already the end of October, and she'd told the truth—she needed every penny to pay for the Christmas presents she'd bought for her sister Coralee, her brother-in-law Ben, and her three-year-old niece Barbara.

She needed some things, too, like dresses for work and a new pair of shoes. So far she'd gotten by with her high school and junior college wardrobe, but it made her appear school-girlish. Being upstairs in the office kept her out of the public eye, and her boss, Mr. Thomas, didn't seem to care what she looked like as long as she did her job.

He wouldn't, either. He liked her and said she was the best assistant bookkeeper he'd had in years, since his wife retired to stay home with their three daughters. Celeste bit into her apple and leaned back in the padded chair Mr. Thomas had scraped up for her.

The work wasn't hard. She was good with numbers and liked seeing them balance out. Working up here instead of down on the floor had a lot of advantages, not to mention a fatter paycheck. She got off at four every afternoon and at noon on

Saturdays.

Today, Friday, she'd done the payroll first thing this morning. With luck, there would be just enough time after work to deposit her check and walk down to the department store to make a payment before she met her father at the bank for her ride home.

She thought, without enthusiasm, of the weekend ahead. Her father would start drinking as soon as they got home. She didn't cook much on weekends because he didn't eat, just holed up on the back porch or in his bedroom with a bottle. It had been that way for as long as she could remember, or, at least, since her mother died when she was five.

Fourteen years. Had it been so long? Though she kept a framed picture of Anne Riley on her dressing table, it was becoming harder and harder to remember the woman she called Mamma. Her older sister Coralee had more memories because she'd been twelve. Though she answered Celeste's questions readily enough, lately Celeste had the feeling there were things Coralee left out.

Sometimes, if she thought about it hard enough, Celeste could pull up vague memories of special occasions like Christmas, when she'd snuggled in her father's lap on Christmas Eve to hear him read *The Night Before Christmas*. The year her mother died, they hadn't even had a tree. In succeeding years, Coralee managed to scrounge a tree and presents, but their father never acknowledged the holiday except with more liquid "holiday cheer."

Too soon, Coralee finished high school and married Ben, who took her to live on his family's ranch in Sterling City. When Ben's parents, Big Ben and Pearl, offered to take Celeste to the ranch, too, her father smashed a vase and a couple of her mother's leprechaun figurines, and yelled, "Hell, no!" before Coralee hustled Celeste off to her room and closed the door.

"Why won't he let me go, Sister? He never pays any attention to me anyway. It's like I'm not even here."

"We'll work it out, sweetie, I promise." Coralee wrapped Celeste in her arms and stroked her hair.

They hadn't worked it out, but Coralee got the last word anyway. She told August Riley she didn't want him to even come to the wedding, much less walk her down the aisle, and he hadn't. Celeste always thought there was more to that decision than the fact he wouldn't let her go to the ranch, but Coralee put her off every time she brought it up.

Celeste shook her head. No use thinking about all that now. She'd been lucky, getting a scholarship to the junior college and being able to work her classes around her job in the notions department at Woolworth. Then, when she finished last spring, Mr. Thomas hired her for the office at a nice increase in salary. Soon afterward, her nights became filled with blue velvet and tears.

Celeste leaned her head back and closed her eyes. *Will it be like this forever? Going to work, going home…going nowhere?*

"Not going out with the others, Miss Riley?"

Celeste startled. "Oh, no, sir, I have my lunch here, Mr. Thomas."

"Seems to me a young girl like you would want to go out and have some fun."

"I go with them sometimes."

"You should go more often."

"Maybe."

"Is it the money? Do you need more?"

"No, sir, I get along fine. It's just that Christmas is coming, and I've got to think ahead."

"Most girls your age wouldn't."

Celeste smiled and shrugged.

"But, of course, your daddy's a banker. I guess he taught you how to handle money."

"Yes, sir." It was a lie. Daddy never taught her anything, and he never paid for anything either except the household expenses. Even then, he went over the grocery bill with a fine-tooth comb and made her justify every purchase, as well as kick in five dollars a week for her board.

Sometimes Celeste wondered if he knew how carefully she planned meals and shopped. Or how she managed to put clothes on her own back, since he never contributed a penny in that direction. By the time she was twelve, Celeste was earning her own money by babysitting and cleaning house for a couple of neighbor women who seemed to know she needed the work. Shortly after beginning high school, she'd gotten the job at Woolworth.

"Well, enjoy your lunch. I'm going to run home for a few minutes. I guess you've already done the payroll."

"Yes, sir. The checks are ready for you to look over and sign."

"Good girl. I'll take care of them as soon as I get back."

Celeste watched him leave, then curled up in a tight ball in her chair and closed her eyes. Everyone thought the banker's daughter lived such a charmed life. She had decent clothes only because she worked to earn the money for them and because Coralee came to San Angelo several times a year and took her shopping.

Celeste always protested that Coralee shouldn't buy her so much, but Coralee always came back with, "Ben's father pays me a salary for keeping his ranch accounts, and I can do what I want to with the money. Ben says I couldn't spend it any better than on you. I want you to have nice things like your friends."

Her father never seemed to know or care how she managed to dress properly or afford things like a class ring or a yearbook or a dress for the senior prom. Actually, she and Coralee made her dress with help from Pearl. Her date, Pete Frame, said she was the prettiest girl there.

Thinking about Pete's open, friendly face still made her smile. He'd gone off to the University in Austin on a football scholarship and was studying to be an engineer of some sort. They didn't keep in touch. Though they'd dated off and on in high school, they both understood they weren't sweethearts. Celeste admired him for a lot of reasons, but she couldn't imagine being married to him the way a lot of her friends were married to the boys they'd dated in school.

She opened her eyes and bit into her apple again, then rose, stretched, and wandered to the window overlooking Chadbourne Street, listening to the silence and regretting just a little that she wasn't sitting in a booth at Concho Drug with Marilyn and the others, eating grilled cheese sandwiches and enjoying a chocolate milkshake.

Balancing the apple on the wide sill, she pushed up the window and leaned out. Too late, she grabbed for the half-eaten fruit now spiraling toward the sidewalk below—and the head of an unfortunate passerby. Celeste's hand flew to her mouth as the startled young man stopped and looked up.

Retrieving the apple from the sidewalk, he held it up with a question in his eyes, eyes that were laughing at her. She felt her face grow hot and ducked back inside, still seeing the amusement in the man's hazel eyes. *Dumb, Celeste! He couldn't be hurt, not by a little apple, but he could come inside and complain. Mr. Thomas will probably think it's funny, but...*

Returning to her desk, she pulled a shortbread cookie out of her bag and unfastened the waxed paper. She really should have gone to lunch with

Marilyn and the others. But this was good enough, and she had the layaway to consider, after all.

****

She loved the lobby of the bank in the next block. It was like a palace, she imagined, as she ran her hand along the cool, satiny marble of the balustrade before she went to one of the windows.

Her father, one of the bank officers, had his own work space upstairs, so she never saw him, which was all right. All the tellers knew her, though, and greeted her like she belonged to them. She stood in line, soaking up the majestic beauty of the lobby, until it was her turn, then handed her check and deposit slip through the window.

"Hi, Celeste, how are you?" Mrs. Banner smiled. "How was your week?"

"Fine, thank you, Mrs. Banner. I had a good week."

"You want ten dollars back, right?"

"Yes, ma'am."

"Hot date tonight?"

Celeste felt her face grow warm, thinking of how her dream lover would most certainly step from behind the blue velvet curtain as soon as she fell asleep. "No, ma'am, unless you count the library book I got yesterday."

"You should get out more, Celeste. A pretty girl like you should be out on the town on Friday night."

"Well, sometimes I go to the movies with a friend."

"But not a boyfriend. What happened to that boy you used to date in high school?"

"He's at the University."

"I remember now. Football player, wasn't he?"

"Yes, ma'am."

"Don't you miss having your boyfriend around?"

"We were just good friends. I'm glad he had the chance for college."

The woman looked like she didn't believe Celeste. "Well, here's your receipt and your money. I'll see you next Friday, I guess."

"Yes, ma'am, thank you."

Celeste turned right outside the door and walked the few steps to Cox-Rushing-Greer. It was her favorite department store, even though Hemphill-Wells had a bargain basement better suited to her budget.

She had her hand on the door when the dress in the window display caught her eye. She froze, eyes riveted on the mannequin wearing the blue dress, blue velvet the color of a starlit midnight sky…the color of the curtain in her dreams. She twisted her head to see a price tag, but it was hidden. Touching the glass with one finger, she almost ached to feel the skirt that fell from a nipped-in waist and swirled at the hem.

"It's new," said the saleswoman when Celeste finally exhaled and walked through the door. "Beautiful, isn't it?"

"It's the most beautiful dress I've ever seen."

"We only got four of them. What size do you wear?"

"Ten, but I couldn't afford it."

"Are you sure?"

Celeste laughed. "I'm real sure."

"You ought to try it on anyway. You'd be a knockout in it, with that peachy complexion and shiny hair."

"No, ma'am, I just came in to pay on my layaway, but thank you."

Celeste took the elevator upstairs and made her payment, gratified that the receipt showed she had only fifteen dollars more to pay before she could take home the carefully-selected gifts and wrap them for Christmas. On top of that, she'd have two nice new dresses and a pair of pumps to change her image from schoolgirl to career woman.

In the empty elevator on the way down, she laughed at herself. *Career woman.* She didn't mind working, but she wanted a home and family like Coralee. Someday she wanted them. She'd taken the business classes in high school and college because she needed them to survive, but she'd always known she didn't want to juggle ledgers for the rest of her life.

The saleswoman who emerged from behind the counter as Celeste stepped off the elevator reminded her of a spider waiting for its prey. "Are you sure you don't want to try it on? There's plenty of time before closing."

Celeste hesitated. Would it hurt to try it on? It wasn't exactly honest, since she couldn't afford it, but...her hands tingled at the thought of touching the alluring material.

"I wouldn't have anywhere to wear it," she said.

"A pretty girl like you?"

"I don't go out much. It's for a formal party or a dance."

"You don't go dancing at the St. Angelus Roof Garden?"

Celeste shook her head.

"You should. I can see you in that dress now, dancing to the music with all those lights sparkling around you."

Celeste's heart sped up. "I couldn't afford it anyway."

"Try it on, honey. You know you love it. I've already put a size ten in the dressing room over there."

Celeste looked at the price tag before she slipped the dress over her head. Forty-nine-fifty—a fortune! She'd never spent so much on anything for herself before and never would. Even if she paid it out, a few dollars a week, she couldn't have it before spring, and by then velvet would be out of season.

The dress molded to her lithe, slender frame as if it had been custom-fitted. She risked a glance in the mirror and gasped. Who was this fairy princess looking back at her? She smoothed her hair, which looked golden in the lights. Coralee said it was their mother's hair. Then she touched the skin of her throat, white above the gently scooped neckline of dark fabric. Her arms floated in the full sleeves ending in tight cuffs at the wrist.

"Come out and let me see you," called the saleswoman.

Celeste stepped from behind the curtain. "It doesn't look so good with my saddle shoes, does it?"

"It was made for you."

"It's a little long."

"We do alterations."

"It's almost fifty dollars."

"There's layaway."

"But I already have some things there."

"Turn around." The saleswoman checked the waist, which hugged Celeste with only enough room left for comfort. She lifted the hair that fell just to Celeste's shoulders and pulled it to one side. "A rhinestone clip," she said. "Right here, and one for the dress. No necklace."

"I can't spend fifty dollars I don't have on a dress I don't have anyplace to wear."

"There's the Roof Garden, honey. You might meet the man of your dreams." She narrowed her eyes in a knowing way. "You just might."

The man of my dreams. Does he even exist in real life? If he does, then where is he, and when will I meet him? Certainly not dropping apples on his head. She giggled at the memory.

"I can't," Celeste said, averting her eyes from the mirror so she wouldn't be tempted further. "I just can't."

She left the dress hanging in the fitting room and walked out of the store, calling a polite, "Thank you," over her shoulder. She didn't dare look back or even glance in the window at the mannequin.

****

Her father, tall and square-shouldered like Coralee, paced the lot behind the bank where he parked his '38 Packard. Coralee had thrown a fit when he bought it new right after refusing to pay for Celeste to go to junior college that year. "Where've you been?"

"I went to pay on my layaway at Cox-Rushing-Greer," Celeste said, sliding into the passenger seat.

Her father grunted and pulled out his keys. "Got groceries for the weekend?"

"Yes, sir." *I don't know why you even ask. You don't eat anyway, just drink.*

He grunted again. They drove home in silence.

****

Celeste made herself a grilled cheese sandwich for supper and offered one to her father who, as expected, declined. He was already slightly drunk, making her wonder—not for the first time—if he kept a bottle in his desk at the bank. Taking her supper into her bedroom, she curled into the deep pink-tufted chair with her library book and put her father out of her mind.

****

Later, after rinsing her dishes and putting them aside to drain, she stepped out onto the back porch after first checking to be sure that her father wasn't there. It was dark, but there was what everyone called a harvest moon already beginning to rise.

"Shine on, shine on harvest moon..." The words slipped unbidden from her lips. She'd sung that song with her friends around more than one campfire. Sometimes Pete had harmonized, barbershop style. He had a nice voice to go with his handsome face.

She shook her head. Why was she thinking about Pete? She wasn't in love with him, never had been, never would be. They'd been good companions, but it ended there. Pete liked team sports, hunting, and fishing, all of which bored her, just like her talk of books and music bored him.

"We're an odd pair," he said once. "Salt and pepper."

"Well, a meal needs both to be seasoned just right," she replied.

"But you don't mix them in the shaker."

"No," she agreed, "you don't mix them in the shaker or you make a mess."

As she stepped back inside, she thought of calling Coralee, but before she could pick up the phone, it rang. "Hi there, little sister."

"Hi, Coralee. I was just thinking about you."

"How was your week?"

"It was good." *I dropped an apple on a man's head, but at least he didn't come after me.*

"Going out this weekend?"

"No, I don't guess so."

"So what are you going to do?"

"My laundry, I guess."

"You ought to do more than that on a gorgeous fall weekend."

"Well, I've got a new library book. I might take it to the park tomorrow after work. It's still warm enough."

Coralee sighed. "I don't know what I'm going to do with you."

"I'm all right, Sister."

"Is he..."

"In his room."

"Cece, you need to get out of there. Find yourself a place somewhere, and a roommate. I'll help you with money if you need it."

"Oh, Sister, I can't do that."

"Why not?"

"What would Daddy do?"

"Hire a housekeeper, that's what. He can afford it."

"He wouldn't like it if I left." *He probably wouldn't even notice I was gone, but where would I go? And what would it be like not to have my pretty pink room to come home to?*

"I guess not. You're free labor. Sweetie, he's not going to change. If you're hanging around waiting for that to happen, you're out of luck."

"I'm not…"

"Oh, all right. So tell me something exciting that happened this week."

"This is long distance, Coralee."

"Ben doesn't care."

"Well, I went to work, and this afternoon after I got paid, I deposited my check and went to pay on my layaway. Wait 'til you see what I got Barbara for Christmas."

"You shouldn't spend your money on her. She gets more than is good for her just from her grandparents here."

"Who else would I spend it on?"

"Yourself, for one."

"I tried on a dress."

"What kind of dress?"

"Oh, Coralee, it was so beautiful! It was blue velvet, but it was for a party or a dance. I couldn't wear it to the places I go."

"Not to church?"

"It's way too fancy for that."

"But you liked it."

"The saleswoman said it was made for me. It's a little long. Most things are long on me. I'm too short, but I guess I'm through growing, huh?"

"You're just right. Tell me more about the dress."

"The saleslady had the idea I could wear it to go dancing at the Roof Garden."

"You should."

"I couldn't. I mean, how would it look for me to go up there alone?"

"You wouldn't need a date. I used to go with some of my friends when I was in high school. Don't you remember? I'd go on the weekends when Ben went home to see his parents. Get one of your friends from work to go with you. It might be fun."

"Coralee, I just couldn't. I'd be embarrassed."

"How much does the dress cost?"

"Too much."

"How much?"

"I'm not going to tell you, because I'm not going to buy it."

"Oh, Celeste, we've got to get you out of your rut."

"I'm fine, Sister. Kiss Barbara for me, okay?"

"I will. Love you."

"Love you, too. Bye."

Celeste stood in the hall savoring the warmth of her sister's voice. Without a doubt, Coralee was the best sister in the world. For awhile, after she first married, she'd bought Celeste a bus ticket to come to Sterling City every weekend. The visits tapered off when Celeste started high school and got involved in other activities, but holidays still meant the ranch and Coralee, Ben, and Barbara, Big Ben and Pearl.

****

A vision of the blue velvet dress swayed provocatively in front of her eyes as she bathed and then got into bed. She almost wished she hadn't seen it, but it was so lovely…so very beautiful…and she'd looked gorgeous in it. Gorgeous beyond belief. Celeste felt herself blushing. She wasn't beautiful at all, but the dress…the dress was miraculous.

****

The young man came across the dance floor holding out his hand, but she couldn't quite see his face. "May I have this dance?"

He moved with the grace of a willow tree blowing in the breeze, holding her at arms' length as they danced and yet with an intimacy that both thrilled and frightened her. "You look like a princess," he said.

"I am a princess in my blue velvet dress. I am a queen."

"And I am a prince. I'll take you away with me."

"Are you really a prince?"

"I really am."

"Then at midnight I'll have to go, or everything will turn back the way it was."

"Not if you go with me."

"If I go with you?"

"Don't you want to?"

"Yes, I want to. I want very much to go."

He took her arm and led her toward an alcove hung with blue velvet like her dress. "If we go through that door, you'll be safe." He didn't say safe from what.

Somewhere a clock began to strike the hour. "Hurry."

Her feet, heavy like lead, refused to move.

"Hurry," he said again.

She tried to move and couldn't. When the last chime sounded, she stood alone, the blue velvet curtains billowing in front of her. And when she looked down, she was wearing her grey wool skirt and matching sweater, with her saddle shoes.

"My dress!" she called out, her voice echoing eerily in the fading light. "My blue velvet dress!"

****

Celeste woke with a start, yearning to be held and loved, aching with desire for even more than that, though she couldn't put it into words. She'd never felt this way when she was with Pete or any other boy in her class. Sometimes a movie or a romance novel could stir vague feelings of longing, but not like these she struggled with now. They consumed her whole body, leaving her confused and ashamed. Without thinking, she stretched her arms into the darkness, wanting to embrace something. The words "warm flesh" came to mind, the same words that had made her return a library book unfinished because of its disquieting effect on her emotions.

You're fourteen, Cece. You're growing up, Coralee said that summer day as they sat on the corral fence watching Ben break a new cutting horse. *You're going to have lots of new thoughts and feelings, but remember—there's nothing wrong with them. Just do what you know is right, even if someone else tries to change your mind.*

Celeste had kept waiting for those feelings, but they'd only surfaced in the last year or so. And, somehow, she questioned Coralee's explanation that there was nothing wrong with them.

Chapter Two

Celeste put the ledgers into the safe and closed it, spun the dial twice, then checked the handle.

"Think they're going to run away over Sunday?" Mr. Thomas asked with a wink.

"No, sir, but you did say to make sure they were locked up before I left."

"Mostly for fire," he said. "Nobody's going to steal them."

"No, sir."

"Well, have a nice weekend, Miss Riley. Got any plans?"

"Just the usual."

The older man chuckled. "The usual. Washing out a few things."

Celeste blushed.

"I beg your pardon if I embarrassed you, Miss Riley. I had three daughters, so I got used to frilly little things hanging all over the place. I used to tease my girls about embarrassing me."

She couldn't stifle the giggle that rose in her throat. "No, sir, that's all right."

He held the door for her. "See you on Monday."

She waved to the girls still working the counters before she stepped through the door onto the sidewalk. Saturday afternoons were busy in town because of all the folks coming in from the surrounding farming communities and ranches. She felt at loose ends, not wanting to go home to what she knew was waiting for her there, but what else was there to do?

She found herself walking toward Cox-Rushing-

Greer instead of the bus stop. From the store window, the blue velvet dress beckoned her, offering no respite, no refusal. She pressed her nose against the glass, trying to drink in every detail of the garment. For a moment, she had a fleeting feeling of being able to reach out and touch something from the past. Then it was gone.

"You look like a princess."

"I am a queen in my blue velvet dress."

Celeste squeezed her eyes shut as if to dispel her dream thoughts. When she opened them again, the same saleslady who had persuaded her to try on the dress waved through the window, motioning her to come in. Against her better judgment, but with a burgeoning feeling of anticipation, Celeste pushed open the glass door.

"It's still the most beautiful dress I've ever seen in my whole life, and I still can't afford it." She spoke the apology with a wistful sigh.

"It's a lot of money, I'll agree, but you looked wonderful in it. Sure you don't want to put it on layaway?"

"I have some things there already."

"Uh-huh, well, I understand."

Celeste hesitated before moving to where the dress was on display inside the store. After a moment, as she touched the skirt with the tip of one finger, something stirred in her again. She tried to examine the thought, but it eluded her. She shook herself mentally.

"If I can figure out a way to do it, I'll be back," she said as she edged toward the door. "But don't hold your breath."

Waiting for the bus at the next corner, she was startled to hear, "Well, well, the apple lady."

She looked up, then back at the sidewalk. "I'm so sorry. I hope you weren't hurt."

"I'm damaged for life since I looked up and saw

you."

She felt the color creeping into her face.

"Ah, she blushes like the apple—or maybe a rose. A rose is better."

"I'm sorry," she said again.

"For blushing? Don't be. I think it's nice. Where are you headed?"

"Home."

"I guess it wouldn't be proper to ask you..."

The bus squealed to a stop, and Celeste jumped on, hoping he wouldn't follow her. When he didn't, she breathed a sigh of relief and dropped into the nearest seat and leaned her head against the window. The boy—no, he was a young man—was flirting with her. She didn't know how to flirt and didn't want to learn. But she had to admit, from the safety of the bus leaving him behind, that she liked it.

She turned her thoughts back to the dress. Fifty dollars! It was insane to even consider it when she made $22.50 a week. Besides, where would she wear it? It didn't matter what she dreamed. Her prince wouldn't be at the St. Angelus Hotel Roof Garden, not in a million years.

****

She washed her lingerie in the bathroom sink and hung it discreetly on a line in the back yard, hidden from view by the boxwoods that made a thick privacy fence between the house and the street. Inside, she ran the carpet sweeper in every room except her father's where, she assumed, he was still sleeping—or drinking—or maybe a little of both, and dusted the unused living room. On her hands and knees, she scrubbed the cracked kitchen linoleum that needed replacing. The one time she'd suggested it, her father flew into a rage and yelled he wasn't made of money. After that, when mopping didn't get the dirt out of the cracks, she took to scrubbing the floor by hand.

The princess in the story Coralee used to read to me scrubbed floors and stairs on her hands and knees and met her prince anyway—or maybe because of her hard work. She earned the right to her happily-ever-after. Maybe I will, too.

In her own room, the one she'd shared so happily with Coralee, she cleaned and straightened her dressing table, wiping her mother's picture with a piece of old dishtowel and then followed up with the collection of leprechauns Coralee had rescued from the mantel after their father's angry outburst about Celeste moving to the ranch. They'd been a set of twelve, but he'd smashed one beyond repair. The other, broken in three pieces, was still missing the end of its pointed cap, but Celeste had glued the rest of it back together.

She spread a fresh dresser scarf and returned the picture and the figurines to their accustomed place. *I wonder why Mamma liked these little things. I keep them around because they were hers, but they're really kind of ugly, especially the one with the long beard and the frown on his face. Did she believe in the luck of the Irish? Did she believe in fairy tales? Was Daddy her prince?*

Later Celeste made a meatloaf and boiled some potatoes to mash in case her father decided he wanted supper. His door remained closed, so she ate alone in the kitchen. The telephone rang while she was rinsing her plate. It was Marilyn, inviting her to a movie.

"*Gaslight* is playing at the Royal. It's Ingrid Bergman."

"We've seen it, haven't we? Wasn't that the one where somebody was trying to drive her crazy?"

"Yeah, but it's been awhile, and I'm bored. My parents are out of town, and I don't like staying by myself. After the movie, you could come back with me and spend the night."

Celeste heard her father stirring. "I might do that, Marilyn, but I have to get up in time for church."

"I know. My parents would kill me if I missed mass, so we'll get up."

"All right. When does the movie start?"

"Seven-fifteen. Plenty of time."

"I'll meet you there at seven." Celeste started for her room.

"Celeste!"

She stopped but didn't turn around. "What is it, Daddy?"

"You fix any supper?"

"There's meatloaf and mashed potatoes in the warming oven."

When he lurched toward the kitchen, she wondered again how he managed to be sober enough to go to work every Monday.

"Put everything in the icebox when you're finished, please. I'm going to meet Marilyn at the movies and spend the night with her."

"This place not good enough for your friends?"

"She invited me, Daddy."

"Always going some place, aren't you?"

"Just to work."

"You meeting some boy?"

"No, Daddy, I told you. I'm meeting Marilyn from work."

"Staying out all night!"

"At her house."

He muttered something under his breath, then loosed a stream of profanity she'd heard before but which always made her feel dirty and slightly sick. "You stay home tonight," he finished.

"No, Daddy, I'm nineteen. I can do what I want to."

"Not and live in this house."

21

"I take care of the house for you."

"You go out tonight, I don't want you back."

She walked on into her room and closed the door. He wouldn't remember what he'd said, of course, but the point was, he'd said it. She didn't know why it still hurt after so long. She could barely remember when he'd spoken kindly to her, taken her in his lap and pretended to make a mustache for himself out of one of her braids. All of that stopped when Mamma died. Thank goodness she'd had Coralee.

She had her pajamas and Sunday clothes packed in a small bag and was on her way out when the telephone rang.

"What are you doing tonight, Cece?" Coralee's cheery voice made Celeste ache to see her.

"You just called last night. Is anything wrong?"

"No, I was just thinking about you."

"I'm going to meet Marilyn at the movies and spend the night with her."

"Oh, good. I worry about you being there by yourself on weekends."

"Why?"

"It's not good for you, being alone so much."

"I'm all right, Sister."

"Did you think anymore about that dress?"

"I went back to look at it, but it's ridiculous to spend so much money on something I don't have any use for."

"You never know."

"Sister, when I was looking at it today, I got the oddest feeling, like I'd seen it before or something."

"We had matching blue velvet dresses when you were about three and I was ten, but I guess you don't remember."

"No. Did Mamma make them?"

"She bought them downtown. At Fine's, I think."

"Where did we wear them?"

"To a Christmas party at the bank. Daddy took all of us."

"Oh."

"He said we were the prettiest girls there."

"He did?"

"Then he took us for hot chocolate at a little café across the street. It's not there anymore, but I remember the wife of the man who ran it happened to be making pies when we came in, and she fried some crust for us. You loved it. Got cinnamon and sugar all over your face. Mamma had to wet the corner of a napkin in her water glass to clean you up."

"I guess we had a really good time."

Coralee sighed. "It was one of the last ones, too. Mamma got sick right after that."

"I don't remember."

"Well, you were only three."

"Coralee, why did Mamma like that set of leprechauns?"

"I don't know. I remember when she bought them at Woolworth, though."

"She bought them at Woolworth? I've never seen them there."

"That was a long time ago, Cece. You weren't even born yet."

"But she liked them."

"Well, she bought them. Listen, you go on to your movie, and have a good time, you hear?"

"Thanks, Sister, I will."

"Love you, Cece."

"Love you, too."

****

She'd just paid for her ticket when she heard, "It must be fate."

"Are you following me?" She lifted her chin and made herself look at him. She knew, when her heart turned over, it was the wrong thing to do.

"Nope, just lonesome on a Saturday night and decided to take in a movie. Are you by yourself?"

"My friend is meeting me."

"Boyfriend?"

"No."

"Is there room for one more?"

Celeste dropped her eyes. "I don't think so. Excuse me."

She shared a box of popcorn with Marilyn, and they sat through the previews a second time before they left the theatre. The young man was nowhere in sight. She wondered if she'd hurt his feelings and made him leave without seeing the movie, but it did seem like he was trying to pick her up. On the way to Marilyn's house, they passed Cox-Rushing-Greer.

"I tried on that dress," Celeste said, stopping in front of the window with the blue velvet dress.

"I'll bet you were a knockout in it. You're really pretty, Cece, but you still dress like you were in school. My father says I should dress professionally even if I do only work a counter at Woolworth."

"I've got some new things on layaway." Celeste put her fingers against the glass and thought of how the dress felt between her fingers. "It costs almost fifty dollars."

"Fifty dollars! Did you strike oil in your backyard?"

Celeste laughed without being amused. "Yeah, think of that on my salary."

"On both of ours put together."

"But it's the most beautiful dress I've ever seen."

"Where would you wear it?"

"That's just it. I don't go anyplace where I'd wear a dress like that. It would be a waste, even if I could afford it."

"You ought to get out more."

"You're the third person to tell me that in two days."

"Don't you want to get married?"

"Someday."

"I'd marry Brad tomorrow if he asked, but he says we have to get ahead first. My parents think he's the most sensible boy I ever dated."

"That's not such a bad idea."

"I guess not, but sometimes I wish he wasn't so sensible."

The bemused look on her friend's face made Celeste laugh. "Well, I'll just wait for my handsome prince, and if he's rich, I'll ask him to buy this dress for me."

****

That night, she dreamed almost the same dream and watched the unknown man fade away as the blue velvet curtains billowed out of her reach. The clock chimed midnight over and over as she listened to him call her name from beyond the velvet barrier.

****

The next morning she left Marilyn in front of Sacred Heart and walked down Oakes Street toward her own church. She'd always loved the square yellow brick building and the way the dark wooden pews were set so there wasn't a center aisle. She liked the corner of a middle pew on the left, where she could watch the organist and see the sun filter through the three stained glass windows above the choir loft.

She'd always felt safe in the church, as if it were her second home or something, and Coralee had made sure they were in Sunday School every week. Now, her class had scattered, so she only went to church, and she missed the group of young people she'd known all her life.

The minister's text that morning was "Ask and ye shall receive." She chewed her bottom lip as she tried to concentrate. *I wonder what would happen if I asked God to give me enough money for that dress?*

I wonder how much of a sin it would be to ask for something material. And even if the money dropped out of the balcony, like manna from Heaven, where on earth would I wear a dress like that? Then, as she closed her eyes when the minister said, "Let us pray," she saw the young man coming across the dance floor again, his hand outstretched. Before she knew it, she'd reached out her gloved fingers but grasped only air.

****

Almost without realizing it, she took the opposite direction after church and found herself standing in front of Cox-Rushing-Greer, her nose pressed against the glass where the blue velvet dress swirled and shimmered on the headless mannequin.

"You'd look pretty in that."

She startled, shying away from the voice so abruptly that she stumbled. A hand grasped her arm to steady her.

"I'm sorry, I didn't mean to scare you."

The hazel eyes meeting hers, the same eyes she'd encountered three times before, held an honest apology. The face they lived in looked honest, too, tanned, clean-shaven, young...and handsome.

"I just wasn't expecting anyone to speak to me," she mumbled, trying to reassemble her dignity.

The hand dropped away from her arm. "It's all right. I'm really not following you."

"I didn't mean to be rude last night."

"It's okay. I wasn't trying to pick you up. Honest."

"I guess it seemed that way to me."

He shook his head. "I still say you'd look pretty in that dress." The young man ran long fingers through his curly hair, the color of the pecans Celeste gathered from the yard on Spaulding Street every fall.

"Thank you. It's the most beautiful dress I've

ever seen."

"But expensive, I guess."

"Very expensive. Forty-nine ninety-five. And then it would need hemming."

"My mother sews for people, but she's in Brownwood, so I guess that wouldn't help, would it?"

"I'm not going to buy the dress anyway. There's nowhere to wear it around here."

"I wouldn't know about that. Like I said, I'm from out of town. I travel."

"You're a salesman?"

"For a plumbing company. I come through here every five or six weeks." He nodded past her. "I always stay at the Naylor over there. Weekends are the hardest, not being home and all. I went to church and then decided I didn't want to go back upstairs and just sit in my room all afternoon."

"Where did you go?"

"First Baptist."

"That's right across from where I go—First Christian."

"I still don't want to go upstairs and do nothing. Would you think I was terrible if I asked you to take a walk with me? Or we could have lunch. I haven't eaten yet."

"Neither have I." *Why did I say that?*

"Then maybe we could get a bite somewhere."

Celeste's heart sped up. "There's the Riverside, across the street."

He grinned, exposing very white but slightly crooked teeth. "Great. I'm Kent, by the way."

"I'm Celeste."

They kept up a steady, impersonal conversation over baked chicken, mashed potatoes, and green beans. She laughed at the stories he told about his travels: unfriendly store owners, secretaries who were too friendly, cats who lived under counters and liked to shred the socks of unwary visitors, and even a parrot who insisted on sitting on his shoulder—and usually relieving himself there. She talked about her job, too, without mentioning where she did it.

After lingering over peach cobbler and coffee, they left the café and turned right toward Twohig Street. "San Angelo is bigger than Brownwood," Kent said. "Did you grow up here?"

"I've lived here all my life."

"Did you ever want to leave?"

"Not really. I couldn't anyway."

"I meant to go to college somewhere."

"I went to the junior college right across the street from the high school."

"So it wasn't much of a change for you."

"I guess not."

"I could've gone to school in Brownwood, I guess, at Howard Payne College or Daniel Baker."

"Why didn't you?"

"I thought maybe I should go to work for a while."

"What would you study? If you ever go, I mean."

"I thought of being a lawyer. Maybe even a judge someday. I was on the debate team in high school. I could come up with some pretty convincing arguments."

"We didn't have a team, but we had some debates in civics class. I liked them."

"What else did you do in school?"

"I made the honor roll every term, but I guess that sounds like bragging."

"No, I was a good student, too. Nothing wrong with taking credit for hard work."

"Did you play sports?" Celeste eyed his broad shoulders.

"Basketball. I always had an after-school job, so football was out. It took up too much time. But a lot of kids had jobs, so we practiced basketball during school hours. We did pretty good, too."

They turned down Twohig Street, passed the telephone office, and went on toward the Texas Theatre. "Do you like movies?" Kent asked.

"I go sometimes."

"With your boyfriend?"

"I did in high school, but he wasn't my boyfriend. We just went around together, that's all."

"Why not now?"

"He's at the University in Austin."

"Who's your favorite actor?"

Celeste grinned. "I think every girl's favorite right now is Clark Gable."

"Oh, sure, Rhett Butler."

She gave an exaggerated sigh. "So dashing, don't you think?"

"I was partial to Ashley Wilkes myself. He was more honorable."

"Well, that's important, too, but he couldn't change with the times. I felt sorry for him."

Kent's eyebrows went up. "Do you think honor and integrity go out of date?"

"I didn't mean that. No, I'll always believe what I do and act that way. But when things change in the world, don't we have to change with them?"

"Give me an example."

"Well, when the depression started, people had to learn to make do. The ones who couldn't didn't get along very well. I heard about people jumping out of windows because they lost all their money."

"That's a good point. Give me another example."

Celeste laughed. "Are we having a debate?"

"Not really, but I like a girl who thinks about something besides the obvious."

"The obvious?"

"How she looks and the next boy she can get to take her out."

"Oh."

They crossed the street and stopped to look at the posters in the glass cases outside the theater. "Hitchcock's *Foreign Correspondent* is coming in two weeks," Kent said. "I want to see that. I read a review of it in *Time Magazine*."

"It's a movie about war, isn't it? Do you think there's going to be a war?"

"There's already a war in Europe. We're just not in it yet."

"Do you think we will be?"

Kent shrugged. "We always end up getting involved."

"It scares me a little. The boys I knew in school are just the right age to go into the army."

"I'm not looking forward to it myself."

"Maybe it won't happen."

Kent shook his head. "It's going to happen. It's just a matter of time."

They re-crossed the street and walked down Irving Street, past Hemphill-Wells, and stood on the corner looking at the county courthouse.

"If you keep going on this street, you'll come to City Hall. It has a beautiful auditorium in it."

"Do you have anything around here that the CCC or the WPA worked on?"

"What?"

"Civilian Conservation Corps. Works Progress Administration. Don't you know what those are?"

"I've heard of them, but I don't know if they did any work here."

"I was part of the CCC for a couple of years. Then I got this job."

"The President put a lot of people back to work with all those programs, I guess."

"The WPA does some work in libraries. Do you have a library here?"

"Right across from City Hall. I go there all the time."

"So you like to read. Let me guess—romance."

Celeste felt herself blushing. "Actually, I read a lot of biographies."

"Come on, a pretty girl like you? No romance?"

"Sometimes I read things like that in a magazine, but the stories aren't very realistic."

"Happily ever after, you mean."

"Not exactly. My sister married someone she met in high school, and they're very happy and always will be."

"How can you be sure?"

"I just know. He's good and steady and treats her like she's really special."

"And you want someone to treat you the same way."

"There's nothing wrong with that."

"Absolutely not. I wasn't baiting you."

"Oh."

"But I'm with you—those kinds of stories and movies aren't the way things really are. Not always. People don't just meet and fall in love and ride off into the sunset."

Celeste giggled, the way she always did when she was nervous. "I don't think I want to ride off into the sunset unless it's in a big car with a chauffeur."

"Good for you. Hold out for the best."

They walked down Beauregard Avenue back to Chadbourne Street and stopped in front of Concho Drug. "I'd better go home now," Celeste said.

"Thanks for having lunch with me. Maybe we'll run into each other again," Kent said. "I'd like that."

Celeste felt herself blushing. "Maybe so." She didn't say she'd like it, too, but she knew she would. She felt him watching her as she crossed in the middle of the block and headed toward Main Street.

You let yourself get picked up, she chided herself. *You talked to a total stranger on the street and even ate lunch with him and walked downtown with him.*

She had insisted on paying for her own meal, and he hadn't argued about it. *He's probably on a budget just like I am. He didn't mention his father. Maybe his mother has to take in sewing to make a living. He was nice enough. We have a lot in common, or maybe I just want to think so. Pete and I were so different.* She glanced at the wristwatch Ben and Coralee had given her when she finished high school. *Almost four o'clock. Daddy'll be sober and wanting something to eat. He'll want to know where I've been. I don't know why he doesn't trust me. He always had something nasty to say when Pete and I went out somewhere, and Pete was a real gentleman. So is Kent, and I guess he didn't really pick me up. Anyway, I'll never see him again, so what was the harm?*

That night, the man who came from behind the blue velvet curtain wore Kent's face.

****

She thought about the dress—and Kent—all week. When Coralee called on Friday, Celeste confessed what she'd done.

"You didn't do anything wrong," Coralee assured her.

"I didn't even know him." *Well, in a way I did. I dropped a half-eaten apple on his head.*

"And you didn't go back to his hotel with him, either."

"Sister!"

"That's how you meet people, sweetie."

"On the street?"

"Anywhere. You aren't in school anymore. You did the right thing going dutch with your lunch, so what's the harm in taking a walk and talking? You were out there in broad daylight. He couldn't have done anything he shouldn't have, even if he'd wanted to."

"It just bothers me a little that I can't stop…"

"Can't stop thinking about him? That's okay,

too. Maybe you'll run into him again."

Celeste couldn't stop the long sigh that escaped. "I'm not that lucky, Sister."

****

That night she fiddled with her meticulously-planned budget and decided she could pay out the dress by spring. But who needed a blue velvet dress in the spring? *I don't need it at all, and that's a fact.*

After Wednesday night prayer meeting, Mrs. Lowe, who had been her Sunday School teacher in the primary department, called to her to wait. "Celeste, I have a favor to ask you, and if you say no, I'll understand."

"I'll help you if I can, Mrs. Lowe."

"My maid quit, just up and quit on me without any reason. You know I always treat my help well and pay them more than they'd get a lot of places."

"Yes, ma'am."

"I've got to give a dinner party in two weeks, and I don't think I can get anyone—or at least train them to suit—in that time. Now, I know you can cook, and you're familiar with all the little niceties. Would you help me out? You know, cleaning, getting things ready, helping in the kitchen? I'd make it worth your while if you'd come in when you get off work at noon on Saturdays for a couple of weeks. We'll have some lunch and then get to work."

"I'll be glad to help you, Mrs. Lowe."

"Oh, Celeste, you're a good girl! How does five dollars an afternoon sound to you?"

"That's fine, Mrs. Lowe."

"You're a good girl," the woman repeated. "I'll pick you up at the store at noon. No need to waste time with the bus."

"Yes, ma'am, that's fine."

On the way home, Celeste did some quick calculations. Ten dollars would be a start on the velvet dress.

Judy Nickles

****

After work on Monday, as she stepped out onto the street, consumed with excitement about her errand to put the blue velvet dress on layaway, she bumped into someone. "Oh, I'm sorry, I..." She looked up into Kent's eyes.

"This isn't a safe place to be when you're around," he teased. "Where are you going in such a hurry?"

"Why are you still here?"

"I stayed an extra day to talk to a prospective customer."

"Oh."

"So where are you going, and can I come, too?"

"No, I mean, I'm going to put that dress on layaway. I got the chance to make some extra money."

"Hey, that's great. I'm glad for you."

Celeste nodded. "So I have to go before they close."

When she started off, he fell into step with her. "You're going my way."

"What?"

"The hotel, remember? It's this direction."

In front of the department store, Celeste paused to gaze at the dress again. "I hope I'm not making a mistake, but it's the most beautiful dress I've ever seen."

"It's not a mistake. You'll be beautiful wearing it."

Celeste chewed her lip. "Well…I'd better do it if I'm going to."

"I'll come in with you. Buy some socks or something." He opened the door for her.

"You figured it out," the saleslady greeted her.

"I've lost my mind," Celeste said, fingering the skirt of the blue velvet dress, "but I'm going to do it. I may be paying for it from my grave, but…"

The woman whisked the dress from the rack. "It was waiting for you. Nobody else has even tried it on, so far as I know. I'll go upstairs with you, and we'll get this tucked safely away right now."

All the way upstairs, Celeste felt sure the prince—or Kent—was holding her hand.

****

Kent grinned at her as the elevator door opened again. "It's a done deal, huh?"

Celeste nodded. "I guess so."

"How about a soda to celebrate?"

She glanced at her watch. "I can't. I have to meet…catch my ride home."

"I see. Well, maybe next time. And don't forget, I'll be back through here next month. I'll count on seeing you."

"Maybe. I've got to go."

She dashed through the door ahead of him and hoped he wouldn't follow her. Standing beside the car, her father scowled. "Who's the man?"

"Nobody, Daddy."

"You were with him."

"He just opened the door for me," she lied. "That's all."

"Well, get in the car, and let's go."

Celeste hurried around to the passenger side and slid in. Turning her face to the window, she thought of how the dress had shimmered in the light and how soft it felt beneath her fingers. Then she thought of Kent and was sure her father could hear her heart beating.

Chapter Three

"I did it," Celeste told Coralee when she called on Wednesday. "I put the blue velvet dress on layaway, though heaven only knows when I'll get it out."

"I'll send you some money."

"No, I'm going to do this myself. That's important to me."

"Why?"

"I'm not sure. It's like, well, maybe like I'm turning over a new leaf for myself. Or something."

"Or something. Are you going to wear it?"

"Sometime."

"Where? Dancing?"

"I was thinking about it. Sister, do you believe in dreams coming true?"

"Absolutely. Mine did when I married Ben."

"You'd known him all your life."

"Half of it, maybe. If he hadn't come to San Angelo to live with his aunt and uncle and go to high school, though, I'd never have met him. I always thought it was supposed to happen."

"You really love him, don't you?"

"More than I have words to tell you, Cece, and I want that for you, too. You've seen how good Ben is to me. His parents are, too. I wouldn't trade my life here on the ranch for anything. The only drawback was leaving you behind."

"I could've come along. Ben's parents offered me a place."

"And Daddy wouldn't let you take it, even though he didn't want you. He didn't want either one of us after Mamma died. I worry about you, Cece."

"Why didn't he want us?"

"He just didn't." Celeste thought Coralee sounded evasive. "But we had each other, didn't we?"

"You took good care of me, Sister, and I'm all right. I'm going to be even better someday."

"Daddy's going to kill himself drinking. You know that."

"He still gets up on Monday morning, stone cold sober, and goes to work. From what I hear, everyone at the bank thinks he's a paragon. Why does he do it, Sister? Why does he drink like that?"

"It started after Mamma died, but there was something…well, never mind. You were too young to see it."

"Is that why? Because she died?" The long silence on Coralee's end of the phone stirred Celeste's curiosity, but Coralee answered as evasively as before.

"No. Things weren't right before that."

"Do you know why?"

"It's not important."

"Maybe it is."

"Forget it, sweetie."

"I'm not a baby anymore, Sister."

"I know. Cece, promise me you'll do something about making a life for yourself away from that house. I just don't like the idea of you there alone with him when he's drinking."

"He says a lot of mean things, I guess, but that's the liquor talking."

"As long as that's all he does," Coralee muttered.

"Why would you say that?"

"Because…I don't know. Never mind."

"Don't worry, Sister. Someday I'm going to meet the man of my dreams." *Maybe I've already met him.*

Coralee laughed. "Especially now, since you have that blue velvet dress."

****

After helping Mrs. Lowe, Celeste paid ten extra dollars on her layaway the following Monday. On Tuesday, Mrs. Lowe called Celeste to thank her again.

"You were wonderful. Where did you learn to do all that? Arrange the flowers and do place cards and make those little appetizers in the shapes of flowers?"

"Coralee taught me everything she learned in domestic science in high school. The rest I just sort of picked up from magazines."

"Well, my friend Ina Smith was impressed. You know Ina, don't you? Her husband is the manager of the gas company."

"I can't place her."

"She's giving a Christmas party and asked me if I thought you'd help her. She'd pay you. In fact, I told her it would cost her ten dollars for one weekend. She can afford it. You're worth every penny, Celeste. She's going to call you."

For the next few weeks, Celeste hoped, in vain, to catch a glimpse of Kent again. By the first of December, she'd paid out her original layaway, and had only twenty dollars left to pay on the blue velvet dress. She could almost see herself wearing it. By doing without movies, lunches out on Fridays, and everything else except her church pledge, she drove her balance down dollar by dollar. On the fifteenth of December, she almost ran to Cox-Rushing-Greer to make her final payment.

The saleslady caught her on her way out with the box under her arm. "You did it. I knew you would."

Celeste felt like her face would split from smiling. "Yes, ma'am, I did."

"I happen to know there's a dance on Saturday night at the Roof Garden. You ought to go."

A new wave of excitement swept over Celeste. "Maybe I will."

"You have some shoes to wear with it?"

"Just my Sunday pumps, but they'll have to do."

"You need silver ones, strappy sandals, I think, and those clips for your hair and the dress."

"I got the clips at Woolworth last week. I work there, so I got a discount. They're cheap, but they don't look it. As for the shoes, maybe I'll find some later."

"You'll have all the young men falling at your feet no matter what's on them."

Celeste laughed. "I doubt that, but it's a nice thought."

****

"What's in the box?" her father asked as she got into the car.

"Just something I had on layaway."

"Seems to me you have plenty of clothes."

"I'm still wearing what I wore in school."

"What's wrong with that?"

"I'm not in school now."

He snorted. "You ought to save your money."

"I pay my own way, Daddy." *I clean the house and cook your meals and still have to pay for mine.*

"You should."

"Yes, sir."

He reached under the seat and pulled out a bottle.

"Can't you wait until you get home?" she asked without thinking.

"Shut your sassy mouth, girl!"

Celeste turned her face to the window to hide her tears.

****

She hung the dress in the back of her closet, reaching in to stroke it every night before she went to bed and again in the mornings as she dressed for work. She asked around at the store and found two of the girls who knew about the Roof Garden dances.

"There's one on Saturday," Veda told her. "Les Green and his orchestra."

"Who?"

"He's been here before, and he's good. Look, my roommate Paula and I are going. Why don't you come with us?"

"I don't have a date."

"Neither do we, but there are always plenty of unattached men around. It's a good time, nothing serious. Everyone's on his best behavior. No mashers to follow you home or anything."

Home. Celeste winced. She might be able to get out of the house dressed for the dance and even back in, but she didn't want to deal with her father in case he happened to see her. He always forgot his threats to kick her out, but they were unpleasant to listen to all the same.

"We share a room in a boarding house over on Harris," Veda continued. "It's not fancy, but we keep it neat, and you're welcome to dress there with us if you don't want to go all the way home."

Veda dropped her eyes suddenly in a way that made Celeste think she knew about her father. But who cared? It had nothing to do with her. "I'd love it," she said. "You're sweet to ask me."

"We'd ask you to spend the night, but there's no room, and the floor's not comfortable, that's for sure."

"No, that's all right. I'll get home afterward." *Daddy'll be good and drunk by then, probably passed out.* Maybe I won't stay very late anyway. Maybe I'll be a wallflower."

Veda narrowed her eyes. "You, honey? We were all glad when you moved upstairs to work, because all the men who came in here couldn't keep their eyes off you. Now we get noticed occasionally."

Celeste flushed. "I didn't do anything to get them to pay attention to me, honestly I didn't."

Veda touched her arm. "I'm teasing you. But you *are* attractive, Cece. I'm serious. And I'm glad you're going with us Saturday night."

****

Celeste packed everything in the dress box and maneuvered it onto the bus Saturday morning. At noon, she asked Mr. Thomas if she could stay upstairs until Veda and Paula got off at five.

"You three have plans?"

"We're going to the dance at the St. Angelus tonight. I'm dressing in their room."

"Good for you, Miss Riley. But you don't have to stay up here all afternoon. I'm short a girl at the hardware counter. Miss Bennett's mother fell and broke her ankle last night. She was pretty upset when she called in this morning, but I told her not to worry about it. If you want to cover for her, I'll pay you."

"Oh, that's awful. I'm really sorry. I'll be glad to cover for her, Mr. Thomas. It'll be nice to have something to do, and maybe you could give Sara a half-day's pay. I'm sure she could use it, especially with Christmas coming up."

The manager looked at Celeste for a long moment. "You're sure about that?"

"Yes, sir. It'll be fun being back on the floor again."

"All right, then. I'll make sure Miss Bennett knows what you did for her."

"You don't have to."

"I wouldn't think of anything else."

****

The store teemed with shoppers all afternoon. Celeste enjoyed waiting on customers again. Just before closing, she tallied her sales and closed out the register, then went with the other girls to take their canvas cash bags upstairs, where Mr. Thomas counted the day's receipts and made out a deposit slip so that he could put the money in the night depository at the bank.

"I think you sell on your smile," he told Celeste as he counted her money.

She blushed. "It was fun being downstairs again."

"Thank you for helping out."

"It's okay, really."

Veda and Paula were waiting for her at the back door. "We usually catch the bus to the Triple Gables for supper, because our landlady doesn't cook Saturday nights and Sundays. She's a good cook, but eating out is a nice break."

Celeste thought of the extra money in her purse now that the layaway was paid for. "I'm starving after working the counter this afternoon."

Reveling in Paula's and Veda's cheerful company, Celeste realized she'd almost forgotten the fun of being part of a group of girls. "I'm going to design school in Dallas someday," Paula offered, studying another customer's stylish dress while they waited for dessert.

"She draws all the time," Veda said, removing the meringue from her chocolate pie. "She's good, too. Me, I want to go to the business college. Didn't you go there, Celeste?"

"No, I took business classes at the junior college. I thought I might go on somewhere else, but I couldn't afford it."

"Money's always the problem, isn't it?" Paula said. "But at least we have jobs. I can remember when they were hard to come by."

Veda nodded. "My dad was out of work for over a year. We barely got by. I always said I was going to marry money."

"I just want someone to love me." The words

slipped out of Celeste's mouth before she realized she'd spoken her thoughts aloud.

"Don't we all?" Paula leaned back in the booth. "But rich wouldn't hurt."

****

The room the girls shared in the boarding house, once the fine home of one of San Angelo's first residents, was neat and clean but small, as Veda had warned. "Bathroom's down the hall," she told Celeste. "And there's a shortage of hot water sometimes. Why don't you go first?"

Paula eyed the dress box. "I'm dying to see what you have."

When Celeste untied the string and lifted out the blue velvet dress, the other girls gasped.

"Oh, my stars!" Paula said. "It's gorgeous! It's the one in Cox's window, right?"

"I've been paying on it since the first of November, and I wouldn't have it out now except I worked for a lady from my church when she gave a party, and then she recommended me to someone else for the same thing. That's how I got enough to finish paying for it last week."

"Oh, it's fabulous." Veda stroked the fabric. "Honey, you're going to take the eye of every man there. Paula and I might as well stay home."

Celeste turned her face away so they wouldn't see her tears, even though they were tears of happiness at being with friends. In school, even though she couldn't invite the other girls to her own home, she'd never lacked invitations to sleepovers. Over the last couple of years she had missed the camaraderie and chatter and the inevitable experiments with hairstyles and makeup.

As if she'd read Celeste's mind, Paula offered to do her hair and makeup tonight. "You don't need much. Just a little powder on your nose and some of your light lipstick. I wear Tangee, too. Looks more natural." She brushed Celeste's hair and pulled it to the side, fastening it with the rhinestone clip so that it fell over her left shoulder. "Do you ever curl your hair?"

"I've tried, but it just goes straight again."

"I saw these," Veda said, fingering the pin and earrings when Celeste came back from the bathroom and took them out of their box. "They don't look like some of the cheaper stuff we have."

"That's why I bought them," Celeste said. "I saw something similar at Hemphill-Wells but couldn't afford them. They gave me an idea of what to look for, though." She let Paula put on her pin while she screwed on her earrings.

"You don't have to have a lot of money to dress well," Paula said. "I learned that from some of the magazines I've read. Like you said, you just have to know what to look for."

"She made me over," Veda said, laughing. "I had some of the gosh-awfullest things you ever saw, when I first came."

"They weren't that bad." Paula readjusted the neckline on her roommate's dress. "That's better."

"See, she's still doing it."

The girls walked arm in arm to the hotel, laughing at nothing and everything. "I couldn't have done this on my own," Celeste admitted as they crossed the lobby. She stopped to stare at the shaggy buffalo head on the wall.

"Him we don't want to meet upstairs," Paula laughed, urging her toward the elevator. "Next stop, paradise," she said as they stepped inside.

Celeste caught her breath and held to the brass rail as the car moved upward. "It's almost magic," she murmured.

Veda patted her arm. "Got your dollar admission ready? Or like magic you'll be on your way back down."

The lights dancing across the polished wood floor almost took Celeste's breath away. "In warm weather, the casement windows are open," Paula told her. "And through those French doors is the garden area."

Celeste pressed her nose to the glass and drank in the tiled roof. "I'll bet you can see the whole town from up here," she said.

"Well, part of it, anyway," Veda replied. "It's beautiful in the spring with all the plants set around the parapet."

Celeste chose a chair near a window and forced herself to keep her eyes down, though she wanted to search the room for her prince, the reason she'd come. She'd dreamed about him again last night. Though he looked like Kent, who wouldn't be there, she knew she'd recognize her real dream prince.

Folding her hands in her lap and crossing her ankles the way Coralee had taught her, she felt inexplicably afraid. *Maybe I shouldn't have come, but please, let him be here. Please.*

****

The familiar voice descending from somewhere high above sent a thrill through her. Her stomach knotted as she lifted her face.

"May I have this dance?"

Kent stood there smiling at her.

"It's you."

"Just got in this afternoon. Pretty lucky, huh?"

Celeste felt the warmth in her cheeks. "I guess so."

"I see you got the dress in time."

"I earned some extra money helping out with some holiday parties," she said, lifting her chin.

"Hey, you don't have to explain it to me. Some things are just meant to be, and that dress was meant for you."

She dropped her eyes. "Thank you."

"So, do you want to dance?"

She rose, feeling the skirt swirl around her. "Yes, thank you very much," she said.

He was clean-shaven and smelled of shaving soap, but the hair curling around his ears announced his need for a haircut. "I'm headed home for Christmas tomorrow. It's been two weeks."

"Your mother will be glad to see you."

"She'll kill the fatted calf—or maybe my brother, if he doesn't clean up our room."

Celeste giggled. "That's nice."

"Have you ever been here before?"

"No."

"I'm glad you're here tonight. You look very pretty."

"Thank you."

When the music ended, he returned her to her chair and lingered as if he were waiting for an invitation to sit down. She swept aside her skirt from where it touched the next chair. "Would you like to sit down?"

"I'd like that very much." He crossed his long legs with the grace of a cat. "You dance very well. Did you do a lot of dancing in high school?"

"In college, too."

He grinned. "When I was in high school, a visiting evangelist came through and told us we were all going to hell in a hand basket if we went to dances."

"So did you go?"

"Just as soon as he left town."

Celeste laughed. "I don't see anything wrong with it."

"I don't either. So, what do you do at Woolworth, if you don't mind me asking."

"I keep books upstairs."

"Do you like it?"

"I always liked making numbers do what they're

supposed to. I have good hours and a good boss."

"Not me. The numbers, I mean. I can do it all in my head, but I always got into trouble for not putting everything down on paper."

"Really? I'm kind of like that, but I use an adding machine, just to be sure."

"Do you think you'll ever finish college with a degree?"

"Probably not."

"My brother Neil is a junior. He'd like to work in a museum somewhere, but he'll probably end up teaching history."

"A lady started a museum here a few years ago. It's small, but it's a start."

"Well, everything has to have a start."

"What about you? If you could go to college, what kind of a lawyer would you be?"

"A good one." He laughed. "And a rich one."

"Well, of course."

"Maybe I'll go someday. Right now, I have responsibilities."

Icy fingers skimmed the base of her neck. Was he married?

He seemed to read her mind. "Oh, I'm not married, if that's what you're thinking. Never have been. I meant I have responsibilities to my mother and brother. See, my dad died ten years ago, when I was fourteen, and Neil, my brother, was just ten. I think I told you before that Mother takes in sewing, but it doesn't pay the bills, not all of them anyway. That's the real reason I didn't go on to college."

"What did you do before you started traveling?"

"Delivered groceries, swept up at the market, had a paper route, mowed lawns. You name it, I did it. Then I went with the CCC for a couple of years. It was the right thing for me at the right time. Then I got this job. It's a good one, but it keeps me away from home a lot."

"You're close to your family then."

"My brother and I are close. Always were. Best friends, you might say."

Celeste didn't miss that he left out his mother. "I have a sister, Coralee. She's still my best friend, even though she's married and lives out of town."

"Where does she live?"

"In Sterling City, about forty miles from here. I spend holidays with her."

"But you're happy here. You like your job."

She ignored the first part of his question. "Sometimes I miss working downstairs with the other girls. I came tonight with two of them. But being in the office pays better than being on the floor."

"Well, that's important. Money's still tight, but I think things are getting better. Do you still live at home?"

Celeste hesitated. "It's just my father and me. My mother died when I was five."

He frowned. "That's tough. Girls need a mother."

"Boys need a father."

They danced twice more, and then Kent asked if she'd like a soft drink. "I'll go down and get them," he said. "It probably wouldn't look right, the two of us leaving in the middle of things."

He brought back two paper cups from the soda fountain downstairs. "I drink too many of these," he said. "On the road, that is. At home, Mother makes the best lemonade you've ever tasted. She's a good cook, too. I get pretty tired of eating out, even if the company pays for it."

"My sister took over the cooking when our mother got sick, and she taught me while she was still at home. I'm pretty good."

"Well, you know what they say—the way to a man's heart is through his stomach."

She blushed.

"I like that. The way you blush, I mean."

"I wish I didn't. All the boys in high school used to tease me to make me blush. In a nice way, of course, but I still didn't like it."

"I'm not trying to embarrass you, but how old are you?"

"Nineteen. Twenty next April."

"You're dancing with an old man then. I've got five years on you."

"That doesn't matter, does it?"

"Not to me. You're young and sweet. Too many girls these days are older than they should be, if you know what I mean."

"Maybe it's because of the hard times they've been through. My friend Veda grew up in a small town and had to leave home to find the job here. She's been on her own since she was barely seventeen."

"Then she's mature. There's a difference."

"But my friend Marilyn still lives at home with her parents. She has a boyfriend in college. They'll probably get married when he graduates."

"You said you had a boyfriend when you were in high school."

"Pete. We were friends, that's all. We enjoyed going around together, but we knew we were too different to think anything could come from it. He got a football scholarship to the University. He's going to be some sort of engineer."

"So you don't have a boyfriend or a broken heart?"

Celeste felt herself blushing again. "Neither one."

The silence that felt between them wasn't totally uncomfortable. "They call this the Roof Garden," Kent said after a few minutes. "But where's the garden?"

"Through those doors."

"Have you seen it?"

"I haven't been out there. It's too cold."

"I think I'll brave it for a few minutes. I've heard a lot about it." He stood up, but he didn't move away.

Celeste hesitated for only a few seconds. "All right. Just a quick look."

They stood by the wall that came just above her knees. Celeste pointed out the buildings she recognized. When she shivered, Kent guided her back inside. "Thanks for the tour."

She didn't look at him. "I've lived in San Angelo all my life, but it looks different from up here."

"You don't see the lights the same way from the street."

"I guess not. It's…"

"Magic?" he finished for her.

"Why did you say that?"

He winked. "I read your mind. Would you like to dance again? *Stardust* is one of my favorites."

****

Veda and Paula didn't lack for dance partners, but they stayed away from Celeste after they saw her with Kent. She caught up with them in the powder room when the band took a break. "He's pretty dreamy," Veda said.

"He's very nice. His name is Kent. He travels."

"Listen, you be careful with a traveling man," Paula said, giving Celeste her best mother-hen look.

"He's very polite." Celeste removed a small tube of lipstick from her purse and applied some, then rubbed her lips together. "Actually, I've met him before."

"Where?" Veda asked.

Celeste recounted the Sunday in front of Cox-Rushing-Greer, leaving out the earlier apple incident. "I probably shouldn't have gone to lunch with him."

"Why not?" Paula readjusted a strand of

Celeste's hair that had come loose from the rhinestone clip.

"I don't know. It was like he picked me up or something."

"Of course he didn't," Veda said. "It was just one of those chance encounters. That's how romances get started." She winked at Paula.

"It's not a romance," Celeste protested. "He's just nice. And he's a good dancer."

"Does he keep his hands where they should be?" Paula asked. She took a small blue bottle of *Evening in Paris* out of her purse and dabbed some behind her ears and then Celeste's.

"Yes, of course he does."

"Just asking."

****

The lights came up as the strains of the last song died away. "Where are your friends?" Kent asked.

Celeste looked around. "Over there."

"You're leaving together." It wasn't a question.

"No, they share a room over on Harris Street. I'm not spending the night, because their room is too small for guests."

"Is it a long way? There's no bus this time of night."

Celeste realized she hadn't thought far enough when she planned the evening. "I'll walk. It's safe enough, I guess."

He frowned. "Look, I have a car the company gave me after I'd been with them a year. I'll drive all of you home—you first, then your friends. That way everything will be proper."

"Proper?"

"I mean you'll all chaperone each other."

Celeste blinked. "Oh…oh, yes, that's a good idea." She waved at Veda and Paula, who were saying goodnight to the two young men they'd danced with most of the evening.

"Kent says he'll take us all home," Celeste said.

"I'll take Celeste first, then the two of you. That way things will be on the up and up."

Suspicion clouded Paula's face. "Up and up?"

"Traveling salesmen aren't to be trusted, are they?" Kent winked at her.

Paula flushed. "You'll do."

Celeste gave directions to her house. As Kent pulled up to the curb, he said, "Are you going to church in the morning?"

Celeste nodded.

"Would it be all right if I met you there? I missed last Sunday, and my mother always asks if I went."

"I'm sure that would be fine," Celeste replied. "Ten-fifty." She glanced over her shoulder at the others in the back. "Do you mind bringing my things to the store on Monday, or should I get them tomorrow?"

"We'll bring them," Veda said.

"Thank you very much for the ride." Celeste slid out of the car before Kent could open his door. "It's all right. I can get in by myself."

Kent frowned. "It was just plain too far to walk at this hour of the night. I'd feel real bad if you didn't get home all right." He looked around at the other girls. "If all of you didn't get home all right."

"Well, thank you again." Celeste closed the door softly and started for the house, hoping that her father wouldn't hear her come in.

Chapter Four

Celeste didn't see Kent when she arrived at church the next morning and decided against waiting outside for him. It would be uncomfortable to explain if someone asked what she was doing. But relief flooded her when he slid into the pew beside her a few minutes later. "I'm glad you came," she whispered.

"I'm glad I came, too," he whispered back. He wore the same suit from the night before, but she noticed he had on a fresh white shirt and a different tie.

"Your mother will ask."

"That's right."

"Do you go every Sunday?"

"I try."

Kent's strong deep voice made Celeste feel as small as his height did. He found the pages in the hymnal and shared it with her for each song. She noticed he didn't take communion, but she'd heard that Baptists didn't do that every Sunday.

As they sang the benediction, "God Be With You," he picked up her coat and held it for her. Threading his way behind her up the narrow aisle, he said, "It's a nice day for this time of year. Picnic weather almost."

"There's the park behind the fire station, but the wind off the river would make it too chilly to sit outside."

"Maybe I'll drive down there and just sit in the car then."

"Alone?"

"I expect you have to go home to dinner."

"No, it's just...just my father, and he...he's not feeling well this weekend. He said he didn't want any dinner."

"Oh? Then maybe we could pick up some sandwiches somewhere and go sit in the car at the park. I mean, if you don't mind riding alone with me. It's daylight, anyway."

Celeste shook her head. "Most of the boys I knew wanted the girls to ride alone."

"Well, I guess I'm no different when there's a pretty girl I want to give my full attention to, but I'm really harmless."

"Your mother brought you up to be a gentleman."

"Yeah, I guess she did."

She caught something in his terse reply that made her wonder again about his mother. "I'd love to have a picnic. If you'll drive me home, I'll make some sandwiches for us."

"I don't want to put you to any trouble."

"It's no trouble, really."

She wondered if he thought it was strange she didn't ask him to come in and hoped he thought it was because she'd said her father was sick. It wasn't entirely a lie. Sunday afternoon was sobering-up time.

She slipped around the house to the back door, where she checked to be sure the kitchen was empty. Then she got the picnic basket from the pantry and threw together sandwiches from some leftover roast. Adding the cookies she'd made earlier in the week, some celery sticks in waxed paper, two glasses, and a half-full bottle of milk, she looked around to see if she'd forgotten anything.

"What're you doing?"

She froze. "Just making a picnic, Daddy." *Please don't let him see the car out front.*

Dancing with Velvet

"Who're you going with?"

"Someone from church."

He jerked open the refrigerator door. "What's there to eat?"

"You can warm up the baked chicken and vegetables."

"That's your job."

Celeste closed the basket and stepped through the back door almost in one motion. "I've got to go, Daddy." She hurried around the house to the street and almost threw herself into the car with the basket in her lap. "Let's go," she said to Kent.

"What's wrong?"

"Nothing. Just...please, let's go."

He started the car and drove away in silence.

At the park, he found a spot partially shaded but still sunny enough to be warm and rolled down his window. "Let me know if you're too cold."

"I'm fine."

"Are you really?"

"Yes."

He seemed to be waiting for her to say more.

"It's just that my father..."

"You didn't want him to see you get in the car with me."

She shook her head.

"Why?"

She turned her face toward the window so he wouldn't see the tears she was trying to hold back.

"He doesn't like you to go out?"

She shrugged.

"He'd have wanted to meet me first. He's protective."

"He's a drunk!" Celeste exploded, then hunched her shoulders and tried not to cry. *I've never told anyone that. Why did I tell a stranger?*

Kent didn't say anything for a few minutes. "I'm sorry, Celeste. I shouldn't have pried." He handed her his handkerchief. "It's clean."

She blotted her face. "I'm sorry I'm acting like a baby."

"I understand. Really." He took the basket out of her lap and put it on the seat between them. "I'll bet you packed a good lunch."

"Just what I had handy."

She unwrapped the sandwich he handed her and took a bite. "Do all the salesmen have cars?"

"No, just a few of us. I got one earlier than usual because the boss says I'm dependable, and I can make more stops if I don't have to take the train."

"It's a nice car."

"I take good care of it, too. It's not really mine, but it's the closest thing to a car of my own that I've ever had. Or probably ever will have for awhile."

"My father has a car. He works at a bank, and I ride to and from work with him every day except Saturday. But the bus stops at the corner, so that's all right."

"How long have you been by yourself? Without your sister, I mean?"

"Since I was twelve. Ben's parents offered to take me, too, but Daddy wouldn't let me go."

"Why?"

"I don't know. He didn't want me." She felt tears welling up again and regretted her words. "Tell me about your family," she said.

"There's just my mother, Neil, and me, but I'd like to have a boy and a girl someday. Of course, you take what you get and like it, don't you?"

"I suppose."

"Two boys or two girls or one of each."

She smiled. "I haven't thought much about it, to tell you the truth."

"Every girl wants a family someday."

"Someday, maybe. I'm not even twenty yet. I've got time."

"So you don't go out much because of your father?"

"Not much."

"Well, you won't always live at home. You'll get out on your own someday."

Celeste turned her face away. "Sure."

"Maybe you'll figure out a way to go back to college."

"I doubt it, but you never know."

"When Neil gets through, I'll think about going. I mean, if he gets a good enough job to help Mother, like I'm doing now. But I'm the oldest, so it's my responsibility to help him go to school and help Mother, too."

"Does he go to school in Brownwood?"

"He goes to Howard Payne so he can live at home. And he has a girl, Kay, who's in nursing school. I'm pretty sure they'll get married someday."

"And then you can do what you want to do."

"I hope so."

Something in the way he looked past her when he spoke the last words made her wonder.

After lunch, Kent helped her re-pack the basket, and then asked if she'd like to take a walk.

"I'll be back through here about this time next month. If there's another dance, maybe I'll see you there."

"I think there's one almost every month, but I'll be sure to check."

"If not, I'll probably see you at church."

"That would be nice."

"And maybe we could go out to dinner on Sunday."

"Maybe."

He took her home just before dark. "Do you want me to let you out at the corner?"

"That might be a good idea."

"I'll wait to make sure you get in all right."

"You don't have to."

"I want to."

They shook hands at the end of the block. "Thanks for today, Celeste. I enjoyed it."

"Me, too."

"I'm looking forward to seeing you again."

She nodded and hurried away without looking back.

****

That night the blue velvet curtains billowed through her dreams again. This time, the breeze became a violent wind that ripped them from their hangings. Her prince—Kent—was nowhere in sight.

Chapter Five

The Christmas card, addressed to "Miss Celeste c/o Woolworth" lay squarely in the middle of her desk when she came in on Christmas Eve morning. Celeste's heart catapulted to her throat, but she slipped the envelope into her desk drawer until the office emptied out at lunch. Then, her hands shaking with anticipation, she took the card out again and opened it.

Kent had signed his first name, then sketched an arrow indicating she should turn to the back.

Dear Celeste,

I hope this will reach you before you go to Sterling City for the holidays. Just wanted to tell you again how glad I am that we met and how much I look forward to seeing you again in January. I hope you'll wear the blue velvet dress. You were beautiful in it. Again, wishing you a Merry Christmas and all the best things in the New Year.

Kent

She read the words three times before she looked to see if he'd included a return address on the envelope. Surely it wouldn't be forward to write and thank him for the card. But the upper left corner of the envelope was blank. She frowned. What did that mean? That he didn't want her to know exactly where he lived?

She considered the fact he'd sent the card to the store, even though he knew her address on Spaulding Street. That was probably a good thing, since her father always walked around the house to the porch and got the mail as soon as he parked the car in the garage. Kent must have considered she'd be better off not answering questions about who she knew in Brownwood.

Oh, Kent, are you the man of my dreams? Is all this going somewhere, or will we just touch each other's lives once a month at the Roof Garden?

She slipped the card back in the envelope and tucked it into her purse before she reached for her lunch.

****

At four o'clock, she stowed the ledgers in the safe and took her coat and suitcase from the corner closet. "Going to Sterling City, Miss Riley?" Mr. Thomas looked up from the stack of dollar bills he was putting into envelopes—small Christmas bonuses Celeste knew came out of his own pocket.

"Yes, sir. There's a bus at four forty-five."

He held out the envelope with her name on it. "Merry Christmas, and my regards to your family."

"Thank you, Mr. Thomas. Merry Christmas to you, too."

"I don't suppose your young man lives in Sterling City, too?"

"My…" Her mouth went dry. She never gossiped with the other girls about Kent and felt sure Veda and Paula didn't either.

He leaned back in his chair and smiled. "I have my spies. Actually, Mrs. Thomas and I have a friend who takes his wife to the Roof Garden whenever there's a good band booked there. They recognized you and told us you were dancing with a very handsome, most attentive young man."

"Yes, sir. I mean, no, sir, he lives in Brownwood, not Sterling City."

"He travels?"

"For a plumbing company. He'll be back in

January."

"I'm glad for you. You're a nice girl. You need to get out more—with the right kind of people, of course."

For a fleeting moment, she wondered if he knew about her father.

"Run along now. If I didn't have to finish these envelopes, I'd drive you to the station myself."

"Oh, no, thank you, Mr. Thomas, I can walk."

"Looks like we might get some snow. Have a good time with your family, Miss Riley. I'll see you on Thursday."

****

As the bus pulled away from the station on Twohig Street, Celeste leaned her head back against the seat, closed her eyes, and let herself think about if Kent really did live in Sterling City. Maybe they'd sit together for the community Christmas Eve service tonight. Maybe he'd invite her home to meet his family. Maybe he'd drive her back to the ranch...walk her to the door...kiss her goodnight. *Stop it, Celeste. You're making way too much out of one chance encounter and a few dances. He's nice, though. And we're a lot alike. I hope he can go to college and be a lawyer. Maybe I'll go with him to the university and finish my degree, too. I'll be a teacher, and I can work while he's in law school...* Celeste pinched herself hard. *You're crazy, Celeste Riley. Meet a man a few times and you're already married to him and planning your lives together. Crazy, crazy, crazy.*

****

After church, Celeste helped Coralee and Ben play Santa Claus for Barbara before going upstairs to the cozy third floor loft that Pearl kept made up for her visits. She was almost asleep when Coralee slipped into bed with her.

"All right, now tell me about that blue velvet

dress and your dreamboat."

"I told you everything, Sister. He's a nice boy...man."

"And you like him."

"Uh-huh."

"So did you get a Christmas card from him? Anything?"

"A card with a note. He's coming back through next month. He promised to come to the dance again."

"Did you tell him about Daddy?"

"I didn't plan to, but it just sort of slipped out. I could tell he wondered why I didn't invite him in and why I didn't want him to walk me to the door. Coralee, did Daddy just change all of a sudden when Mamma died? I mean, I don't have many memories before that, but it seemed like we were happy."

Coralee didn't say anything for a few minutes. "They separated for a while before you were born. Mamma and I went to Bronte and lived there with one of her friends."

"How old were you?"

"I went to all of first grade there."

"So was Mamma...expecting me in Bronte?"

"You were born after we went home."

The realization of what her sister wasn't saying hit Celeste like a fist in her stomach. "I'm not really Daddy's. That's it, isn't it?"

Coralee rolled over and put her arms around her sister. "He was crazy about you, Cece. Passed out cigars when you were born, the whole bit."

"Why, if I wasn't his?"

"Maybe he thought you were, I don't know. I mean, they got back together and you were beautiful, just like Mamma. Look at your baby pictures sometime."

"He wanted her back, so he took me, too."

"That's not the way it was."

"Then how was it?"

"He came to Bronte and begged Mamma to come home with him. The friend we were staying with really needed us out, so Mamma packed up and left with him."

"When was that?"

"Right before school started. I threw a fit because I couldn't go back to second grade there with all my friends."

A chill engulfed Celeste's body despite the two blankets and down comforter. "Who was my father?"

"Mamma went out with a lot of different men. I never knew any names."

"Why did she and Daddy separate?"

"She was only fifteen when they married. Didn't even finish school. I remember hearing her tell people how much she'd missed, and that she shouldn't have married an old man."

"Was Daddy old?"

"Thirty, I think."

"So why wouldn't he have been glad to be rid of me when you married, and Big Ben and Pearl offered to bring me to the ranch?"

"Big Ben said it was his way of getting back at Mamma."

"They know? Big Ben and Pearl and Ben and everybody knows about me? Knows that I'm..."

Celeste felt her sister's hand cover her lips. "Don't you say that, Cece. Don't you dare say that or even think about it anymore."

"How can I help thinking about it?"

"I didn't mean for you to ever know. I shouldn't have told you."

"So I've just lived with everybody knowing about me except myself?"

"It wasn't that way, sweetie. We lived here in Sterling City then. That's how Big Ben and Pearl knew, and maybe a few other people. Daddy got the job in San Angelo and moved us there in February, right before you were born in April."

"I feel so dirty," Celeste whispered. "Oh, Sister, I'm not even a real person. I told Kent about Daddy, but I can't ever tell him about me. Not ever."

So now I know. It all makes sense now. No wonder Daddy hates me. Only he's not really my father. I just call him that because I always have. What would Kent think about all this? Would he care? His mother probably would. She sounds like a real prim and proper lady.

The blue velvet curtain filled her dreams. Shimmering in the soft light of the stars, it billowed and beckoned to her, and this time her feet moved toward it. When it parted suddenly, Kent stood there holding out his hand, but when she reached for it, he snatched it away. The curtain fell between them, hiding him from her sight. She tried to find her way through, but her fingers clawed a solid, unmovable wall. Exhausted, she fell to her knees, weeping and calling Kent's name, but no sound came from beyond the curtain.

****

As Celeste moved through the end of December and into January, she felt as if she were a stranger to herself, as if the body she lived in didn't belong to her. Coralee called almost every night for two weeks. "I don't want to talk about it, Sister. Not now."

"Don't say anything to Daddy, Cece. Confronting him would just make things worse."

"I'm not going to tell him anything." *I never tell him anything. I don't have anything to say that he wants to hear except "Dinner's ready" or "Your dry cleaning came."*

"Maybe this is the time to think about getting out on your own."

"Maybe I will." *Where would I go? I'd have to leave my room with all my things.*

"Have you heard from Kent?"

"No."

"When is the next dance at the Roof Garden?"

"I don't know. I'm not going anyway."

"Cece, don't be that way."

"Kent would know something was wrong the minute he saw me. We were just getting acquainted, and now I don't even know who I am."

"You're my baby sister, and I love you."

"But he wouldn't, if he knew about me."

"Then he's not worth your time. Real love doesn't have anything to do with circumstances."

"Would Ben have married you if things had been turned around?"

"He said so right out when I told him that you knew."

"Why did you even tell me?"

"I don't know. I wish I hadn't. But Pearl always said you needed to know when you grew up, and maybe she was right. The point is, now you know, and you have to deal with it. Frankly, if it loosens the hold Daddy seems to have on you, it's a good thing."

"He doesn't have a hold on me."

"Look, sweetie, go to the dance. Wear the silver sandals I bought you for Christmas. Hold up your head and be the same person you've always been. Think about the dress and Kent. Think about all the positive things that will make you feel better."

Celeste didn't say that nothing could make her feel better right now. After Christmas Eve, she'd even stopped dreaming about the blue velvet curtain.

****

The January dance fell near the end of the month, about the time Celeste calculated Kent should be back in San Angelo. When Paula and Veda invited her to dress at their place again, she almost said no. *How can I look at Kent and wonder what he'd think of me? Maybe Ben wouldn't have cared if it had been Coralee, but Kent would. He's not like the men Mamma went out with, the ones who... How could Mamma let someone do that to her when she was already married and had Coralee? Kent said I was young and sweet, but now he might think I was like Mamma. I look like her. Maybe all those feelings I've been having means I'm like her in other ways, too. Kent wouldn't want anybody like that. Never in a million years.*

But when Saturday came, with hope welling up from deep inside, she got on the bus carrying the box with her blue velvet dress and the new silver sandals.

****

The Roof Garden was as beautiful as she remembered it, but Kent was nowhere in sight. When the band took a break, she wandered down to the lobby to get a soft drink.

"Hey, Miss. You in the blue dress."

Celeste followed the sound of the voice to the desk clerk. "Are you talking to me?"

"You wearing a blue velvet dress?"

Yes, and silver slippers, she thought unhappily, *much good they're doing me.*

"Your name Celeste?"

She nodded.

"Have a letter for you. Just saw it in the box." He held out an envelope. "Yeah, it's for you."

Celeste turned the envelope over in her hands. It was addressed to the hotel, but just below the address were the words, "For Celeste, the girl in the blue velvet dress."

Retreating to a secluded corner behind a potted palm, she tore open the letter with trembling fingers and unfolded the paper.

Dear Miss Celeste,

My route has changed, so I won't be back in San Angelo again. I can't complain, since it's a promotion and more money, but I was counting on seeing you.

Like I told you, I have responsibilities yet, and I can't even think about what I want right now, but if I could, I'd want you to be part of my dreams. Maybe someday our paths will cross again.

You take good care of yourself, and don't stop going dancing or wearing that blue velvet dress. I'm sure somebody else will ask you to dance. A lot of somebodies. I just wish one of them could be me.

*Sincerely,
Kent*

Veda and Paula found her curled in the deep leather chair, weeping quietly, and got the story out of her. Though she protested she didn't want to ruin their good time, they insisted on walking her home, where they hugged her and told her everything would be all right. She'd meet somebody else next month. At least Kent had been gentleman enough to write and explain why he didn't show up.

Before she got into bed, she hung the dress in the back of her closet and returned the silver slippers to their box. If she hadn't walked home in them, the soles would hardly be scuffed.

Sitting on the edge of the bed in her pajamas, she read Kent's letter again. What had she expected from him? He'd been honest from the beginning about not being free to make a commitment. Besides, what kind of commitment did she expect him to make after they'd met only a few times? *Anyway, things have changed. I'm not who he thought I was, and no blue velvet dress and silver slippers can ever make me the same person again.*

She slipped the letter under her pillow. *Maybe*

it's better this way. I spent fifty dollars on a dress I'll never wear again. I could've had three new outfits for work. Serves me right for being so silly.

She sat up, plucked the letter from beneath her pillow, and held it briefly against her cheek. Then she got up and tucked it into the box Pete had made for her in wood shop when they were in high school. Her fingers skimmed the polished lid. Another memory put away. *Is that all I'll ever have—memories? What about a life?* She got back into bed and switched off the lamp.

All over. All her bright dreams. They were silly dreams anyway. Kent wasn't her dream prince after all. Maybe princes didn't exist, at least not for her.

He'd been so nice, so thoughtful the way he'd driven her home first, before Veda and Paula. She'd felt so proud sitting next to him at church the next morning. Maybe pride was the problem. Maybe only her pride was hurt.

She turned over and buried her face in the pillow, trying to quash her thoughts. She and Pete had some good times in high school, but this was different. Kent was different.

Oh, Kent, why did it turn out this way? Why couldn't we have had just one more night, one more weekend? Then I could've made some excuse about why we shouldn't see each other again or keep in touch, about why I can't be part of your dreams.

She flopped over on her back. *Why am I such an idiot?*

For the first time since before Christmas, she dreamed about the blue velvet drape billowing in an unseen wind. But this time, no one came out from behind it…and her beautiful dress hung around her in tatters.

Chapter Six

Winter dragged on through February and March, cold and wet, the dreariness of the days matching Celeste's spirits. Her twentieth birthday fell on a Saturday in April. At Coralee's insistence, she took the bus to Sterling City for the weekend, but she continued to refuse all invitations to return to the dances at the St. Angelus.

"Maybe you went for the wrong reason," Veda ventured over lunch one Friday. "I mean, did you go to have a good time or to find a husband?"

Celeste tried to hide her irritation at the question. "Why do you and Paula go?"

"To have a good time, that's all. Paula's set on that design school in Dallas, and I'm not going to clerk at Woolworth all my life either. We're not old maids because we're past twenty, and neither are you. If I meet someone special there, fine, but for now, it's a safe, clean, good time."

"I just don't want to go back, Veda."

"Then I won't nag you about it, but if you ever do, don't be afraid to say so."

"Sure, I'll let you know."

****

"I'm worried about you, Cece," Coralee told her when Celeste came for another visit at the end of May. "You're drooping."

"I'm all right."

"Honey, Kent isn't the only man in the world, and you only saw him three or four times. You put all your eggs in one basket."

"Is that what I did?"

"I think so."

"Maybe. I don't know."

"Maybe after you'd gotten to know him better, you wouldn't even have liked him."

"I guess that's possible. But he was so nice, Sister. He was nice to me."

"You said he was a good dancer and a perfect gentleman, but you've dated a lot of boys like that."

"He wasn't a boy, Sister. He was a man."

"Is that what you liked about him?"

"I think so. It was like the dress…different, you know?"

"And you were really attracted to him, the way a woman is attracted to a man. Do we need to have a talk?"

"You had a talk with me when I was twelve, remember?"

"Well, yes, but I only went so far. Maybe it's time for another one."

Celeste giggled. "I know about the birds and the bees, Sister."

"It's a lot more than that, sweetie. Marriage is a whole lot more than just wanting to be physically close to somebody."

"You and Ben are really happy, aren't you?"

"I love him more than I did when we got married ten years ago, if you can believe that. We were just kids, for heaven's sake. Seventeen and eighteen."

"And even then you knew you wanted to spend the rest of your life with him."

"Sure, I did. Young as we were, we meant for it to last forever, and it's going to. But we both had a lot of growing up to do even after we married. Living here with Pearl and Big Ben helped. We saw the kind of give and take relationship they had and learned from it. Still, it's a good thing we didn't have Barbara right off the bat. We weren't ready to be parents."

"You and Ben are good parents."

"We try. She's the only chance we'll get."

"I'm sorry about what happened when she was born."

"Well, I am, too, Cece, but we both came out all right, and maybe one child is enough, with the way things are going in the world."

"The Sunday we walked around town, Kent said there's going to be another war."

"I think he's right. Big Ben says things are sure heading that way."

"Would Ben have to go?"

"Probably not. Ranching is what they call a *war-necessary business*, and since it's just his dad and him, well, he'd probably get exempted."

"I hope so."

"But there'll be a lot of others who have to go."

"Like Kent."

"Your Kent would be a prime candidate at his age with no dependents."

"He's not *my* Kent."

"But you still kind of think of him that way, don't you?"

"I need to stop thinking about him at all."

"Yes, you do. Get out and have some fun, Cece. Big sister says so."

****

Spring was late, and when summer came, it was hotter than Celeste could remember. Mr. Thomas brought up an extra fan from the stockroom and kept the windows wide open, but nothing helped very much. By noon, Celeste felt like a hothouse plant someone had overwatered by mistake.

She made a conscious effort to put Kent out of her mind, chiding herself for expending so much effort and emotion on someone she'd seen twice. She didn't even know his last name, just Kent from Brownwood. They'd kept it impersonal for a reason, and now she was acting like a silly schoolgirl.

Still, every time she went to the window to find some fresh air, she couldn't help watching the sidewalk below, hoping against reason to catch a glimpse of him. Once she thought she did, but when the man took off his hat to wipe his forehead with a handkerchief, she felt foolish and drew back inside so quickly she bumped her head hard enough to bring tears to her eyes.

She caught a summer cold and had to stay home for two days. Her father—though she'd tried without success to stop thinking of him that way—didn't ask how she was feeling and complained that dinner wasn't ready when he got home. Feverish and miserable, Celeste told him he could afford to eat downtown. He slammed out of the house mumbling something about not paying for her keep.

Maybe it was the fever that made her dream, but she woke one night calling Kent's name. He'd been so real, so close, and now he was gone. She wept with frustration, closed her eyes, and tried to call him back.

She did her Christmas shopping in July so she could put things on layaway. One Friday, the saleslady who had talked her into the blue velvet dress waylaid her on her way out of the store.

"I'm dying to know what happened to you in that dress."

"Nothing happened," Celeste replied, resenting the intrusion into her private life. "I went dancing once or twice, that's all."

"Only once or twice?"

"I didn't like it."

"Didn't like it? Every girl likes to dance with a handsome man."

"Maybe there weren't any handsome men," Celeste said. "Excuse me, I've got to catch my ride."

All the way to the bank, she berated herself for

her rudeness. If things had been different, she might have told the friendly clerk about Kent. But things weren't different, and it hurt to remember how she thought they had been.

****

At the end of August, Paula received word she'd won a scholarship to the design school in Dallas and would be leaving at Christmas to enroll for the second term. Veda asked Celeste if she wanted to share the room.

"I can't afford it on my own. If I can't find a roommate, I'll have to quit and go back home. Not that home's a bad place, but there aren't many jobs in a little place like Winters. Besides, I like San Angelo. I'm even thinking about taking a night class at the business college."

Celeste was tempted. *I could manage half the rent, and Coralee would say I should do it.* Then she thought of her own spacious room and how she'd have to fit into half the cramped one in the boarding house. Though she'd shared space happily with Coralee for years, she'd settled into her own way of doing things now that she had the room to herself. "I couldn't leave my father to do for himself," she fibbed. "He depends on me."

"Is he going to depend on you for the rest of his life?" Veda asked.

Celeste shrugged. "If I left...well, I just can't, that's all. Not right now."

Coralee didn't even try to hide her irritation when Celeste told her about turning down the offer. "You can stay with Daddy until the day he dies, and he'll be the same as he is right now. What do you think is going to happen?"

"It's not Daddy. It's leaving my room and all my pretty things. He might, well, get rid of them."

"Ben and I will go down and get your bedroom suite and anything you can't take with you and store it at the ranch."

"Daddy wouldn't let you."

"He owes me. He owes *you*, for that matter."

"I'm going to stay for now, Sister. Maybe one of these days I can have my own place."

"I think you're making a big mistake. This is a golden opportunity."

"Then it's my mistake," Celeste snapped, instantly regretting her words. "I'm sorry. I didn't mean that."

"I almost stayed home longer because of you. Ben understood. He really did. But I knew if I didn't get out when I had the chance, I might not ever get out. Then, when Big Ben offered you a place here, I knew I'd made the right decision."

"But I didn't go."

"No, you didn't. Do you know what Daddy said when I told him Ben and I were getting married?"

"I guess I don't remember."

"Because you didn't hear. I sent you across the street before I told him. He called me a name I won't repeat and asked me if I was pregnant."

"Oh, Sister."

"Didn't you ever wonder why he didn't walk me down the aisle? It wasn't just all that stuff about not letting you go with me."

"I guess I was having too much fun being a bridesmaid to wonder where he was."

"You didn't care where he was. Neither did I. I really worried about leaving you there afterward."

"I've been all right."

"How long are you going to be all right, Cece? Nothing's going to change."

Celeste sighed. "I'll think about it again, Sister. I promise." But they both knew she wouldn't.

****

September was muggy and wet. People talked about the flood of 1936 and wondered aloud if another one was due. Celeste packed a small bag and kept it under her desk in case she got caught downtown some afternoon and couldn't get home.

The weather finally turned cooler in mid-October, and November brought the first frost of the season. She went to Sterling City for Thanksgiving. It was a quick trip, there and back in one day, because she had to be at work on Friday.

After work that Friday, with her layaway paid out early, she used some of her savings to buy a new winter coat at Levine's and wore it to church on Sunday. Mrs. Lowe told her she looked like a blooming rose in the bright red wool.

The next week seemed to drag. Veda found a new roommate, which eased Celeste's conscience, and the girls at the store began planning a going-away party for Paula. Mr. Thomas said they could use the employee lounge after work if Celeste would be responsible for locking up.

She overslept the following Sunday and was almost late to church. She wondered if she was going because it was the thing to do, because she was enjoying her stylish new coat, or because it was simply a habit.

Just after twelve, as the congregation began to exit the church, she sensed something wasn't right. Several cars parked along the street had their radios turned on with the volume up louder than necessary. As she walked down Harris, she heard the words *Pearl Harbor* repeated over and over. Finally she stopped beside one of the cars to listen.

"What does it mean?" she asked an older man leaning on an open car door.

"It means we're at war, little lady."

"War? Why?"

"The Japs finally did it. They bombed our bases at Pearl Harbor."

"Where's that?"

He spat a brown stream of tobacco juice into the gutter. "Hawaii," he said. "In the Pacific Ocean. Our boys are floating around in the Pacific Ocean like dead fish."

****

On Monday, Celeste sat in the office with Mr. Thomas and Marilyn and listened to President Roosevelt ask Congress for a declaration of war against Japan. She thought of Pete and hoped he'd be able to graduate from the university before he was drafted. Then she thought of Ben, hoping Coralee was right about him not having to go. And then she thought of Kent and knew he would.

****

As the country geared up for war, Celeste threw herself into the local efforts by volunteering with the Red Cross on Saturday afternoons. When the small local airport became a bombardier training school, Mrs. Lowe and some of the other ladies in town decided that two bases warranted a Canteen for the servicemen who would be arriving to learn to fly or to drop their bombs with deadly accuracy.

"We want nice girls, Celeste. Girls who remind the boys of their sisters and girlfriends back home. Girls that the married men, if there are any, can sit and talk to about their wives and children."

Celeste recruited Veda, whose brother had enlisted in the Marines the day after Pearl Harbor. "I can't do anything for Bobby," Veda said, "but maybe being nice to some of these other boys will help him somehow."

"I'm sure anything we can do will help *all* our boys," Mrs. Lowe assured her. The day before the doors opened, she called in all the volunteers and laid down the rules.

"This is their home away from home, so to speak. We're going to have good food, good conversation, games, dancing, a place for them to write letters, listen to the radio, and read. Anything they need, we're going to provide if at all possible.

"What they don't need—and neither do we as an organization—is any kind of activity that even hints at being improper. I'm not saying that you young ladies might not get interested in a serviceman and want to go out on a date, but you won't do it from here. You don't leave the Canteen with a serviceman at any time. He can pick you up at home like a gentleman. If you break the rules, you won't be allowed back, and that would be a shame. We need all of you. We have to work together to win this war. If you keep that in mind, it shouldn't be too hard to follow the rules."

The field commander agreed that the first group of trainees who arrived in September could attend the grand opening of the Canteen on the third Saturday night after their arrival. Half a dozen girls turned out to decorate, while Celeste and Veda fried doughnuts all afternoon, and a local band set up to play. At six o'clock, when the mayor opened the doors, the boys poured in.

Celeste, hot and disheveled after her stint in the kitchen, announced her intention to stay there. "I don't think I'll go out," she told Veda. "Next week, maybe."

"Just go wash your face and powder your nose, honey. And take off that apron." Veda reached to untie the strings at Celeste's waist.

Celeste shrugged. "Oh, why not? I'm not going to know anyone anyway." She spent a few minutes in the ladies' room making herself presentable. A little powder, a little lipstick, and a brush through her hair helped more than she anticipated. Feeling excited in spite of herself, she pasted a smile on her face, squared her shoulders, and stepped out into the main room.

"I thought I recognized you."

The voice just behind her sounded eerily familiar. She whirled. "You!"

"Yeah, me, Kent. Remember? The victim of your half-eaten apple." He winked at her.

Celeste stared at the crisp new uniform in which he looked more handsome—and more vulnerable—than ever and blinked back tears.

"Once I knew I was being sent here, I decided to look you up. You're not married or anything? Or engaged?"

She shook her head.

"Good. I've thought about you a lot."

"You have?"

"Told my brother all about you."

"You did?"

"But it wasn't fair to you to start something, like writing letters or anything."

"It's all right. I understood." *No, I didn't. I waited and waited to hear from you. Anything would've been better than nothing.*

"Well, I'm not sure I did. I had to take the new route because of the money, but I didn't like it. I mean, I didn't like not coming back here." He turned his cap in his hands. "How've you been?"

"All right."

"Go dancing again?"

"No. Not since I got your letter."

"I'm sorry." He grinned suddenly. "Well, maybe I'm not sorry at that. Music sounds good in there. Want to give it a try?"

She lost the battle with her tears. "I'm so glad to see you," she said. "I'm just so glad."

"Hey, don't cry, kid."

"I'm sorry."

"I'm glad you're glad to see me, but I don't like to see you cry."

He pulled out a clean handkerchief and offered it to her. "I'll have to keep a supply of these for you, I guess." Then he took her hand and led her out onto the dance floor.

****

Kent held her closer than she remembered him doing before. "Can we talk?" he asked as the dance ended.

"I'm supposed to be mingling," she said.

"Then I'll follow you around like a lost puppy."

She smiled. "Let's go sit at the table over there. If one of the chaperones gives me a look, I'll have to get up."

He brought two cups of coffee and some doughnuts to the table. "Veda and I fried those things all afternoon," Celeste said, wrinkling her nose. "I don't even want to look at them."

He tossed a paper napkin over the plate. "Sorry."

She giggled. "They're good though. Go ahead and eat."

"Have you really been all right, Celeste? You look, well, thinner."

"We've been busy getting the Canteen up and running. And before I forget, the rule is, no girl leaves here with a serviceman."

"What about seeing one on the outside?"

"That's all right."

"Good, because I plan to see a lot of you."

"Do you?"

"I sure do."

"How are your mother and brother?"

"Neil's taking extra classes to finish college early."

"So he can enlist?"

"No, he's 4-F. He was born with a club foot the doctor didn't correct right off the bat, and he still has a limp. I'm glad he's not going."

"Did you enlist or get drafted?"

"I didn't want to wait around, so I just went

down and signed up. It was only a matter of time anyway. Mother will get my allotment. She says they'll manage all right, and when Neil finishes school, he'll get a job."

"What made you decide on bombardier training?"

"I wanted to fly, but they said I'd be better at dropping bombs. I guess it's all the same, pushing the button or flying the plane. People are going to get killed."

"Well, we're at war."

"That doesn't make me feel any better about killing people."

"I didn't mean that it should. I'm sorry."

"Hey, I know you didn't mean it that way. I'm just touchy about it. I hear after you've been at it awhile, it'll get to be routine."

"How long will you be here?"

"Probably until December. We're the first class to go through, so I guess we can expect a few hitches. Are you still working at Woolworth?"

"Yes."

"Why didn't you go dancing anymore?"

She shrugged. "I just didn't want to."

"Because of me?"

She didn't look at him. "Maybe."

"I'd have hated it if some other Romeo had carried you off."

"Romeo wasn't a very steady fellow, killing himself and all. I always imagined a handsome prince would come along one day and carry me off."

"How about a handsome airman?"

She felt her cheeks grow warm. "That would be all right."

"After I took you home, your friends did a lot of talking about you. They made sure I knew you were a nice girl, and they wouldn't appreciate it if I didn't treat you right. I promised them I would, except I never got the chance."

"It's all right."

"I thought about you a lot, Celeste. I really did. I always pictured you in that blue velvet dress. You looked real pretty."

"Thank you."

"I knew you were somebody special."

"Did you?"

"Yes, I did. Remember how I said you were young and sweet and not old before your time? I did say something like that, didn't I?"

"I remember."

"Do you really, or did you just forget about me?"

She knew he was teasing her again. "I thought about you a lot, too, Kent. I...I even dreamed about you sometimes."

"Does that mean I'm the man of your dreams?"

She felt herself blushing.

"There you go blushing again. Hey, doesn't every girl need a man of her dreams?"

"I suppose."

He touched her hair with the tips of his fingers, then let his hand fall away. "Do you look like your mother?"

"Coralee, my sister, says so. She says maybe that's why my father..."

"Why your father what?"

Celeste shook her head.

Kent covered her hand with his. "Come on, you told me about him, remember?"

"It's not important."

"It is to me."

She took a deep breath and looked away. "Nothing's changed, and it never will. I had a chance to move out and didn't take it."

"Why?"

"I have a nice room at home. When it came right down to it, I couldn't give up all the things I grew up with."

"Nothing wrong with that."

"Coralee said I should have gone, but I didn't, so that's that."

His fingers tightened around hers. "I'm sorry, Celeste."

"Let's don't talk about it, Kent."

"Kent Goddard. I remember we didn't exchange last names. Jonathan Kent Goddard, Jr."

"Celeste Riley."

"Celeste…celestial…heavenly. Are you an angel?"

"I don't think so."

"What do people call you?"

"My sister and some of my friends call me Cece."

"Then I'll have to come up with something else."

"Why?"

"So it'll be special between you and me."

"You still have responsibilities, don't you?"

"They're not quite the same anymore. When you put on a uniform, you get the idea that life isn't forever."

"Oh, don't say that. Don't even think it." Her eyes filled with tears again.

"It's true. Sure, I want to come back, and I want something to come back to. I want a reason to come home." He put one finger under her chin and made her look at him. "I wasn't sure just what that reason was until I saw you again."

"I'll be here," she said so softly he could barely hear her. "I'll always be here."

****

He left ahead of her and waited at the corner. "I have to get my ride back to the base," he said. "I wish I could walk you home."

"I understand."

He took her hand and moved her from the streetlight into the shadows. "I'll come to church tomorrow if I can get into town."

"You know where to find me."

"Left front, sixth pew from the back."

"Yes." She felt his arms slip around her and knew what was coming.

"I'm glad you're still here," he murmured, brushing her lips with his. "Really glad."

Mrs. Lowe calling, "Celeste? Are you out here?" interrupted the second long kiss.

"I'm here, Mrs. Lowe," she said, moving into the light again.

"I'll drive you home. It's too late for you to walk by yourself."

Kent came out, too. "I agree."

"You met Kent when he came to church with me," Celeste said.

Mrs. Lowe studied his face. "You look familiar."

"It was a long time ago, but I'll be around a lot now," Kent said, grinning.

"Did Celeste tell you the rules?"

"Yes, ma'am, she sure did."

"They're not negotiable."

"No, ma'am." Kent winked at Celeste. "See you tomorrow, I hope."

Later, in her room, she threw herself on the bed and relived the moment his lips had fastened on hers and how she wished he hadn't had to let her go.

Chapter Seven

The next morning they met in front of the church. Kent took her arm as they walked up the steps and through the center doors. As he'd done before, he held the hymnal for her, but he didn't take communion even though she whispered to him that it was "open."

They were almost up the aisle when Celeste saw Mrs. Lowe edging her way toward them. "I see you got here, young man," she said. Her voice was pleasant, but her eyes held a question. "We haven't really been introduced."

"This is Kent Goddard from Brownwood, Mrs. Lowe. We met a couple of years ago at a dance at the St. Angelus. I was surprised to see him at the Canteen last night."

"I was traveling then, and my route was changed, so I never got back. I was sure glad to see Celeste last night."

"I'm sure she was glad to see you, too."

Celeste felt the color rising in her cheeks. "Yes, ma'am."

Kent took her arm. "I'll only be here until I graduate, but it makes me feel better to know you'll be keeping an eye on Celeste for me. Making sure nobody gets fresh or anything like that."

"You can be sure of that, young man. I've known her all her life. Most of it anyway."

"She was my Sunday School teacher," Celeste murmured.

"It was nice to meet you, Mrs. Lowe," Kent said. "The Canteen is terrific. All the guys said so on the way back to base last night."

"We worked hard on it. Well, you two run along. I expect you have plans."

"We're taking a picnic to the park," Celeste said. "I left the basket in the Sunday School superintendent's office. We were just going to get it."

"Well, you don't need to walk all that way carrying a basket. Mr. Lowe and I will run you over there."

Celeste glanced at Kent who nodded. "Thank you, Mrs. Lowe. We really appreciate it."

****

"She's the one I worked for to get money to pay on my dress," Celeste explained after they'd thanked the Lowes for the lift and waved goodbye.

Kent set the basket on a table. "I'm starving to death."

"Don't they feed you well out there?"

"It's not Mother's home cooking, that's for sure."

"I've got fried chicken and hot rolls. Well, they were hot when I took them out of the oven this morning."

"You got up early to do all this?"

"Yes."

"What about your father?"

"I left a plate for him. He doesn't get up until noon anyway, and he's never hungry. He's got to sober up for work tomorrow."

"What does he do?"

"He's a banker."

"Why does he drink?"

"I don't know. Neither does Coralee." *I do know, but I'm not going to tell you.*

"Can't have been easy for you."

"I got used to it. I do the cooking and general housekeeping."

"For room and board, so to speak."

She shrugged. "That's money in the bank for

me."

"A banker should be able to hire someone to keep house and take care of his meals."

"I guess he could. Maybe he would if I moved out, but I'm not ready to do that."

"Just because of your room?" He helped himself to a piece of chicken. "Is that the only reason?"

"It's the only one I can come up with for now."

"Are you scared of being on your own?"

"I've been on my own for a long time."

"Not like you'd be if you moved out. I'm not trying to convince you, Celeste, just give you something to think about."

She passed him a paper napkin. "You like the chicken?"

"It's got a spice to it that I don't recognize."

"It's my secret ingredient. I made a lemon pound cake, too."

"So you really do believe that the way to a man's heart is through his stomach."

"I might."

After lunch, they took a walk by the river and sat on the bank. "I used to fish with my dad before he died," Kent said. "We had some good times."

"I don't remember my mother very much. I wish I did."

"You said your sister says you look like her."

"That's what she says."

"She was pretty, then."

Celeste didn't reply.

"I've been thinking about something to call you."

"Why do you have to call me anything except my name?"

"I told you, I want something special that's just between you and me."

"Did you think of something?"

"Maybe. I'll let you know when I'm sure. I bet you had a lot of boyfriends in school."

"A few. I dated one boy pretty steady through high school, the one I told you about, Pete. He went to school all last summer so he could finish college early, before the draft got him."

"Did it?"

"No, he graduated and then enlisted in the army. I ran into him when he was home before he left for basic training. He said the same thing you did, that it was just a matter of time, so he might as well go on. But I'm glad he got to finish school anyway."

"You said he was going to be some sort of engineer."

"Electrical, I think. What about you? Didn't you ever have a special girl?"

"Not really. Couldn't afford one. Didn't have the time or the money." He turned to look at her. "Still can't, but I think I've got one now."

"We barely know each other."

"We'll get acquainted."

"I hope so."

Later, he carried the empty picnic basket in one hand and held her hand with the other while he walked her home.

****

Kent came to the Canteen every Saturday night, and almost every Sunday he managed to hitch a ride into town to meet her for church. When the weather turned colder, they gave up picnics in favor of a small café where they went dutch.

Sometimes they went to a movie at the Texas Theatre or just window-shopped downtown. They furnished their dream house from Shepperson's and discussed the features they liked best in the fine houses along Twohig Street.

There were fewer dances at the Roof Garden these days, so sometimes they snuck through the lobby of the St. Angelus and sat on the empty dance floor, talking, holding hands, and sharing a few brief kisses.

"I'll be gone before Christmas," Kent told her at the end of November. "If I'm lucky, I'll get a pass home. Maybe you'd come with me."

"I always spend Christmas with Coralee and her family. I don't get any extra days off."

"I really want you to meet my brother."

"How about your mother? You never mention her, not really."

He sighed. "Her, too, but…"

"But?"

"To tell you the truth, she never liked anyone I dated in high school."

"Why not?"

"Well, I was the oldest, and she depended on me after Dad died." He sighed again. "I don't know…she's a little, well, possessive, I guess you'd say. When she said she was going to talk to one of Dad's friends on the draft board about getting me exempted, I just went down and enlisted."

"She didn't like that much, I bet."

"She didn't like it at all."

"Then this might not be the time for me to meet her."

He pushed back the hair that fell over her face despite the barrette holding it and brushed her cheek with the tips of his fingers. "She's going to have to meet you sometime, because I like you a lot, more than I ever liked anyone else."

For a moment, the pit of Celeste's stomach burned, and her knees felt like jelly. "I like you, too, Kent."

"I wish there was some place we could be by ourselves and have some real privacy," he said. "Besides the dance floor at the hotel. I'm always looking over my shoulder for some hotel employee who might have seen us come up here."

"I know a place." As soon as the words were out of her mouth, guilt kicked in.

"Where?"

"I have a key to the store. Mr. Thomas told me to keep it after we had the going-away party for Paula in the employee lounge. He said somebody ought to be able to get in if there was an emergency, and he was out of town or something."

"I don't want you to get in trouble."

"He won't know." *What am I saying? Mr. Thomas knows everything that goes on in that store.*

"He might find out."

"Then I'll explain it to him. He'll understand." *He'll understand, but he won't like it. But Kent's leaving soon, and this might be our only chance to be alone. Really alone.*

They cut through the alley to the back of the store, where Celeste let them in with her key. "There aren't any windows in the lounge, so we can turn on the light in there."

Kent made sure the door was locked behind them before he followed her down the dim corridor.

"This is it," Celeste said, opening a door and flipping on the light. "Such as it is."

They sat discreetly apart on the cracked leather sofa. "It's hard to talk when there're people around," Kent said after a minute.

"Yes."

"I've decided what to call you."

"Did you? I thought you'd forgotten."

"Well, I had to make sure it was just right."

"So what is it? What's my new name?"

"Can't you guess? It's Velvet."

"Velvet?"

"Sure. That's how I always think of you. Soft and pretty in that dress."

"Velvet."

Kent reached for her hand. "You're real special,

Velvet."

Before she realized it, she was in his arms, and he was kissing her harder and more intimately than ever before. "Oh, Velvet," he whispered, "you're so beautiful." His hands caressed her back and slipped down to her waist, then around to her stomach and down. "So, so beautiful."

She knew he was way past *too familiar*, as Coralee used to say, but she didn't care, not until he slipped one hand up under her sweater. "Kent, don't…"

He didn't seem to hear her as his fingers crawled down the top of her slip until they were on her bare flesh.

The next thing she knew, she was flat on her back on the sofa with her sweater up around her neck. He began to tug the straps from her shoulders. She felt his lips, moist and searching, where they had no right to be.

"Kent, stop." She struggled to sit up. "We're going too far."

He sat back, a look of confusion on his face. "I thought you liked it."

"I did…I do, but it's wrong. You know it's wrong."

"I wouldn't hurt you, Velvet. I'd know when to pull back."

Moving away from him, she straightened her sweater. "You were way past that."

His mouth twisted briefly, then relaxed. "You're right. I'm sorry."

"I was wrong to suggest coming here. We should go."

He stood up. "Right."

"Don't be mad, Kent."

"I'm not mad."

In the alley, when she turned to double-check the door, Kent's hand went to the knob, too. "It's locked good and tight."

Celeste nodded. "This wasn't a good idea. You know that as well as I do."

He took her hand. "I'll walk you home."

At the end of the block, he kissed her goodnight. "I'll wait 'til you get inside," he said, the way he always did. "And I'm sorry things happened like they did."

"It's all right."

He squinted at her in the light from the street lamp. "I'm a man, Velvet."

"What does that mean?"

"It means that maybe you're still a little girl."

A knot of fear formed in the pit of her stomach. "Maybe I am," she managed to say. "I've never been that far before."

"I could tell." He made no move to touch her. "But you liked it. And I meant what I said, I know when to stop."

She felt her mouth tighten. "So you've done this before."

His jaw hardened. "I'm twenty-six, almost twenty-seven years old, Velvet."

"What does that have to do with it?"

He shook his head. "You really are a little girl."

"You said you liked me being young—and sweet."

"I know what I said, and I meant it, but there comes a time when you have to grow up."

"Grow up as in forget what I believe is right and what's wrong?"

"Not exactly. A lot of girls—a lot of your friends, I'll bet—don't let a guy get started and then put the brakes on like you did."

She had to swallow the lump in her throat before she could answer him. "I wouldn't know."

"Anyway, I'm sorry. It won't happen again." He touched her hair. "Goodnight."

Her eyes fell on her mother's picture as soon as she turned on the light in her room. "You didn't put the brakes on," Celeste said aloud. "I'm proof of that. And I'm not like you, Mamma. I'm not."

Chapter Eight

Celeste had to re-do her ledger sheet three times on Monday before she got it to balance. Her mind was too full of Kent, the feelings his touch had stirred up, and even a few regrets that she hadn't let things go on a little longer. *If they'd gone on much longer, they'd have gone too far, and he wouldn't have pulled back, like he said. I knew what I was doing when I used that key. Maybe I even wanted it to happen. Now I'm not sure. Has he been with a girl—really been with her—before? More than one? Does he think being twenty-six years old gives him the right to do everything he wants to do—even that?*

"Miss Riley?"

She started. "Yes, sir?"

"I've spoken to you twice. Is everything all right?"

"I just had a little trouble with these figures, but they finally tallied."

"That doesn't sound like you."

"No, sir."

"Want me to go over them for you?"

"They're all right now."

"I wondered if you'd like to work downstairs on Saturday afternoon. This is the second girl I've had to hire since Paula left, and she's not doing much better than the first one. Maybe you could help her a bit."

"I'd be glad to, Mr. Thomas."

"You don't have any plans with your young man?"

"I'll see him at the Canteen Saturday night."

"If you're sure."

"I'm sure." *But I'm not. Maybe he won't even show up, and if he doesn't...* Quick tears sprang to her eyes, and she turned her head to hide them. *If he doesn't, it will be my fault. But I can't give him what he wants. I just can't, no matter what.*

****

Claudia Peters reminded Celeste of a movie starlet. "There's just so much to remember," the girl said, tugging at her turquoise sateen blouse.

"Not really," Celeste said, wondering if the girl knew she looked cheap with her skirt and blouse too tight and her makeup too thick and inappropriate for the workplace. "Let's go over everything again. You'll catch on."

When Claudia finally managed to close out her register, Celeste walked upstairs with her to turn in the money to Mr. Thomas. "You're not from around here, are you?"

"Oh, no. I'm from Brownwood. My boyfriend is out at the airfield."

"Is he part of the bombardier class? They're going to graduate and leave soon."

"I know, but I just had to come be with him."

Celeste had a feeling she didn't want to know what *with him* meant.

"We've been together since we were in high school."

"And you're not married yet?" slipped out before Celeste could bite her tongue.

"I thought we would be, but, well, he wants to wait."

Wait for what? To get older? For the war to be over?

"But we'll get married before he goes overseas, I'm sure."

"That's nice." *Does Kent want us to get married before he leaves? Does he want to be sure I'm waiting for him, or does he just want to…* Celeste fought the feelings that threatened to take over her body. *What's wrong with me? I didn't used to think about things like this.*

"Kenny's wonderful. I'd wait for him forever."

****

Relief washed over Celeste when Kent showed up at the Canteen just after it opened that night. "I was afraid you wouldn't come," she said, when he'd maneuvered her to a table in the back and sat down across from her.

"To be honest, I wasn't sure you'd want me to."

"It was my fault as much as yours."

He shrugged. "How was your week?"

"Busy. I worked the floor this afternoon, trying to break in Paula's second replacement. But she'll leave, too. Her boyfriend's out at the field with you, and she only came to San Angelo to be close to him."

"What's his name?"

"Claudia just called him Kenny."

"Claudia? Her name is Claudia?"

"From Brownwood, like you. Do you know her?"

"Bleached blonde?" His brows came together in a scowl.

Celeste nodded.

"Yeah. Yeah, I know her." He rose so hastily that he almost overturned the chair. "Come on, let's dance."

****

When the evening ended, Mrs. Lowe caught Celeste at the door and pulled her aside. "I know you meet your young man at the corner every Saturday night," she said.

"He walks me home when he can get another ride to the field besides the bus he comes in on."

"It's not really… It's bending the rules a little."

"I don't leave with him."

"I know you don't. I'm not criticizing you,

Celeste. He seems like a nice boy, and the fact that he comes to church with you every Sunday speaks well for him." She hesitated. "It's just that a few of the other ladies have noticed."

"I can tell him not to wait for me anymore."

"You'd do that?"

"I wouldn't like it, but he'll be leaving in a few weeks anyway, and I want to keep helping out at the Canteen."

"He seems like a nice young man."

"Yes, ma'am."

The older woman patted Celeste's cheek. "I'll explain things to Ina and Pauline. They'll understand. We just don't want anything to upset all the hard work we've all put in to get this up and running."

"No, ma'am, I don't want that either."

Mrs. Lowe nodded. "Run on then."

****

Kent kept his arm around Celeste's shoulders as they walked through the light mist. "I guess I ought to tell you about Claudia."

Celeste stiffened. "Are you Kenny? Her boyfriend? Is she here because of you?"

"She won't leave me alone." He pulled her closer. "We need to find somewhere to talk."

"I didn't bring the key to the store, and I wouldn't use it if I had it." Anger—or was it fear—made her not want to hear what he had to say.

"I didn't mean that," he snapped.

She bit her lip as the rebuke drilled into her. "We could go sit in the lobby at the Cactus Hotel, I guess."

"It would be warmer, for sure."

"All right, for a little while."

****

Except for a man reading a newspaper in a chair near the elevators, they were alone. Cigar smoke drifted up from behind the paper into the light from the chandelier. "My father smoked cigars," Kent said and fell silent.

"Claudia said she and her boyfriend had been together since high school," Celeste prompted.

"We went to high school together. She was wild, one of those girls who…" He touched Celeste's hair. "Not like you, Velvet."

Again, Celeste waited, not because she wanted to but because she didn't know what to say.

"She started acting interested in me during our senior year. Hung around the locker room after basketball practice, changed desks with someone in a couple of classes so she'd have the one next to mine. I felt sorry for her, to tell you the truth. The other guys said awful things about her, and they probably knew what they were talking about. The girls, most of them anyway, wouldn't have anything to do with her."

"Can you blame them?"

"I don't know how girls think, Velvet, but they can be mean. I caught her crying once—I mean, really crying her eyes out one day after school. She showed me a note one of the girls had left on her locker. It was so bad I wouldn't even tell you what it said. Anyway, I tried to be nice to her, even invited her to our church youth group."

"Did she come?"

"Oh, yeah, she came, but not for the reasons I wished she would. I'd walk her home afterward. A time or two we stopped for ice cream at a little stand near the church." He sucked in a long breath and blew it out. "And I took her to the senior prom."

"Why?"

"She wasn't all bad. Nobody is, you know."

"I know." August Riley's face flashed across Celeste's mind.

"After that, I went off to the CCC, but she

always seemed to know when I was home and called or came over. Mother didn't like it. Didn't like Claudia." He took Celeste's hands between his. "She went off for a while, too, but then I ran into her again just before I came up here. That's how she knew where I was."

"Why does she think you're her boyfriend?"

Kent didn't meet her eyes. "I don't know. I guess she needs to feel like somebody cares about her."

"What about her family?"

"Her father took off when she was little. There's an older brother and a younger one. But I'm not her boyfriend, Velvet. Never was, never will be."

"All right."

"But if she knows we're seeing each other, she'll make trouble for you."

"I can take care of myself."

"You don't know Claudia."

"And I don't think I want to. I'll make some excuse if Mr. Thomas asks me to help her again."

"That's probably a good idea."

"What about you? What are you going to do if you run into her?"

"I don't know. But I'll be leaving here in December."

"December's almost here."

He squeezed her hands. "I wish…I wish we could settle things between us before I leave."

"Settle things how?"

"I love you, Velvet. I know it's too soon to ask you to marry me."

"Are you asking?"

"I guess I am."

She gritted her teeth against the uncomfortable stirring deep inside her body. "I don't think either of us is sure enough of our feelings to get married. Mrs. Lowe says there'll be a lot of broken marriages after the war is over." *I don't want ours to be one of them, but what if you never come home? What if we never have another chance to be together?*

"She's probably right. Like I said, when you put on a uniform, you understand everything that means. I'm going to go drop bombs on people, and they aren't going to like it, so they'll shoot back at me and maybe..."

"Don't, Kent."

"I better get you home."

"We'll work things out. The war won't last forever."

He gave her a hand up and buttoned her coat under her chin. "It hasn't even gotten started," he said. "We're in for a long haul."

****

Celeste tried to sleep, but at four o'clock she was still awake. No matter what Kent said about his feelings toward Claudia, the girl felt otherwise. *It's not Kent's fault, but she's here, and she's going to be a problem.* Celeste turned over and scrunched the pillow under her face. *We've already had one problem. If he got so...so serious with me, what did he do with a girl who let boys do that sort of thing?*

She sat up and switched on the lamp beside her bed. "What did you let someone do, Mamma? Or a whole lot of someones?"

Her mother's face, forever young, smiled from the frame on the dressing table.

What was it like to be married when you were only fifteen? And to a man twice your age? Did you love him, or did you just want something from him? What did you want—a home? Babies? Or something else?

At six-thirty, still sleepless and knowing everyone on the ranch would be awake, she managed to stretch the phone cord inside her room and shut the door.

"Cece, what in the world..." Coralee's voice,

tinged with panic, didn't even make Celeste feel guilty.

"Tell me about Mamma, Sister."

"What are you talking about?"

"Why did she marry Daddy when she was fifteen? Did she have to?"

Static crackled along the line, but it didn't mask Coralee's silence.

"She did, didn't she?"

"Yes."

"Did she love him?"

"I don't know."

"Did he love her?"

"Yes."

"Did she love us?"

"Yes."

"And Daddy loved her so much that he took me just to get her back."

"She was a good mother, Cece. She took good care of us."

"You're not like her, and neither am I."

Coralee's voice seemed purposefully muffled. "Ben and I were never together until we married."

"And I'm going to be the same way. He's not going to…I'd never let him…"

"Did Kent try something?"

"Things just got a little out of hand last week."

"But you still want to be with him."

"I think so. No, I'm sure I do."

"Be careful, sweetie."

"Don't you worry about me. I know how to take care of myself."

"Do you want me to come down this afternoon?"

"No, I'm all right. I just had to know about Mamma."

"Nobody's perfect, Cece. She did the best she could. And I can't imagine not having you."

"I love you, too, Sister."

"I'll call you tomorrow night, okay?"

"Sure, okay."

After sneaking the phone back to the stand in the hall, Celeste locked herself in her room again and crawled back into bed. At eight-thirty, mostly out of habit, but also galvanized by the fact that Kent would be waiting for her, she got up again and began to dress for church.

Chapter Nine

On Sunday night, lulled by the memories of a Sunday afternoon spent at the Royal in the circle of Kent's arm, Celeste slept better. The next morning, since she didn't hear her father stirring, she left breakfast in the warming oven and caught the bus at the corner.

The piece of toast she'd eaten turned to a boulder in her stomach when she saw Claudia Peters waiting outside the employee entrance. "Good morning, Claudia." Celeste tried to step past the other girl, who blocked her way.

"I'm only going to tell you this one time—stay away from my boyfriend. Stay away from Kenny."

Celeste could almost taste the garish red lipstick on the mouth that spoke scarcely an inch from her face. Her knees went weak, but she straightened her back. "We're going to be late clocking in," she said.

"You only get one warning, *Miss* Riley. You better pay attention, or you'll be sorry."

Celeste sidestepped the slight body that seemed larger and more menacing as it quivered with rage, and slipped through the door. She shied away as the door opened behind her, but it was Veda. "I heard what she said. What was she talking about?"

Celeste took her time card from the rack and inserted it into the machine before she said, "She and Kent went to high school together in Brownwood. She has the idea he's her boyfriend."

"So that's why she's here. Does Kent know?"

"Yes."

"And?"

"And he says he's not her boyfriend. Never was. I've got to go, Veda." Celeste's new pumps clicked on the bare wooden risers of the stairs as she fled to the safety of the office.

Half way up, Veda caught her arm. "Listen, Cece, you don't know him, not really. You don't know what he did before you met him."

"He's nice to me. I like him."

"Okay, but be careful."

"I've got to go, Veda. If you brought your lunch, come upstairs and eat with me."

****

"I hear you had a little problem this morning," Mr. Thomas said as Celeste returned the ledgers to the safe at four o'clock.

Thinking about going downstairs and running into Claudia again on her way out, Celeste had only picked at the raw vegetables and cheese and crackers she'd packed for lunch, and now her stomach rumbled embarrassingly. When she bent over the safe, she felt dizzy, and the necessity of answering Mr. Thomas's question didn't help.

"Would you like to tell me about it?"

"No, sir." Celeste straightened and began to clear her desk.

"Well, you don't have to, because Miss Sawyer did."

"She shouldn't have done that."

"I disagree. I'm responsible for the profitability of this store, and if my employees don't work to capacity, losing money is inevitable. Everyone has to get along in order to do his or her job."

"I'm sorry."

"It doesn't appear that you have anything to be sorry about, Miss Riley. Threats are unacceptable anywhere and especially in the workplace. I'm going to let Miss Peters go."

"Please don't do that."

"Why?"

"Jobs still aren't that easy to find. I wouldn't want to be responsible for anyone losing one."

"She's not doing hers here very well. Perhaps something else would be a better fit."

"I'll come in early so we won't run into each other."

"That doesn't seem like a fair arrangement for you."

"Please, Mr. Thomas, let me try to work things out."

The chair protested as he leaned back and looked at her over his rimless glasses. "If you're determined, I'll give things a while. But you understand I won't give them forever."

"No, sir."

He glanced at his watch. "Then go on, now, before the girls on the floor start closing out their registers."

Celeste gathered up her coat and purse and left without another word.

****

She knew it was only a matter of time before Claudia figured out she was coming in early to avoid her. By Friday, the girl was waiting at the back door again. "Trying to get me fired is a pretty lowdown trick," she hissed, her penciled brows coming together over her nose.

"I didn't..."

"And so is telling the other girls how awful I am. I have to work with them."

"Veda heard you threatening me on Monday."

"Oh, I know, but you put her up to spreading the word."

A feeling of weariness started in Celeste's toes and crept to her knees and shoulders. "I don't want to fight with you, Claudia."

"I told you to leave Kenny alone, and I meant it.

You better listen."

Celeste tried to move past her, but Claudia's fingers closed around her upper arm, her long painted nails digging sharply into Celeste's flesh even through her thick red coat. "Leave him alone. We were all right until you came along."

"Please take your hand off my arm."

"Please take your hand off my arm," Claudia mimicked in a high, sing-song voice. "Little Miss Holier-Than-Thou." But she dropped her hand.

Upstairs in the empty office, Celeste sank into her chair and buried her face in her hands. *I don't need this, any of it. I'm not even sure Kent is worth it. I wish I'd never bought that dress or gone to the dance. I'm going to get out of here. Get another job in another town. Leave Daddy and his bottle, and Kent and Claudia and...*

"Miss Riley."

Her head came up with a jerk that made her neck twinge. "Good morning, Mr. Thomas," she said, hating the unsteadiness in her voice.

"Is everything all right?"

"Yes, sir." Celeste rose and took off her coat. "Everything is just fine."

****

By noon on Saturday, while she waited for her bus, she had almost made up her mind not to go to the Canteen that night. But by the time she stepped off the bus a block from her house, she knew she couldn't stay away.

Thinking of Kent and hoping that her father had already drunk himself into a stupor, she unlocked the kitchen door and stepped inside. The unexpected blow that landed across her shoulders sent her reeling into the sharp edge of the cupboard. She tasted blood.

"Whore! Slut!" August Riley's open hand slashed Celeste's bleeding cheek.

She threw up her hands to shield her face. "Daddy, don't!"

He advanced, backing her against the sink. This time his fist connected with her jaw. The sound as much as the force triggered nausea. She turned, retching into the sink. "Get out of my house! Get out, and don't come back!" He raised his fist to strike her again, then whirled and stumbled away.

Celeste heaved again before falling into a chair at the kitchen table. As she reached for a paper napkin to stanch the blood on her cheek, her eyes fixed on the single sheet of torn notepaper imprinted with Claudia's bright red lipstick.

Just thought you'd want to know your daughter is sleeping with my boyfriend.

****

Behind the locked bathroom door, Celeste bathed her face in cold water and inspected it in the mirror over the sink. The gash above her right eyebrow wasn't deep, but it would most certainly leave a scar. She dabbed it with peroxide and noticed the beginnings of a bruise around her eye. A cut could be easily explained away, but not a black eye. *Why did you do it, Claudia? Is this what you wanted?*

She locked her bedroom door and slid the dresser across it before collapsing onto the bed. Pulling the quilt over her face, she listened to her father screaming her mother's name, over and over and over again. Somewhere a door slammed, and then there was only empty silence.

When she woke later, the room was dark. She switched on the lamp to see the time. Six o'clock. She was due at the Canteen in half an hour. She tried to remember whether she was making sandwiches or arranging tables. It didn't matter. She couldn't go.

When she moved the dresser, the muscles in her shoulders screamed. At least nothing was broken, but she knew she could count on being sore, probably for several days. She maneuvered the phone into her room and dialed Mrs. Lowe's number.

"It must have been something I ate," she said. "I've been throwing up all afternoon."

"I understand, dear. Just take care of yourself, and I'll see you at church tomorrow if you're able to come."

Celeste crept around the house in the dark, listening for her father. The single bulb left burning in the open, empty garage explained the lack of sound or movement in the house. Even so, she locked the bathroom door before lowering her aching body into a tub of water as hot as she could stand. While she dried herself, she checked her face in the mirror again and gasped. She could stay home from church on Sunday, but she had to go to work the following day. Wishing wouldn't heal her face by then.

****

She slept late on Sunday morning and woke to a gnawing hunger. Wrestling the dresser aside one more time, she tiptoed into the kitchen. From the window above the sink, she saw the garage still sat empty. Relieved, she put on the coffeepot and scrambled some eggs. Back in her room, she locked but didn't barricade the door and sat down by the window to eat her breakfast.

The afternoon wore on in an odd, lonely-but-comforting way. She treated herself to another hot bath, which eased the stiffness and pain in her shoulders, if only temporarily, but she took only a cursory glance at her face, knowing it looked the same. She had just finished her library book when she heard the doorbell.

The look that spread over Kent's face when she opened the door changed from anticipation to horror. "My God, Velvet!"

She turned her face away. "You shouldn't be

here, Kent."

The latch came loose from the door facing as he jerked open the screen door and grabbed her.

"Kent, you can't stay." She twisted to free herself from his hands wrapping her upper arms.

"Where's your father?"

"I don't know."

"He did this, didn't he?"

She shook her head.

With one hand, he cupped her face and turned her toward him. Pushing back the collar of her blouse, he saw part of the bruise on her shoulder. When she winced at his touch, his hands flew up as if they'd been burned. "That bastard beat you up!"

She cringed at the word. "Just leave, Kent. You'll only make it worse."

"Fine, I'll leave, but you're coming with me."

"I can't. Where would I go?"

"Anywhere. Get the key to the store and lock yourself in the lounge." He pulled her against him and stroked her hair. "When you didn't show up last night, I asked Mrs. Lowe about you, and she said you were sick."

"That's what I told her."

"And then when you didn't come to church, I got worried." He held her away from him again, this time with more care. "Why did he do this?"

She shook her head.

"Do you know?"

She shook her head again.

"You're lying, Velvet. I talked to Veda, and she told me about your run-in with Claudia. Did she have anything to do with this?"

Celeste tried to pull away.

"She did, didn't she? By God, I'll..."

"It's done. You're going to graduate and leave in a couple of weeks, and then she'll probably leave, too."

"Tell me what she did."

"I can't."

"Then I'll ask her."

Celeste let her head fall back against his shoulder. "She must have found out where I live. There was a note on the kitchen table." She stopped and pressed her lips together.

"What did it say? Something about me? About us?"

Celeste nodded.

He cradled her against him, his lips against her hair. "Go get your coat, Velvet. We'll get out of here, for a little while, at least."

Kent was trying to push the latch back into the splintered wood when she came out of her bedroom. At the same time, her father burst through the swinging door from the kitchen and grabbed her arm. "I told you to get out, you whore, but you just brought that lousy sonofabitch you're sleeping with here into my house!" He shoved her against the wall hard enough to tilt the pictures hanging there.

Celeste watched as Kent sprang to his feet. "Don't you touch her." The way his lips pulled back from his teeth reminded her of a snarling dog. "Don't you ever touch her again, you lousy, filthy bastard!"

He hurtled across the room, all but on top of August Riley before he finished speaking. When his hands closed around her father's throat, Celeste threw herself against him. "Stop it, Kent! Stop it! You'll get yourself into trouble you can't get out of. Please, stop!"

She wasn't sure when he turned loose or how she got him out of the house and down the sidewalk to the street. The harsh sound of her father's rage followed them until they turned the corner, but she didn't care, as long as they were leaving it behind.

Chapter Ten

"You can't go back there," Kent said. "We'll find a pay phone and call your sister."

"It's not that easy, Kent."

"She'd be up here in a minute if she knew what happened."

"I don't want her to know."

"Why not, for pity's sake? She's your sister. You can't be thinking about going back to that house tonight."

"Just for tonight. I'll figure something out."

"He'll kill you."

"I don't think so. He's got a reputation to protect."

"Dad tanned my britches a time or two, but he never beat me."

"Daddy never spanked Coralee and me when we were growing up. After she left, he mostly just ignored me."

"What would make him believe you were doing things you shouldn't be?"

"I don't know." *I do know, but I'm not going to tell you. You're the last person I'd tell. I'm not my mother, but you'd probably think so. You don't really know who I am, any more than I know who you are.*

"Look, go back after dark and pack a suitcase. I'll wait for you. There's got to be a cheap hotel where you could spend the night. I've got a little extra money this month."

"I can lock my door and put the dresser in front of it again. I'll be all right. I don't want you coming back to the house with me. He might call the police, and then you'd really be in trouble."

"Let him. I don't care."

"You know you do. You've come this far. Why would you want to sit out the war in a military jail?"

"You could go to the police and show them what he did."

"No."

"I don't know why you want to protect him."

"I'm protecting myself."

"I don't understand that."

No, and you won't, either.

"Is there anything open on Sunday? A coffee shop or a soda fountain?"

"There might be something on Main. I think I've seen the light on in a little place on Sundays. It's not too far." She tucked her hand through his arm, more for security than warmth.

****

They sat drinking coffee in the tiny café until dusk, when the owner said she was closing up. "Don't like to run off a soldier and his girl, but I gotta get home to my own kids." She eyed Celeste. "What happened to you, honey?"

"I fell," Celeste said and added, "I was trying to change a light bulb, and the chair tipped over. I hit the cabinet on the way down."

"You need to be careful. You could've done a lot worse."

"I told her that," Kent said. "I should've been there." He paid the ticket, and Celeste slipped some extra change under her saucer for a tip. "I don't feel good about this," he said as they started back toward Spaulding Street.

"You've got to get back to the base."

"I'm already late."

"Will you be in trouble?"

"They won't hang me. Besides, I doubt they've even missed me. Things are pretty loose on Sunday afternoons."

"How will you get back? It's too far to walk."

He grinned. "I have a buddy who has a girl here, and if I know him, he's still at her house. I'll just give him a call and get him to pick me up."

At the end of the block, he took her in his arms again. "Promise me you won't spend another night there after tonight."

"Promise." *But I will. What else can I do?*

"I love you, Velvet."

She nodded against him. "Thank you."

"That's an odd thing to say."

"I just meant it feels good to know you care about me."

"I hope you're right about Claudia leaving after I'm gone, but meanwhile, stay out of her way."

"I'm trying."

****

After several long kisses, she left him standing on the sidewalk and walked the rest of the way home. Skirting the front, she climbed in through the bedroom window she'd left unlocked. Then she barricaded her door again and sat down on the bed. *Kent doesn't understand. Where could I go besides here? Veda says there's hardly a room to be had in town these days, with both bases filling up. Maybe she'll know of something, though I doubt it. At least I won't have to explain my face to her, but...oh, Lord, how am I going to explain it to Mr. Thomas?*

****

She caught the early-morning downtown bus and let herself into the building with the key she'd meant to get rid of but was glad she hadn't. In the employee lounge, she set the coffeepot on the gas ring and curled up on the shabby couch to wait until she could clock in. Veda found her huddled over a cup of coffee gone cold.

"Celeste, honey, what happened?"

"I'd rather not talk about it."

Veda sat down beside her and pushed her hair back to inspect her face. "You'll have to do some fast talking when Mr. Thomas sees you."

"I was wondering…you know a lot about makeup. Is there anything I could put on this?"

"I think that black eye is beyond hiding, kid, but I'll see what I can find on the floor. Does it hurt?"

"Some."

"It was your father, wasn't it?"

Celeste put her lips together.

"Oh, come on, Celeste, everybody knows about him."

The words jerked Celeste from her apathy. "How do they know?"

"He's a bigwig at the bank. People know him. They know what he does."

"You never let on to me."

"Of course I didn't. Why would I want to hurt your feelings? Listen, you've got to move out. I wish I still needed a roommate, but I'll ask around and see what I can turn up. Does Kent know?"

"He came over yesterday afternoon. I thought…Veda, I really thought he was going to kill Daddy."

"Any man who'd beat up on a woman, much less his own daughter, would've deserved what he got, but it wouldn't have done Kent any good. I'll go see if I can find something to patch you up a little, but you're not going to fool the boss."

A few minutes later, Paul Thomas walked into the lounge behind Veda. Her mouth twisted. "Sorry, kid, he saw me poking around behind the cosmetic counter."

"Let me see your face, Miss Riley."

Celeste turned her head away. "I'm all right, sir."

"Your face, Miss Riley."

She complied.

"I want you to go over to my doctor's office in the McBurnett Building. I'll call and tell him you're coming."

"No, please, I'm all right. Really I am."

"I can't force you to go, but…your father did this, I presume."

Celeste glanced at Veda and frowned. She threw up her hands. "I didn't tell him anything."

"Why did he do it? Not that there's any justification for physical violence against a woman."

"He found out I was seeing Kent." *It's only half a lie.*

"I see. Does Kent know?"

"He came over yesterday."

"Well." The man seemed to be considering his next words. "I'll drive you home after work. My wife will go in with you and help you pack. You can stay in our guest room until you find something." He held up his hand as Celeste opened her mouth to protest. "And if I have to make that a condition of keeping your job here, I will."

****

Kent called at noon. "I've only got a few minutes, Velvet. Are you okay? I hope I'm not getting you into trouble calling you at work."

She told him about Mr. Thomas's edict.

"That takes a load off my mind then. You didn't run into Claudia this morning, did you?"

"I don't want you to say anything to her, Kent. It won't help."

"Somebody needed to take a strap to her years ago, but I guess it's too late now."

"I've been thinking about how mad you got at Daddy."

"I admit I lost control for a second."

"It was more than that. I thought you were going to kill him."

"I thought about it."

"You don't mean that…do you?"

"Well, not literally, but I was so mad when I saw what he'd done to you."

"I never thought I'd see you act like that."

"What did you want me to do, Velvet?" The fury in his voice came through the phone. "Smile and shake hands with him?"

"No, but…"

"Look, I told you, I'm a man, not a kid like you dated in high school. And if you knew much about them, you'd probably find a fight or two in their backgrounds, too."

"You think I'm still a little girl."

"Are you trying to pick a fight with me?"

"No. But what you did yesterday scared me as much as Daddy did."

"I'm not sure I like that comparison."

"I'm not… I'm sorry… I just meant…"

"I'll try to get a pass sometime this week. Things are winding down a little now that we're getting ready to take exams. I'll call you again tomorrow, if it's okay."

"Mr. Thomas went home to lunch. He's probably telling his wife about this mess. I'm so embarrassed."

"It's a mess all right, but it's not your fault, and you're going to get out of it pretty quick. Listen, I've got to go. I love you."

Celeste made a sound of what she hoped signaled agreement and said goodbye.

****

At three-thirty, Coralee burst into the office, with Ben following, and wrapped Celeste in her arms. "Oh, sweetie, oh, what did he do to you?"

"Mary and I discussed everything at noon and made the decision to call your sister," Paul Thomas said. "We felt it was best."

Coralee patted and caressed Celeste like she would a child, murmuring reassurances and reproaches in the same breath. "You should have called us when it happened."

"We're taking you to the ranch for a few days," Ben said.

"I have to work. You know that."

Mr. Thomas shook his head. "You have some time coming, Miss Riley. My wife can help me with the books. She used to do it before our family came along."

"But the payroll's due."

"Mary was doing payroll before you were born."

"You're coming home with us tonight," Coralee said. "That's all there is to it."

"I want you to leave now," Mr. Thomas said. "Go home and pack before your father gets there."

Suddenly too tired to argue, Celeste took her coat from the closet and let herself be shuttled down the stairs and out the back door. Claudia, smoking a cigarette in the alley, smirked as Celeste passed her.

****

Ben brought boxes from the grocery market. Coralee and Celeste had one left to pack when Kent showed up. "I don't know how he did it, but your boss got me an instant pass," he said, reaching for Celeste's hand. "I ran into your brother-in-law outside, and he said I could bring some boxes out to the truck if you have them ready."

Coralee glanced up. "So you're Prince Dreamboat."

Celeste gasped. "Sister!"

"It's okay." Kent winked at her and then at Coralee. "Only problem is, you're the one carrying off the princess instead of me."

"I'll be back, Kent." Celeste moved closer to him.

Coralee muttered something that sounded like *over my dead body.*

"Better make it soon, Velvet. Two more weeks, and I'm gone. We got the word right after I talked to you."

Celeste blinked back tears. "Do you know where?"

"The big bombing's going on in Europe."

"Oh, Kent."

He pulled her into his arms. "It's okay. I'll have some leave to go home before we ship out They won't put us on a boat right off the bat. We'll have some time together."

"Take these," Coralee said, indicating four soap boxes stacked on the cedar chest.

Kent let Celeste go. "Sure."

"Be careful. They're full of breakables."

He winked at Celeste again. "I'll treat them like I do my bombsite—like pure gold."

****

Ben suggested supper before hitting the road and invited Kent to come along. "But you'll have to ride in the back with the boxes."

"No colder than a cockpit at thirty thousand feet, or so I understand."

Coralee stuffed Celeste in the middle and crawled in after her, slamming the door. "Maybe you shouldn't get involved, sweetie. He's leaving soon, and what he's going to do isn't the safest job in the world."

"He'll be back," Celeste said, though a knot of fear had formed in the pit of her stomach. "He will, Sister."

"I hope so, for your sake."

Ben reached across her to pat Coralee's knee. "I like him."

"I don't like anybody right now," Coralee snapped. "It's a good thing we missed Daddy."

****

Kent and Celeste held hands under the table

while they ate supper at Twin Gables. Celeste wished her sister would warm to Kent as Ben had, but she had to settle for polite. "I can get back to the base," Kent said as they emerged into dropping temperatures.

"You sure?" Ben asked.

"Somebody's always going out that way this time of day. I'll hitch a ride. Just drop me in front of Ma Goodwin's."

Coralee's eyebrows went up.

"It's an okay place," Kent said. "And busy. Almost like a station or something."

When Ben stopped in front of the popular nightspot, which was already filling up, Coralee let Celeste out of the truck to say goodbye.

"They'll take care of you," Kent said as he took Celeste far enough away so they couldn't be heard.

"I've taken care of myself since I was eleven," Celeste said.

"I know, but you need somebody. I wish you needed me." He curled a strand of her hair around the tip of one finger.

"I do need you, Kent."

"I don't think you do, not yet. Not like I need you." He kissed her forehead. "But I can wait."

"Promise me you'll stay away from Daddy."

"Him and Claudia both. I sure hope you're right about her leaving after I do."

"She can't do anything more to me than she's already done."

"Don't count on it." His lips drifted down past her bruises to her chin. "I promise I'll see you before I take off for good."

"I'm coming back before you leave the base, if I can find a place to stay."

"That might not be so easy."

"I'll find something."

"You looking for a ride, soldier?" An older man

in a thick twill jacket and sweat-stained felt hat motioned to Kent.

"Yeah, thanks. Just a second." Kent held Celeste against him. "Gotta go, Velvet. I'll see you. I'll see you every night in my dreams, wearing that blue velvet dress and smiling at me." He brushed her lips gently, trying to avoid the bruise that had spread almost to her chin. "I'm meant to have you, just like you were meant to have that dress." He kissed her again, harder this time. "You take care, you hear?"

Celeste wanted to cry as she watched him sprint for the battered truck where the other man waited. But, though it occurred to her that watching him hanging out the window, waving as the truck rattled away, might be the last time she'd see him, something inside her hurt too much for tears. She waved once more before she walked back to Coralee and Ben.

Chapter Eleven

No one talked much on the drive to Sterling City and not at all about what had happened to Celeste or about Kent. Pearl put her lips together in a tight line when she saw Celeste, but she didn't say anything except, "Your room is ready, honey." Coralee went up with her and saw her settled, kissed her goodnight, and left.

At breakfast the next morning, Big Ben weighed in. "You can't go back, Celeste, at least not to live in your father's house. We'd all like for you to stay here."

"I have to work." Celeste didn't meet his eyes.

"Understood, but it's not like you'll go without if you don't work for a while."

Pearl kept Celeste busy all day, helping with the cooking in progress, sorting quilt squares, ironing pillowcases, tablecloths, and napkins, even dusting the little-used dining room. No one said anything else about her going or staying.

Kent called that night. "I got the number from information. Hope nobody minds."

Celeste noticed that the kitchen emptied out, leaving her alone to talk. "Nobody minds."

"How're you doing, Velvet?"

"Okay. How about you?"

"I found out we'll be graduating at the Roof Garden, and there'll be a dance afterward."

"I wish I could be there."

"I do, too. Maybe it'll work out."

"What am I going to do, Kent? I don't want to lose my job."

"That's one of the reasons I called. One of the guys in my squadron—his wife came with him and has a room over on Preusser that she'll be giving up next week."

"There's probably a long waiting list."

"Well, there is, but he called his wife and sort of explained the situation and she talked to her landlady."

"Oh, Kent, I didn't want it spread all over town."

"Wait a minute, Velvet, it's not all over town. No names, no details, just that you need a place. Anyway, it's all arranged. You can have the room if you'll call the landlady first thing in the morning and send her the first week's rent. Seven-fifty a week."

"That's a lot." She thought of the five dollars she gave her father each week and did some quick calculations.

"Yeah, but you get kitchen privileges. You can eat cheap and not starve."

"I don't know." Celeste, her knees wobbling out of control, sank into the nearest chair.

"My friend says it's a nice room, furnished and all that, and the landlady's friendly, too. The city bus stops at the end of the block."

"I don't know," Celeste repeated.

"Velvet, it's a sweet deal, and it's the only one you're going to get. There'll be a new class coming in here right after graduation, and there aren't enough rooms in town to hold all the wives coming along with their husbands. My friend says that women are already sharing four deep around town."

Celeste almost dropped the phone as the necessity of making a decision, the biggest decision she'd ever made in her life, swept over her, leaving her weak.

"Look, I can give her the seven-fifty tomorrow if you want the room."

"I…"

"What are you going to do? Sit in Sterling City for the rest of your life? Go back home and let your father beat you up again?"

"Don't yell at me." Celeste burst into tears.

"I'm not yelling. Well, maybe I am, but I love you, Celeste. I want you to be happy, but right now, I just want you safe. I hate the idea I can't stay here and take care of you."

"I ought to talk it over with Coralee."

"Why? It's not her life. She's doing okay."

"Why are you being so mean to me?"

"You think I'm being mean just because I found you a good place to stay so you can keep your job? Listen, I talked to a guy from Sterling City. He says there aren't any jobs there. Come on, Velvet, this is a good deal."

"It's a big decision."

"You're a big girl now, aren't you?"

"I don't know. I guess so. I…"

"Yes or no, Velvet?"

Her breath came faster, and she could feel her heart beating beneath her sweater. Kent was right. There were no jobs here, and she didn't know anybody except Coralee and Ben and his parents. It was a dead end, like Kent said, so why was it so hard to decide? *I've never been on my own before, not really. Daddy didn't take care of me, but he was there. I like my job. I'd miss the church and Veda and Marilyn and the rest. I know I'm welcome here, but I don't want to be the poor relation. I don't want to depend on Big Ben and Pearl for what I need.*

Her fingers began to cramp from clutching the telephone receiver so tightly. "Okay. Yes."

"Good girl." The approval in Kent's voice warmed her. "I'll tell the woman you don't know exactly when you'll move in, but she won't care, not if she's got her money. Listen, there's a line waiting to use the phone, so I've got to go. I'll call you again tomorrow night." His voice dropped to a whisper. "Love you, Velvet."

"I love you, too." She wasn't sure she'd spoken the words aloud before she heard a click breaking the connection.

****

Only Coralee expressed reservations about Celeste's decision. "I was counting on having you here for a little while," she said, her mouth trembling.

"She'll be back for Christmas," Ben said. "Won't you, little sister?"

Celeste nodded.

"Are you sure Kent didn't talk you into something you don't want to do?" Coralee said.

"He… No, it's the only thing to do…isn't it?"

"You know you're welcome here," Big Ben said.

"I know, but my job… I don't want to lose my job."

"And there aren't any here," Ben said, cutting off Coralee's reply. "She'll be fine, Coralee sweetheart. August Riley isn't going to risk his job by breaking and entering. Besides, he won't even know where she is."

"Preusser is pretty close to Spaulding," Coralee argued, "and who knows what he'll do when he's drunk."

"Don't borrow trouble," Pearl said. "I think a chance to be on her own is exactly what Celeste needs. And we're not that far away if she needs us."

Maybe she's right. Kent thinks I'm doing the right thing. Celeste took a deep breath. "I'll be okay, Sister. Really, I will."

****

"I'm proud of you," Kent said when he called the next night. "You're going to like being independent. It's a good feeling."

"It's scary, if you really want to know."

"I'll be here a while longer, and your sister's only a phone call away."

****

Ben and Coralee drove her back to San Angelo and helped carry her things upstairs to the small back room overlooking a trashcan-filled alley. Coralee stripped the bed and remade it with the sheets, blanket, and chenille spread Pearl had packed. Ben took down the empty curtain rods over the venetian blinds so Celeste could hang the sky-blue sheers Pearl had helped her sew just the day before.

"It's all right, I guess," Coralee said as she put four hooked rugs on the bare hardwood floor. "It's clean, anyway."

"I could go get her furniture," Ben said.

Celeste shook her head. "No. Daddy might say you stole it."

"He wouldn't dare," Coralee snapped. "But we'll talk about that later. You might find something better than this." She opened the box in which Pearl had packed half a dozen thick towels and washcloths.

"Those were for Barbara's hope chest," Celeste murmured.

"She's five years old," Coralee said. "She'll have more than she needs when she gets married."

"Which won't be until she's thirty-five," Ben said and grinned.

Their laughter broke the tension. A few minutes later Mrs. Clay, the landlady, came upstairs. "Your young man called. He was in a hurry but wanted to make sure you got here all right. He said he'd see you at the Canteen on Saturday night."

"Thank you for taking the message," Celeste said.

"Can't do too much for our boys," Mrs. Clay said,

her face suddenly shadowed. "I lost a brother in the first big war, and his sons are in this one. You need anything?"

"She's fine," Coralee said. "But I'd like to leave you my name and telephone number, just in case."

****

Everyone at Woolworth welcomed Celeste back. If the girls on the floor, besides Veda, knew why she'd been gone, they didn't mention it. Claudia kept her distance, but Celeste thought she looked pleased with herself.

"I've already given Miss Peters a warning," Mr. Thomas said after greeting Celeste in the upstairs office.

"Maybe you shouldn't have done that."

"You're not to come in early to avoid her."

"I think she's already figured that out."

"How's your young man?"

"He'll be graduating soon."

"What about your new room?"

"It's very nice."

"You'll be all right, Miss Riley. Please don't forget that Mary and I are here if you need anything."

Celeste sat down and opened the daybook. "Thank you, Mr. Thomas. I'll be fine now."

Chapter Twelve

Veda helped her shop for a formal to wear to the graduation ceremony and dance. "I shouldn't spend the money," Celeste protested while she tried on dresses at Levine's.

"Sure you should. You admitted you had some saved up. This is exactly what you were saving it for."

"Kent likes for me to wear the blue velvet dress."

"It's not formal enough." Veda said as Celeste emerged wearing a black dress with a lace bodice that came to a V just below the waist. "But this one is. You look terrific."

With something akin to fear, Celeste looked at herself in the full-length mirror. "I don't even look like myself."

"You look grown up."

"Have you been talking to Kent?"

"No, why?"

"He said I needed to grow up."

"Well, that's exactly how you look. We'll pull your hair back and up on each side with some eighth-inch velvet ribbon, and I have some mid-length black gloves." Veda adjusted the neck and short sleeves. "This is very modest, too."

"I didn't dare look at the price tag."

Veda reached for the piece of pink cardboard dangling from the back of the bodice. "Thirty-eight ninety-five."

Celeste stiffened. "Veda, that's…"

"Do you have that much in the bank or not?"

Celeste nodded.

"Is your Christmas layaway paid out?"

"One more payment."

"Do you want to make Kent proud?"

"You know the answer to that."

Veda squared her shoulders in triumph. "She'll take it," she said to the saleswoman waiting near by.

****

The instant she glimpsed Kent in his dress uniform, waiting with the other members of his class, Celeste put away her last regret at dipping into her nest egg to buy the dress. He signaled her with his eyes—eyes shining with pride for her as much as for his own accomplishment. As she slipped into a chair and folded her gloved hands in her lap, her lips relaxed in a smile.

When the ceremonies were over, Kent found her in the crowd. "You look beautiful, Velvet."

"Veda said the blue velvet dress wasn't formal enough for tonight."

"You look so grown up I can hardly realize it's you." He touched one lace sleeve and let his hand slide down her arm to circle her wrist.

"I wanted you to be proud of me tonight." *The way you're looking at me is worth every penny I took out of my savings account.*

He leaned closer. "I love you, Velvet. The dancing will start as soon as they clear the floor. I can't wait to hold you in my arms, hold you like I can't do at the Canteen."

She shivered and dropped her eyes.

****

Kent had arranged a ride for both of them back to her boarding house. "I can't stay," he said, as he walked her to the door. "And I have to leave tomorrow."

"Tomorrow? Oh, Kent, I thought you'd be here another few days."

"We have to clear out to make room for the next

class. But I'll call you from Brownwood."

"I'm sorry your family couldn't come tonight."

"I'm not. Neil is taking exams, and Mother doesn't drive on the highway. Anyway, I didn't want to have to look after them instead of being with you." He folded her in his arms. "I love you so much, Velvet. I wish we were married, and this was our house so we could go in together...go upstairs."

She felt her face grow hot.

His hands slipped down her shoulders to her back, and pressed her against him. "Someday," he murmured, kissing the tip of her ear. "Someday."

"After the war."

"I hope it won't be that long." He moved his lips along the line of her jaw toward her chin, then up to her mouth. "You're all I'll ever want, Velvet, and I want you so much."

Only later, after she'd hung up her dress and gotten under the covers, did she let herself think of the long, passionate kiss they'd shared before Kent went back to his ride waiting at the curb. His hands on her back under her coat, his warm breath on her neck, his lips possessing hers as they never had before, stirred a longing in her for something she now recognized and understood.

Hugging the extra pillow to her breast, she let the longing fill her. *Kent, oh, Kent, how I wish you were here with me. I understand now about wanting...and I want you, too, so much...so much.*

****

"I've got thirty days, as it turns out," Kent said when he called from Brownwood the next night. "I'll make sure Mother and Neil are okay, and maybe I can get back down there to see you before I ship out."

"I hope so, Kent. Do you know where you're going?"

"Europe. The bombers fly out of bases all over England."

"I wish you didn't have to go."

"The sooner we go and get this thing over with, the better."

"I'll write to you every night."

"And send me a picture? One in the blue velvet dress?"

"I'll get one made as soon as I can."

"I love you, Velvet, and when I come home, well, we'll just pretend all the bad things never happened."

She sat holding the phone long after he'd hung up. *Pretend all the bad things never happened. Mamma didn't run off and end up with me. Daddy didn't hit me. The man I love isn't going to war and maybe get killed.*

The blue velvet curtain filled her dreams that night. When she woke the next morning, she only remembered the silence beyond it.

****

Mrs. Clay had shown her where to look for her mail on the long foyer table. "You already know about the phone in the little closet under the stairs. You'll have plenty of privacy."

Celeste blushed, but when Kent called again on Saturday night, she welcomed the seclusion. "I think about you all the time," he said.

"I think about you, too."

"But not all the time."

"Well, not at work."

"I don't have much to do here. Neil's sort of taken over."

"That's good, isn't it?"

"Oh, sure. Makes me feel good that he can do it."

"How is your mother?"

"Not very happy about me shipping out."

"Neither am I."

"I'm going to try to hitch a ride up next weekend and meet you at the Canteen.""Where will you stay?"

"With a friend's aunt. She said anytime I wanted to bunk there, it was okay." His voice dropped. "I want to hold you again, Velvet."

She tried to stop the feelings threatening to take her over. "It'll be safer at the Canteen," she said.

"I don't like that, but it'll have to do. Have you had any trouble with Claudia?"

"Not since Mr. Thomas warned her not to bother me."

"She doesn't listen very well. I hope she'll leave pretty soon."

"I guess I do, too, but she's not bothering me."

"I wish I could kiss you right now. I'd start at your forehead and move down. Nibble your ears and your neck."

Celeste felt her face grow hot.

"You're so nice to kiss, Velvet."

"Next weekend maybe, if you can get a ride."

"At least we'll have your room for some privacy."

"That's not a good idea, Kent. Besides, my landlady told me in no uncertain terms that she doesn't allow men upstairs."

"She didn't tell me that."

"Did you ask her?"

"No, just about calling."

"We don't need the chance to get carried away."

"We could get married."

"Married!"

"That way I'd know you'd be waiting for me."

"You should know that now."

He blew out his breath in a long sigh.

"I don't want a hurried-up wedding, Kent. I want a real wedding someday. A honeymoon that lasts more than a weekend. A marriage that lasts more than a few days."

"Isn't a few days better than nothing at all? What if…"

"You'll come back, Kent. I know you will."

****

By noon the following Saturday, Celeste's excitement at seeing Kent again had reached a fever pitch. Then she ran into Claudia in the corridor on her way out. "I thought you should see this," Claudia said, pulling a framed picture from a paper bag.

Celeste shook her head. "I don't think we should be talking."

"Then don't talk, but look. Look good." Claudia thrust the photograph in front of Celeste's face. A little boy, perhaps three or four years old and dressed in a sailor suit, smiled at the camera while clutching a model airplane. "This is my little boy, Jonny. Jonathan Kent Goddard, the Third."

Celeste grabbed for the wall to keep from toppling over. Then she rushed for the door as bile rose in her throat.

****

I won't go to the Canteen tonight. I'll call Mrs. Lowe and tell her I'm sick again. No, I can't do that. She'll think... No, she wouldn't think that. Or maybe she would. Oh, Kent, why did you do it? How could you have a child with that girl? Celeste sank down on the bench at the bus stop and tried to stop her mind from racing as fast as her heart.

No, I know how. You were on your way to the same thing with me the night we went to the store lounge. You said you were a man, and I was still a little girl because I wouldn't let you go any further. But you were wrong. You're the little boy, thinking about what you want and not about what happens to the girl.

As the bus rolled to a stop, the doors opened with a soft swoosh. Celeste stepped on and deposited her fare before taking a seat near the front. *Did you have a special name for Claudia? Did you tell her the things you've said to me, that you liked kissing her, that you just wanted to hold her?* She leaned her head against the window. *You aren't my prince after all. Coralee found hers, and I thought I'd found mine, but I was wrong. I was stupid to think that anybody who picked me up off the street and at a dance could be the right sort of man. I'm no better than Mamma, just lucky that I stopped in time before I ended up with a baby.*

****

By five o'clock, Celeste knew she would go to the Canteen, though she wasn't quite sure why. *Maybe Kent couldn't get a ride, so he won't be there. Even if he is, I don't have to meet him at the corner afterward. I don't have to talk to him and dance with him all evening. There are other soldiers who need company, and that's why I'm there, isn't it? To be nice to all the servicemen?*

She took the last bus back to Main Street. A scared, sick feeling engulfed her when she saw Kent waiting at the Canteen door as she stepped off the bus. She stiffened as he threw his arms around her. He stepped back immediately. "What's wrong, Velvet?"

"Why didn't you tell me about Claudia and you? About your little boy?"

She thought he looked like someone had knocked him back a few feet.

"Oh, my God, she didn't pull that, did she?"

"She showed me the picture of him. Jonathan Kent Goddard, the Third." Celeste glanced around at the other girls arriving. "I've got to go inside."

He caught her arm. "Not until we straighten this out."

"Let go of me."

He didn't. "You believe her? You believe I fathered her child?"

"What am I supposed to believe?"

"I told you—she let everybody."

"You're not everybody."

He dropped her arm. "You believe her and not me."

"I know what happened the night we went to the store lounge. I know the way you've touched me and kissed me, the things you've said."

"I told you I knew when to pull back, and it only happened once."

"You went way too far with me."

"I said I was sorry."

"Sorry for what? That you're a man, and I'm still a little girl?"

"I shouldn't have said that."

"You were right. You're a man, and you do the things a man does, only I thought you were different."

He looked at her for a long moment. "I thought you were different, too, Velvet." Then he turned and walked away into the dusk.

Veda found her crying in the bathroom and managed to elicit the information that it was over between Celeste and Kent but not why. "He's not the only fish in the sea," she said with a heartiness that Celeste didn't find comforting. "Wash your face and powder your nose, and go play on the beach."

When Veda had gone, Celeste stared at herself in the mirror. *You really hurt him. Maybe he deserved it and maybe he didn't, but it wasn't up to you to be his judge and jury. Even if he's not everything you wanted him to be, he's not a bad person, either. He made a mistake. And you made a mistake, too. Now he's gone, and so are you. Velvet's gone forever.*

Chapter Thirteen

Mrs. Clay didn't comment on Celeste's empty mail tray. Veda didn't ask questions when they ran into each other at work. Claudia's expression, like a cat replete with cream, made Celeste wonder if she knew what had happened between Kent and her.

The following Friday, Celeste paid out her Christmas layaway, managing to struggle onto the bus and finally up the stairs to her room with the huge box. Before she could open it, Mrs. Clay called her to the telephone.

"I'm sorry, Velvet."

Celeste's heart turned over at the sound of Kent's voice. "I'm sorry, too."

"Are you okay?"

"I'm all right."

"I'm not. That's the other thing I called to tell you."

"What's wrong?"

"My mother knows someone… Well, she's from a family that had pull in a lot of places. She's still got it, and she used it. I'm not shipping out with my squadron. I'm coming back to San Angelo as an instructor."

Relief washed over Celeste like a giant wave before she realized what his return would mean.

"I don't mind telling you I'm pretty teed off about it."

"Your mother just wanted to help."

"No, it's not like that. You wouldn't understand."

"Why?"

"She ran Dad's life, and she wants to run mine,

too."

"Oh."

"Anyway, I'm coming back after Christmas."

Celeste tried to think of something to say and couldn't.

"But I won't bother you if you still feel the same. I won't come to the Canteen or to church."

"I shouldn't have judged you."

"The boy isn't mine."

"All right."

"Do you believe me?"

"I want to."

"I love you, Velvet."

She wanted to say that she loved him, too, but the words stuck in her throat.

"Well, that's it, I guess. I just wanted you to know I'm coming back."

"Maybe you'll like being an instructor."

"I'd like being with my squadron better."

"At least you'll be safe."

"Training accidents happen. I'd rather buy it from German flak than with a wet-behind-the-ears student pilot."

A long, uncomfortable silence followed.

"When you get back," Celeste began, then stopped.

"When I get back, what?"

"I don't know, Kent. I'll see you sometime at the Canteen...or at church."

"You mean that?"

"Yes."

"I love you."

"I know."

"Well, goodnight."

"Goodnight, Kent."

She let the phone fall back into the cradle. *If he comes back...when he comes back, it'll be like it was before. I can't do anything about it. I couldn't make*

Daddy love me, and I can't make myself not love Kent. If only I hadn't seen that picture. Maybe it's really true that what you don't know doesn't hurt you.

Upstairs she began to wrap Christmas gifts, but her heart wasn't in preparations for the holiday. *Now Claudia will stay. I wonder if she has the little boy here with her? What does he do while she's at work? Has she told the other girls at Woolworth? Do they all know that I'm going out with the man she says is the father of her child?*

She laid down the scissors she'd just used to cut ribbon for Barbara's gift, a pair of pink pajamas with satin trim around the boat neck, and matching fuzzy pink slippers, and perched on the end of the bed. *Why is everything such a mess? If I hadn't gone back to look at that blue velvet dress after church...if I hadn't gone to the dance at the Roof Garden...*

She lay back against the two new pillows she'd found on sale in Hemphill-Wells' bargain basement. *I don't want Kent to go to war and get killed, but why couldn't he have been sent to instruct anywhere but here?*

****

Celeste hadn't told Coralee about her fight with Kent, but she did tell her he was coming back to San Angelo.

"You don't sound very excited about it."

"He's not happy that his mother pulled strings to keep him out of going overseas."

"I guess not. Ben wants to enlist, and Big Ben told him to follow his conscience, that we'd get along all right."

"Is he going to?"

"He knows I don't want him to."

"But you wouldn't do or say anything to keep him from doing what he felt was right."

"No. I told him I'd support whatever decision he

made."

"Good for you."

"It wouldn't be good for me if he got himself killed, but I love him too much to fight him on it. Pearl says I'm supposed to be his partner, not a millstone around his neck. She doesn't want him to go either, but she'd never say so, not out loud. On a happier note, when will you be here for Christmas?"

"Mr. Thomas decided to close at noon on Christmas Eve this year, so I'll get the early bus. And I don't have to go in on Saturday morning."

"It'll be a nice long weekend for you."

"I can't wait, Sister."

"You're really doing all right?"

"Mrs. Clay is wonderful to me, and the other roomers are really friendly. Most of them have husbands at Goodfellow Field or Concho Field."

"And Kent's coming back after Christmas."

"That's the plan."

"Cece, you aren't thinking about getting married?"

"Not yet. Someday, but not yet."

"I'm not against it, but you haven't known him very long."

"I guess I'll get the chance to know him a lot longer and a lot better, won't I?"

"That's a good thing. Be sure."

"Like you were sure about Ben."

"I want you to be happy, Cece, as happy as I am."

"That's what I want, too."

"Okay then. I'll see you Thursday. Love you, baby girl."

"Love you, too, Sister."

Celeste hung up and opened the phone closet door. Mrs. Clay stood there holding out an envelope. "Someone left this for you."

"Who?"

"I don't know. I found it on the floor. Someone slipped it through the mail slot."

Celeste took the envelope between two fingers. Claudia. That was her way. Sneak around and do the damage and then move on. "Thank you, Mrs. Clay," she said as she moved toward the stairs.

"Are you all right, honey? You just turned real pale."

"I'm okay. Just tired, I guess." She hurried up the stairs, feeling like she was being smothered in a heavy blanket. Inside her room, she leaned against the door and slipped a single sheet of paper from the envelope.

I know you went to the graduation dance with Kenny. It should've been me, not you. Leave Kenny alone. You'll be sorry if you don't.

Chapter Fourteen

With deliberate effort, Celeste managed not to think too much about Kent while she was in Sterling City. He didn't call, which the others might have thought odd, but no one said anything. On Sunday afternoon, she took the last bus back to San Angelo and found Veda waiting at the station. "I figured you'd come back at the last minute," she said.

"Why are you here waiting for me?"

"Because I need to tell you something before you come to work in the morning."

A feeling of dread, colder than the December wind whipping around the building as they emerged from the station, chilled Celeste despite her heavy red coat. "Claudia."

"Let's get your suitcase. I borrowed a car to take you back to the boarding house. We can talk in your room."

On the way, Celeste told Veda about the picture Claudia had shown her and the note slipped through the mail slot. "Kent says the little boy isn't his."

"But you don't believe him. That's what you were crying about that night at the Canteen."

"I don't know what to believe. He called later to tell me his mother managed to pull some strings to get him reassigned to Concho Field as an instructor. He won't be going overseas."

"How did she do that?"

"Family connections, he said. I get the idea that she meddles in everybody's lives."

"Not promising for a future mother-in-law."

"No."

Veda helped Celeste carry everything upstairs to her room and sat down on the end of the bed to watch her unpack. "Well, at least I don't have to tell you about the kid."

"Was that what you thought I should know?"

"There's more. She cornered a couple of the girls from cosmetics on Christmas Eve, after you'd gone, and told them you were a home-wrecker. She said you were trying to break up her marriage."

"Marriage!"

"That's what she said. Anyway, Mr. Thomas had come downstairs to find Betty because she hadn't picked up her bonus check yet."

"How can you forget your Christmas bonus?"

"She got busy with some old biddy who wanted a certain kind of lace. Betty told her four times that we didn't have it, but the gal was convinced Betty wasn't showing her everything. Can you beat it? Anyway, when Mr. Thomas brought the check downstairs, he overheard Claudia and told her right in front of everybody that he'd warned her, and now he didn't have any choice but to fire her."

"In front of everybody? That doesn't sound like Mr. Thomas."

"Our mouths were hanging open, I can tell you. But Claudia just laughed and said she wasn't surprised that he'd stick up for you, that you were probably making it with him, too, and…"

Celeste collapsed on the bed. "I can't believe she said that to him."

"Oh, she did. He told her to see him on the twenty-sixth, that he'd have her final check ready. He was mad. Red-in-the-face mad."

"So she'll come upstairs tomorrow." Celeste squeezed her eyes shut. "Oh, Veda, I don't think I can face her."

"You haven't done anything. It's her own fault. Can you imagine talking to your boss that way?

Especially one as nice as Mr. Thomas."

"I don't know."

"Miss Riley." Mrs. Clay knocked and called name from the hall. "Telephone."

Celeste got up. "I hope it's not Kent."

"Want me to wait or leave you alone?"

"Stay here, if you don't mind."

The voice on the other end of the line belonged to Mr. Thomas. "I have a bit of unpleasant news," he said.

"It's okay, Mr. Thomas. Veda met my bus and told me what happened."

"Oh. Well, that's good, that's good. I just didn't want it to hit you when you came in tomorrow."

"I'm so sorry."

"You have nothing to be sorry for. Miss Peters caused her own problems. But I don't want you in the middle of what promises to be an unpleasant interview tomorrow, so don't come in to work until nine or later."

"But..."

"I mean it, Miss Riley. My wife is coming with me tomorrow morning to witness everything."

It was on the tip of Celeste's tongue to ask why he needed a witness after he'd already fired Claudia in front of the whole store, but she swallowed her curiosity. "Thank you, Mr. Thomas. I'll be in at nine."

"All right. I'm not doing this for you, Miss Riley. I have a business to run, and I can't afford to let anything interfere."

"I understand." *I don't understand any of it. How did things get so tangled up? The dress, that's what it was. Wanting something I didn't need, doing things I shouldn't have done. Maybe I should quit, too, but what if I can't find anything else? What if Claudia can't find another job? Will she go back to Brownwood? What will happen to her little boy?*

She filled Veda in on the conversation. "Somehow I can't help thinking this is my fault."

"That's crazy, Celeste. Besides, nobody liked Claudia. She's a cheap floozy, and you know it. She couldn't ever close out her cash drawer without someone helping her, and she left customers standing around while she took a break in the powder room four or five times a day or went out back and smoked."

"Maybe she never worked a counter before."

"Why are you making excuses for her?"

"She has a child to support."

"That's not really an excuse. She should have thought of that herself and been more responsible." Veda got up and reached for her coat. "I've got to get the car back to my friend."

"Thanks for meeting my bus. Thanks for being a good friend."

Veda put one finger under Celeste's chin. "Listen, I don't really know Kent. He seems like a nice enough guy, but you better take things slow until you know him a lot better."

"I will, Veda. Really."

"Okay. I'll see you tomorrow."

****

With Claudia gone, Mr. Thomas hired the wife of a serviceman, even though she told him she might be temporary. He assigned Veda to train her. Celeste thought it was as if Claudia had never worked a day at Woolworth. Betty and Ellen made a point to tell Celeste privately that they never believed what Claudia said and were glad she was gone. She didn't hear from Kent.

On the second Saturday night in January, when sleet made the streets and sidewalks treacherous, he showed up at the half-empty Canteen, greeted Celeste with the allowed handshake, and asked if they could sit at their usual out-of-the-way table and talk.

"I just got in this morning," he said.

"You didn't call."

"I was trying not to pressure you until you'd had time to think about things."

"Do you know about Claudia?"

"What about her?"

"Mr. Thomas fired her the day after Christmas."

"Why?"

"She talked too much."

Kent's face contorted almost as if he were in pain. "What now?"

"It's not important."

"I'd like to know."

Celeste lowered her voice to a whisper and gave him the gist of what Claudia had said.

"That sounds like her. She's obsessed with the idea that we're…that I'm going to change my mind about her." He leaned forward. "I never cared about her, not that way. I just felt sorry for her. But I'm crazy about you, Velvet."

Celeste felt her face grow warm. "What's done is done."

"You still aren't really sure about me, are you?"

"I'm sorry I said what I did. I shouldn't have just thrown all that in your face with no warning." She chewed her lip, tasting Tangee along with the doughnut she'd nibbled on earlier. "Did you know about the little boy?"

He sat there looking at her for a long moment. "I'd seen him."

"In Brownwood?"

He nodded. "She brought him by the house one day. Mother told her to get out and not come back."

"Where do you think she is now?"

"I really don't care."

"Not even about the little boy?"

"How many times do I have to tell you he's not

mine?" He crumpled a paper napkin in his fist.

"You could care about him anyway, couldn't you? It's not his fault."

"Let's just drop it, okay?"

She nodded. "Sure. Okay."

He waited for her on the corner. "I'll walk you home," he said.

"How will you get back to the field?"

"I ran into one of the guys in my training class. He ended up getting assigned back here, too, because they found a problem with his eyes when they rechecked him. He has a car, and his wife is staying with a friend in town. He'll come by and pick me up—unless your landlady will throw me out of her parlor."

Celeste giggled. "How do you know she has a parlor?"

"Every house has a parlor, doesn't it?"

Mrs. Clay clucked over Kent like a mother hen, insisting that she'd bring hot cocoa to warm him up from his walk. "You, too, Miss Riley," she said. "The two of you can have the parlor to yourselves until your young man leaves."

"So where are we, Velvet?" Kent asked when Mrs. Clay had left them alone with a pot of cocoa and a plate of oatmeal cookies.

"We haven't known each other all that long," she parried. "Maybe we just need to get to know each other better."

"Okay. Then what?"

"Then whatever happens, happens."

"Okay. But I still love you."

"We have to be sure."

"I'm sure." He reached for her hand. "But you're not, are you? Not since Claudia showed you that picture."

She took back her hand. "I wish it hadn't happened."

"What does your sister say?"

"She doesn't know."

"No?"

Celeste shook her head. "It would just worry her. Besides, it's something I have to work out for myself."

****

Just before midnight, Kent's friend, whom he introduced as Perry Davidson, arrived. Kent kissed her goodnight. "I'll see you at church tomorrow, unless the roads are bad."

"I won't be there either, if the sidewalks are icy."

"Even if I don't see you, I'll call you during the week." He rested the tips of his fingers against her cheek. "I love you."

Chapter Fifteen

Celeste woke to the sound of tree limbs cracking under the weight of ice and knew she wouldn't be leaving the boarding house for church. She wondered if the city buses would run on Monday so she could get to work. At ten, Mrs. Clay knocked on her door and said she had a pot of coffee and some rolls in the kitchen. "Come down in your robe if you want to. It's just us girls."

Celeste and the six other women living in the house sat in the kitchen visiting until noon. Mrs. Clay suggested a potluck meal for mid-afternoon. "Everybody can throw in whatever she has in the ice box or stored in your rooms." Celeste was beating eggs for an omelet when Mrs. Clay appeared in the kitchen door with Perry Davidson behind her.

"Go up to the parlor," the landlady said.

Celeste sat in a ladderback chair, her fingers locked together to keep them still.

"Kent said you knew about Claudia," Perry began, going on only after Celeste nodded. "There's been an accident."

"Kent?"

"He's going to be okay." Perry squatted down by the chair. "I don't know how she got on base this morning, but the CO called Kent in and said she'd given him quite an earful. Then he suggested that Kent take her back to wherever she was staying in town. There's an old car that's been there for a while. Don't know where it came from, but it runs in an emergency, and the CO keeps the keys. So Kent put Claudia in the car and started for town. Just the other side of the Lone Wolf Bridge, he must've hit a patch of ice and rolled."

"You said he was going to be all right."

"Broken collarbone."

"Claudia?"

Perry covered Celeste's hands with his. "Snapped her neck. She was DOA at Shannon Memorial Hospital."

****

Perry took Celeste to the hospital to see Kent and let her go into his room alone. He lay strapped in thick bandages, his face toward the window, but he turned his head when he heard her come in. "Hi, Velvet."

"Hi."

"I guess Perry told you what happened."

She nodded.

"I told them how to get in touch with Claudia's mother in Brownwood."

"Is that where her little boy is?"

"That's what she told my CO. She told him we were married and that I refused to let her get my allotment, but when she couldn't produce a marriage license, he called me in and told me to get her off the base."

Celeste approached the bed. "Does it hurt?"

"Yeah. A lot."

"I'm sorry."

"Me, too."

"How did she know you were back at the base?"

"She said she went home for Christmas and ran into Neil. He didn't tell me about it."

"I guess not."

"She has...had a way of getting things she wanted out of people. Information, favors, you name it."

"So what's going to happen now?"

"They'll send me back to the base tomorrow

sometime. I can still sit at a desk and teach, even like this."

"I meant about Claudia."

His face twisted. "I don't know. Her mother will have to arrange for her...body...to be sent back to Brownwood."

"Will she blame you?"

"How do I know? It wasn't my fault. That old car ran, but that's about all. The brakes were bad. When I realized I was sliding, I pumped them, but they didn't grab."

"Do you want me to call anyone for you? Your brother, maybe?"

"I'll call him tomorrow." Kent held out his hand, the movement causing him to wince. "Velvet, I'm sorry."

She curled her fingers inside of his. "It's not your fault."

"I just keep hurting you."

"I'm sorry for Claudia. I didn't have a good situation, but maybe hers was worse."

"She ran wild from the time she was twelve years old. Mrs. Peters couldn't do anything with her. I'm not sure she even tried."

"You tried."

He looked away. "Yeah, and look what it got me."

Perry put his head in the room. "I've got to get back to base, so I'll need to run you home, Celeste."

"Thanks for everything, Perry," Kent said.

"Sure. Ready, Celeste?"

Kent tried to pull her closer, but she freed her fingers and stepped back. "Call and let me know how you are," she said.

****

"Kent's a good guy," Perry said as they drove on streets that were beginning to thaw a little. "He's crazy about you."

"I like him, too."

"Is that all? I thought you two were pretty serious."

"I don't want to rush into anything."

"Well, that's understandable. My wife was the girl next door, so we'd known each other all our lives."

"I haven't known Kent very long." She hesitated. "Do you think anything will come of this?"

"I don't think so. Slick streets, bad brakes. It was an accident. You don't think he did it on purpose, do you?"

"No, of course not!"

"It's a wonder he's not dead, too. You should see the car—or what's left of it."

Celeste shivered.

"But he's going to have to live with it. I mean, he didn't ask Claudia to come out to the field and make trouble, and he was doing what Major Beeman told him to do, but Kent's a responsible guy. This is going to eat on him some."

"It's not fair."

"No, it's not." He eased to the curb in front of the boarding house and stopped. "Will you be okay?"

"I'm fine. Listen, let me know how Kent's doing."

"He said he'd call you, didn't he?"

"Yes, but that won't tell me how he really is, will it?"

"Maybe not. Sure, I'll keep in touch."

"Thank you for what you've done today."

"Anytime."

Celeste slid out of the car and picked her way past the remaining icy spots on the sidewalk.

Chapter Sixteen

Celeste almost hoped for more ice the next morning so the buses wouldn't run, but when they did, she dragged herself in to work and hoped no one would notice her somber mood. She thought she noticed Mr. Thomas watching her from time to time, but he didn't ask any questions.

That night, she was on her way upstairs to her room with a bowl of soup when Kent called. "I'm back at the field."

"How are you?"

"Okay, I guess. How about you?"

"Okay."

"Major Beeman talked to the police. They're calling it an accident."

"You didn't expect anything else, did you?"

"I didn't roll the damn car on purpose!" he exploded. "Sorry, about the language."

"It's all right."

"I talked to Neil and Mother. Neil's beating himself up for telling Claudia I was coming back to San Angelo."

"You said she'd have found out one way or the other."

"I guess so. Mother's going to see Mrs. Peters and offer to help with the arrangements."

"That's nice of her."

"She's not doing it to be nice, but never mind. Listen, I can't get into town all week. Maybe Saturday. You'll be at the Canteen, I guess."

"I'll be there."

"I love you, Velvet."

"I know."

"You just don't know if you love me."

She searched for the right words and didn't find them.

"I shouldn't have said that. I promised I wouldn't put any pressure on you."

"Thank you."

"I've got to go, Velvet. I'll call again in a couple of days and try to get into town on Saturday."

"Be careful, Kent."

"Sure. Goodnight."

She reheated the cooled soup and took it upstairs. It cooled again as she sat by the window and tried to sort out her feelings. *Did I love him, or was I just looking for a way out? What's wrong with me that I can't forget he's not perfect? Nobody is. I'm not. If it had just been Claudia talking about them together... But when she showed me the picture of the little boy, that changed things. Kent keeps saying he's not the father. The problem is, he never came right out and said he couldn't be.*

Celeste made herself swallow a few spoonfuls of vegetable soup, then pushed the bowl away. *How far would he have gone that night in the employee lounge if I hadn't stopped him? How far did he go with Claudia? I know he said she let everybody, but I thought...I want to believe he's better than that.* A picture of the innocent little boy in the sailor suit flashed across her mind. *What will happen to him? None of this is his fault. His father, whoever that is, doesn't want him, and now his mother's dead. Poor little boy.*

She glanced toward the framed photograph of Anne Riley. *Who was my real father? Did Daddy ask you that? Did you know? Did he want you back so much that he was willing to love me? I know he really did love me once. I remember how it used to be. Can love stop, just like that?* She pressed her fingers against her eyes. *Maybe it can. I really thought I loved Kent, and now I'm not sure. Either I didn't love him, or I've stopped loving him. Either way, it's a mess. A terrible, tangled, awful mess.*

****

Kent showed up at the Canteen on Saturday night. Mrs. Lowe and the other chaperones, seeing his sling, fussed over him, but Celeste could tell he didn't like it. She was thankful war news had crowded the accident out of the paper, so they didn't know about Claudia.

When Celeste wasn't dancing with the other soldiers or serving coffee and doughnuts, she sat with Kent at the back table. "At least it was the left side," she said.

"Yeah, but I need two arms for most things. I have to have help getting into my uniform."

She smiled. "Somebody tied your tie very nicely."

"Perry."

"I like him."

"He's been a good friend."

"Have you heard anything from your family?"

He grimaced.

"You don't have to talk about it if you don't want to."

"Mrs. Peters brought Claudia back to Brownwood. There wasn't a funeral."

"Why?"

"Everybody knew what she was." He shook his head. "No, that's not all of it. I think my mother had something to do with the decision. She doesn't want anyone to know I was involved."

"I guess she's protecting you."

"She protected me into ending up back here. If she hadn't, Claudia wouldn't have gone out to the field, and she'd still be alive."

"I hadn't thought of it that way."

"I've already talked to Major Beeman about

going overseas as soon as this class graduates."

"That's really what you want to do?"

"I didn't want to come back here, that's for sure. I don't mean because of you, Velvet."

"I know what you meant."

"Do you ever see your father?"

"No."

"Does he know where you are?"

"He might. I had my mail forwarded, not that I get much, and changed the address on my bank account."

"It's better if he doesn't know."

"He was drunk, Kent. He wouldn't have hit me if he hadn't been drinking."

"That doesn't excuse it."

"Besides, I..." She stopped. *Maybe I should tell him about myself. Maybe he should know I'm not exactly who he thinks I am, that I'm like Claudia's little boy. How would he feel if he knew my mother was like Claudia?*

"What?"

"Nothing."

"I wish we could dance. I need to hold you. I can't even hold your hand while we're in here."

She looked at him in the dim light, trying to remember what she'd felt the first time she saw him. "Kent, if we'd never met that afternoon in front of Cox-Rushing-Greer...or at the Roof Garden...if the war hadn't happened...do you think we'd have been attracted to each other?"

He grinned. "Not if we'd never met."

"It was a silly question."

"I think meeting each other was meant to be. You thought so, too, at least you used to."

"I think you were right, that night when you said I'm still a little girl. My head's still too full of dreams."

"Dreams are all right."

"Nobody's perfect, Kent, not you, not me, not anybody."

"At least you know that."

"If I was really mature, what Claudia said wouldn't have made any difference."

"I wish it hadn't."

"I wish it, too. I'm trying, Kent. I want to grow up and look at things the right way."

"I don't mind waiting." He stretched his hand across the table.

She touched it quickly, then pulled back. "Will you wait for me on the corner?"

"I'll wait for you forever, Velvet."

Chapter Seventeen

As soon as she came out of the Canteen, Celeste saw Kent standing at the corner under the streetlight and started toward him, then stopped dead in her tracks when Coralee and Ben emerged from the shadows. *Not something else,* Celeste thought, fighting the urge to turn and run. *Oh, please, no more.*

Coralee came toward her, arms outstretched. "It's Daddy, baby girl."

"Daddy?"

Ben put his arms around both of them. "Let's go where we can talk." He nodded at Kent. "You can come, too."

In the parlor at the boarding house, Coralee sat with her arm around Celeste. "When he didn't show up at work on Friday, they sent someone to the house to look for him."

"But this is Saturday night."

"He wasn't at the house," Ben said, "so they didn't know where else to look." He moved to sit on Celeste's other side. "Someone saw the car near the Bell Street crossing this afternoon."

"What happened?"

"The temperature at night has been below freezing all week. He wasn't wearing his overcoat," Ben said.

"But they don't know."

"They know he didn't...do anything to himself," Coralee said with difficulty.

"Kill himself, you mean."

Coralee nodded. "But there was an empty bottle

on the front seat."

"He got an early start, I guess," Celeste said, glancing at Kent.

"We hadn't heard from him since you moved out," Ben said. "Coralee called a couple of times, but he wouldn't talk to her."

"He knew what he'd done," Coralee said. "I'd like to think he was ashamed of himself."

"He wouldn't have done it again, Sister."

"Sure he would," Kent blurted. "It's like an animal tasting blood."

Ben shook his head. "That's pretty extreme."

"I'm still glad she moved out," Kent said.

Coralee smoothed Celeste's hair. "She had to."

Kent stood up. "I think I hear Perry's car outside, so I've got to go."

Celeste broke away from her sister. "I'll be back," she said.

In the foyer, Kent took her in his good arm. "I'm sorry, Velvet. Maybe it's for the best."

"I don't know." *I don't know about anything. About you and Claudia and that poor little boy. About Daddy. Even about myself.*

"I'll get Perry to drop me here instead of at the church tomorrow."

"Thank you." His wool topcoat scratched her face as she leaned against him.

He kissed her head and rubbed her cheek. "It'll be okay, Velvet. Everything'll be okay."

****

"We're going to stay at the house," Coralee said. "Do you want to come with us?"

"No."

"Are you okay, baby girl?"

"I'm okay. I guess I lost Daddy a long time ago, didn't I?"

"Are you and Kent all right?"

"Why wouldn't we be?"

"He said he was in a car accident," Ben said. "Last weekend when it was icy."

"Well, I'm glad he wasn't hurt worse and that you weren't with him," Coralee said. She hugged Celeste. "I don't know what we'll do about a funeral, but Daddy was pretty well-known around here, so we'll have to do something."

"Not just because of that," Ben said. "It's the right thing to do."

"The right thing to do," Celeste echoed.

"Are you sure you don't want to come with us?" Coralee asked.

"Kent's coming over here tomorrow."

"All right. We'll be back sometime, too."

****

Celeste watched them drive away before she went upstairs to her room, where she undressed in the dark and slid into bed. *Do I even care he's dead? What's wrong with me? Maybe he wasn't my real father, but he was all I had, and I should at least care that he's gone. Coralee was right. I could've stayed around forever, and he wouldn't have loved me. But I should still care. He did a lot of things he shouldn't have done…maybe Kent did, too…or maybe he didn't. Maybe I wanted Kent to be perfect because Daddy wasn't.*

She turned over and hugged the extra pillow, and her eyes closed. The blue velvet curtain billowed in an icy wind. Beyond it, Kent, Claudia, and her father stood together laughing. Laughing at her.

****

On Monday, even though August Riley hadn't darkened the door of the church since his wife's funeral, the minister preached a short service at the funeral home and prayed briefly at the open grave beside Anne Riley's. All the bank officers and their wives came and said how sorry they were. Afterward, the Christian Women's Fellowship had lunch for the family in the second-floor church parlor.

Celeste felt relief when Kent called to say he couldn't get to town. The more she thought about it, the more humiliated she felt. She wished he didn't know everything about her. Almost everything, that is. He didn't know about her mother.

Mr. Thomas insisted she take Tuesday off, too. Coralee and Ben came by the boarding house to say goodbye before they drove home. "We'll be back to see about the house," Coralee said. "I talked to Daddy's lawyer. He had a will, so we'll get everything straightened out eventually."

Ben took an envelope from his pocket and put it into Celeste's hands. "He had a paycheck coming from the bank. They gave it to us in cash."

Celeste shrank back. "I don't want it."

"Lord knows you've got it coming, baby girl," Coralee said. "The bills for the house are paid through January. You take the money."

When they'd gone, Celeste took the envelope to her room and emptied the money onto the bed. Seventy-eight dollars. A fortune. She sat smoothing the bills in her lap. *Is this what they call blood money? It's not mine, and no matter what Coralee says, I don't have it coming. Daddy didn't owe me anything, not really. He kept a roof over my head, even if he only did it so I'd cook and clean for him. I've never done without anything I really needed.* Her fingers tapped the bills into a neat pile. *Any other time, I'd enjoy spending some extra money, but not this money. Not now, anyway.* After a while she put the cash in a shoebox on the top shelf of the closet and closed the door.

****

Kent called and said he'd see her at the Canteen on Saturday if she was going. "Why wouldn't I? Daddy's dead and buried, but the soldiers still need cheering up."

"That's one way of looking at it."

"I'm going back to work tomorrow. I didn't need an extra day off, but Mr. Thomas insisted."

"Things will catch up to you. I remember when my father died."

"That was different."

"Maybe it was. Anyway, I'll see you on Saturday. Sunday we'll go out to eat and spend the whole afternoon together."

"That'll be nice, Kent."

"Things have to get better for both of us now."

"I guess they do."

"I love you, Velvet."

She was thinking of saying that she loved him, too, but he hung up before she could get the words out.

Chapter Eighteen

"It was nice of you to come to Daddy's service," Celeste said to Mr. Thomas as she hung her coat in the office closet on Wednesday morning.

"Mary and I came for you." He shuffled some papers on his desk. "I also know what happened to Miss Peters."

"How?"

"I have a friend at the police department. He thought she still worked here, so he called me."

"She went to the field to make trouble for Kent, and his CO told him to take her back to town."

"It's too bad."

"Did you know she had a little boy?"

He looked up, a frown creasing his forehead. "No, I didn't."

"She says…said…he's…Kent's." Her voice broke.

The wooden swivel chair creaked as he sat down. "I see."

"Kent says he's not, that she…that Claudia…"

"You needn't explain." He put his hands over his eyes. "I might not have let her go if I'd known about the child, but my policy has always been to discourage gossip and backbiting among my employees."

"There's nothing wrong with that."

"Yes, well, I might have given her a second chance if I'd known she had a child to support. Where is he?"

"With her mother in Brownwood, I think." Celeste stooped to take the daybook from the safe. "I'll stay late to catch up. I didn't really need time off."

Mr. Thomas lifted one hand as if to wave away her offer. "Mary came in and posted the accounts," he said. "Everything's current."

"She didn't have to do that. Please tell her I appreciate it."

"She likes having something to do outside the house, now that the girls are grown and gone."

Celeste sat down and uncovered the adding machine. *I'm so tired of thinking about all this. I need to work and forget.*

"Miss Riley."

"Yes, sir?"

"I hope things will be better for you now."

"Yes, sir, I hope so, too."

****

Kent didn't call, but he showed up at the Canteen on Saturday. Celeste thought his face looked drawn and a little pale.

"Does your shoulder still hurt a lot?"

"Not as much. The medic at the field said I'd have to wear the sling another three or four weeks. It's driving me nuts." With his hand on the small of her back, he urged her toward the table where they always sat. "Did you have a lot to do when you went back to work?"

"Mr. Thomas's wife had kept things caught up." She wondered if she should tell him what Mr. Thomas had said about Claudia and decided it would serve no purpose.

"Major Beeman is doing what he can to get me overseas by summer."

"Does your mother know?"

"I haven't talked to her but once since the accident. She chewed me up and spit me out."

"Because of Claudia."

"Right."

"Does she know about me?"

"Sort of. Neil knows."

"Would she like anybody you went with?"

"Probably not. When Dad died, she just sort of decided I was the man of the family and always would be."

"You were only fourteen."

"I grew up fast."

"Coralee was only twelve when Mamma died, but she'd been taking care of me for a while before that, ever since Mamma got sick."

"But she didn't have any trouble breaking free, so to speak. Marrying Ben and moving to Sterling City."

"Ben's parents offered to take me, too, but Daddy wouldn't let me go."

"You told me that. Why?"

Celeste shook her head as if to say she didn't know, even though she did.

"Velvet, when the war's over, we need to get out of here. I mean as far away as we can. You can visit your sister whenever you want to, but we need a fresh start away from here."

"San Angelo's all I've ever known."

"I was born and raised in Brownwood, but that doesn't mean I have to live and die there." As he bit off the words, she caught a flash of the anger she'd seen when he confronted her father. She wondered what had sparked his anger now, though at the same time she realized it wasn't directed at her.

A young soldier approached their table. "Can I borrow your girl?" he asked Kent with a grin. "Promise not to move in on you."

Kent nodded. "Sure, go ahead. I'm grounded, as you can see."

When she came back to the table, Celeste said, "He's just eighteen. He has a girl back home in Kansas."

Kent's mouth twisted. "I hope he makes it to

nineteen."

****

After church on Sunday, they ate at the little café on Chadbourne where they'd shared their first lunch. Then they walked to the St. Angelus and snuck up to the empty Roof Garden, where they sat on the floor in a corner, holding each other hungrily and sharing kisses that grew more passionate by the minute.

"Do they still have dances up here?" Kent asked when they came up for air.

"I think so."

"We need to go to one when I get out of this contraption. You can wear your blue velvet dress."

"Veda will know if there's a Valentine dance. We could go to that."

Kent found her mouth again. "I've missed this, Velvet."

I've missed it, too, but I wish I could stop thinking about you and Claudia.

As if he'd read her mind, he pulled back. "What's wrong?"

"Nothing's wrong."

"You're thinking about Claudia and me, aren't you?"

She dropped her eyes. "I guess I do sometimes."

"Look, Velvet, I'm twenty-seven years old. I haven't lived in a monastery."

"You wouldn't look very good in a long brown robe with your head shaved," she said, trying to lighten the mood.

He straightened, letting his arm fall away from her shoulders. "I'm not going to do anything you don't want me to, but you need to grow up."

"I'm sorry, Kent."

He blew out his breath as if it were his last. "Yeah, me, too. Come on, I'll walk you home."

"Now?"

"Why not? We can sit in Mrs. Clay's parlor and play checkers or something."

"Don't be mean to me."

"I'm not being mean, Velvet. I'm being realistic. You're who you are, and I guess that's part of why I love you."

****

Coralee called on Monday night to say that she and Barbara would be staying at the house in San Angelo for at least a week. "I'm going to get rid of Daddy's stuff. The house is pretty clean. I guess he hired someone to come in after you left."

"What are you going to do about the house?"

"That's the other thing I want to talk to you about. The lawyer is filing Daddy's will for probate. He left everything to me."

"You're his daughter, and I'm not."

"Well, you know I'm going to split everything right down the middle with you."

"You don't have to do that, Sister."

"And there's something else, too. We've all talked about it and we think you should move out of that little room and back into the house. It's paid for, and there's money invested to pay the taxes and enough in savings to pay the water, gas, and electricity for a couple of years. By then, you may be married and gone, and we can decide what to do with the house. But it doesn't need to sit empty 'til then."

Celeste caught her breath as the rooms on Spaulding Street flashed through her mind like a kaleidoscope. Home to her own room, the sunny kitchen, a porch to sit on in warm weather, something outside the windows besides an alley full of trash cans. "Oh, Sister, do you mean it?"

"You know I do. That way, Ben and Barbara and I will have a place to visit you whenever we want to."

Excitement all but choked her. "Oh, Sister. Oh,

Sister."

"Then you'll do it?"

"I'll start packing up right now. I'll help you clean out everything."

"I'll pick you up at the store when you get off work at noon on Saturday. Be sure to tell Mrs. Clay right away. She won't have any trouble renting the room. Not with a war on and two bases in town."

Chapter Nineteen

"I think it's the right thing to do," Kent said when he called later. "You'll be a lot happier at home."

"A lot cozier, certainly, and it'll really be home now."

"You might even rent out the second bedroom for some extra money and the company."

"I thought of that."

"I'm glad for you, Velvet."

"Coralee's picking me up at noon on Saturday, so I won't be at the Canteen. You can come to the house if you want to."

"I'm not much use with one arm, but maybe I can find something to do to help."

"Just be there, Kent. That's all I need."

****

Kent made himself useful by entertaining Barbara until Coralee put her to bed at eight. "I'm going to send all the clothes to the Salvation Army," she said. "There's not much else to dispose of."

"Where are Mamma's things?" Celeste asked.

"When I married and moved out, I took what I could sneak past Daddy. Personal stuff like jewelry, and some scarves and a few keepsakes. The jewelry is just dime store stuff, but that's what she liked. I left the leprechauns in your room because you always loved them. The rest is in the attic, unless he got rid of it."

"Do you want to look?" Kent asked.

Celeste shook her head. "It's too cold up there now. Maybe later." She curled up on the yellow-and-white-flowered settee and looked around. "I'm going to use this room every single night. Do you think the radio still works?"

Kent went over to the wooden table radio and turned it on. When he twirled the dial, music replaced static. "It's an Emerson. They make good stuff."

"That's Glenn Miller's 'Moonlight Serenade,'" Coralee said. "I heard he joined the army and got a band together to play for the soldiers."

Celeste closed her eyes. "I'm going to sit here every night and listen to the radio. Veda and Marilyn will visit, too."

"You should, baby girl." Coralee leaned over the back of the settee to hug her sister. "You just do anything you want to do, and I'm going to be so happy thinking about you doing it."

****

"I'm not going to take advantage of you living here alone," Kent said as they walked out on the porch when Perry honked.

"You're welcome here, Kent. You know that."

"I do want to check all the door locks next time I'm here. Make sure they're good ones. With so many new people in town because of the bases, it's a good idea to lock up pretty tight when you're gone and especially when you're home alone at night."

"All right."

He put his good arm around her. "Will you be at church tomorrow?"

"If I'm not, come here afterward. Coralee and I'll have something for lunch."

"You sure?"

"I'm sure."

He brushed her lips so lightly that she hardly felt his kiss. "Night, Velvet. Sweet dreams in your own bed tonight."

****

The first of the week, Coralee set the boxes of August Riley's clothes on the porch and went inside and shut the door like she was closing a finished book. When Celeste said as much, her sister laughed. "I guess I am. In some ways, I need to put all this behind me as much as you do."

Sometime during the day, the Salvation Army sent a truck for the boxes. "Get the laundry to pick up all the sheets and things we took off the bed," Coralee said to Celeste. "Does that old machine on the back porch still work?"

"I used it sometimes. Daddy sent his things to Model Laundry downtown."

"I wish you had a car. How will you get groceries home?"

"M System used to deliver the big things, and I picked up bread and milk at a little place up on Main Street sometimes."

"Daddy just took it for granted you'd manage and never offered to help."

"It's done, Sister."

"Maybe Kent can help you when he has two good arms again."

"He's trying to get overseas duty. His CO promised him."

"How do you feel about that?"

"I want him to be happy."

"Just how serious are things between the two of you? I know I've asked before, but you've sort of hedged your answers."

"We've talked about getting married after the war."

"After."

"I want to be sure, Sister. I want to be married forever."

"Then be sure, baby girl. Making a quick decision in the middle of a war isn't the thing to do. A couple of the high school girls in Sterling City have run off and married, and I hear one already has a baby on the way. She could end up raising it by herself."

"I'm not going to do that."

****

By the end of January, Celeste felt at home in a way she'd never experienced before. She opened the drapes in the parlor every morning and turned on all the lamps there at night. Veda said she'd keep her ears open for anyone who might want to rent the extra bedroom, but Celeste wasn't sure she was in any hurry to share her nest.

For the first week, she woke a few times in the night and thought she heard August Riley stumbling around in the hall, but even that ended. She was alone, in her own home, and enjoying every moment of her independence. Marilyn and Veda dropped in with or without an invitation. More often than not, they came home with Celeste to spend the night after Canteen duty.

"I love it," she told Coralee during one of her sister's regular phone calls. "I love having a real home where I can invite my friends."

"Maybe I shouldn't ask, but…"

"Kent doesn't come over. I meet him at the Canteen on Saturdays and at church on Sundays. He walks me home, but Veda and Marilyn are usually with me, too. Then his friend Perry picks him up."

"It's none of my business."

"Sure it is, Sister."

"I just don't want to see you get hurt."

"Kent wouldn't hurt me." *Not intentionally, but he'd take what he wanted if I'd let him. Maybe all men are that way. Lord knows, I've had little enough experience with them to know for sure.*

"Just enjoy your new life, baby girl. You've had it coming for a long time."

****

Kent bought Celeste a corsage of red roses for the Valentine dance at the Roof Garden. With his arm finally free from the sling, he could hold her close in her blue velvet dress. They rode with Perry and his wife Sue, so Kent kissed her goodnight on the porch and didn't move to come in. She invited them all for lunch on Sunday. "I had enough ration points for a nice roast, and I'll make yeast rolls, too." She liked feeling part of a couple while they spent the afternoon in the parlor working a jigsaw puzzle and listening to the radio. When Kent had to leave with Perry, Celeste balanced disappointment with relief. *We don't need to be alone here in the house. Mrs. Aikman next door isn't a gossip, but she knows everything that goes on here, and it's not a bad idea to have someone looking out for me. Besides, when Kent and I get too cozy, we always end up in an argument about how much is too much.*

In March, Perry got his orders for overseas duty and took Sue back to Fort Worth to live with her parents. Kent bought his car and gave it to Celeste. "I can't take this," she protested, shocked at the size of his gift.

"You need it more than I do. I can get the bus in to the Canteen and again on Sundays, and you can drive me back to the field on Sunday nights if you want to."

The new freedom of being able to come and go as she pleased gave her a heady feeling, and she liked the extra time with Kent when she drove him back to Concho Field on weekends.

They didn't talk about Claudia or his mother, and he didn't do more than hold her hand and kiss her goodnight. They spent most of their time just talking, something Celeste said they needed to do. She didn't think Kent really agreed, but he didn't argue with her.

He got his orders in May and asked her to drive

Dancing with Velvet

to Brownwood with him to meet his mother and brother. "I have to admit I'm not anxious to meet your mother," she said. "Not after everything you've said."

"I'm not anxious for you to meet her, either, but it's got to be done."

"For the sake of good manners."

"That, and just so she can't say I snuck around behind her back."

"What if she doesn't like me?"

"She probably won't, but it doesn't matter. I love you, Velvet. And you'll like Neil and Kay. I worry that they're not married yet because of Mother, and I plan to talk to him about it while I'm home."

"Will it do any good?"

"I hope so." He caught her hand and squeezed it. "Things are going to work out for us, Velvet. We've got to keep believing that."

****

"Don't go if you're going to feel uncomfortable," Coralee counseled. "I just wish you were going to have a mother-in-law like Pearl."

"I don't think there's anyone else like Pearl."

"She's one in a million. That's what Big Ben always says. She's started a hope chest for you, by the way."

"For me?"

"Right alongside Barbara's. When is Kent leaving for good?"

"The end of June, he thinks."

"And you're still going to wait. I mean, wait for *everything*."

"He doesn't want to, but maybe men don't see anything wrong with it."

"They do if they're the right kind."

"Well, I'm waiting, Sister, and like you said, a hurry-up wedding in the middle of a war isn't a good idea, not for me."

"Well, you're sensible, baby girl. You stick to your guns. When he comes home again, if you're sure you want to marry him, you'll have the biggest wedding First Christian Church has seen in years."

Chapter Twenty

Coldly polite were the words Celeste used to describe Kent's mother to Coralee. "She looked me over like I was something he'd found on the street somewhere. Not just on the street, but in an alley maybe. A garbage can. At meals, she talked to Kent and Neil and ignored me."

"Doesn't sound promising, baby girl."

"Oh, Kent and I spent most of our time out of the house. His mother didn't like that either, of course. Neil's girlfriend Kay is nice. Neil's determined to marry her, but she put her foot down about living in the house with his mother."

"I don't blame her."

"I wouldn't do it either."

"Did Kent tell her that the two of you are engaged?"

"We're not exactly engaged. We have an understanding, that's all."

"You're planning to get married, so you're engaged."

Celeste didn't tell her sister about the humiliating scene on their last morning in Brownwood when Mrs. Peters stormed up the walk and demanded money from Kent to support Claudia's little boy. "You owe it to her," the stringy-haired woman insisted. "You're the reason she's not here to take care of him."

"She didn't take care of him anyway," Kent retorted. "She left him with you from the time he was a baby. And I'm not going to be responsible for him, because he's not mine."

Celeste, trying to make herself invisible, felt sorry for Claudia's mother, despite the fact she appeared as cheap as Claudia had, though in a tattered sort of way. *I hope they get enough to eat. Especially the little boy.*

Overhearing the argument—Celeste thought maybe everyone in the neighborhood heard it—Mrs. Goddard stormed out of the kitchen and told Mrs. Peters to get out and not come back. Claudia's mother left, spewing threats of taking Kent to court for child support and worse.

On the drive to San Angelo, Kent refused to talk about it, except to repeat, "He's not mine, so I'm not responsible for him."

Celeste let it go at that because she knew she didn't want to hear anything different. *Kent's right about me needing to grow up and face reality, but I'm just not ready. At least, not as far as he's concerned. Anyway, he's leaving, and I don't have to make a decision right away.* She did wonder about the little boy, though. Had anybody ever really been responsible for him? What was his life like?

****

She begged off from the Canteen and made baked chicken and dressing for their last evening together, putting aside her qualms about being alone in the house with Kent and trying not to think of Claudia and her little boy. They ate by candlelight, and afterward he dried the dishes as she washed. "We're playing house," he said.

"Or something."

His hand caressed her shoulders and moved low on her back. "Or something."

She shivered. "We can go sit in the parlor and listen to the radio."

"If we were married, we wouldn't have to sit in the parlor."

"We're not married."

"I love you, Velvet. I need you. Need you like a man needs a woman."

She moved away from him a few steps. "Don't, Kent."

He picked up the dishtowel again. "I'm not going to attack you," he said. The bitterness in his voice unsettled her.

"I know that."

"But I meant what I said. A little hand-holding and kissing doesn't go a long way toward…"

"Stop it."

He tossed the dishtowel on the cabinet and stalked out of the kitchen. She found him leaning on the porch railing, staring into the dusk. "Maybe we should go to the Canteen and dance," she said.

"Maybe you should just drive me back to the field."

"It's your last night, Kent. I don't want to spoil it with a fight."

"That's what I'm fixing to do, you know, fight. Maybe it'll be from an airplane where I can't see them, but I'm still going to kill people, and they're going to try to kill me."

She slipped her arms around his waist from behind him. He jerked away. "Don't be a tease, Velvet. Claudia sure was."

Celeste froze. "I thought you said…"

"I said the boy isn't mine."

She sucked in her breath. *I don't really know you, do I? And if I don't know you, how can I think I'm in love with you?* "I want to hear that he *couldn't* be yours, but you can't say that, can you?"

His silence answered her question.

"Why weren't you honest with me?"

"If I'd been honest, would we be having this conversation right now?"

"I don't know."

"I think you do. All right, she kept on and on,

and got me going so bad I didn't want to stop, and then she laughed at me."

"So you...you..."

"Yes, I did! That's what she wanted. Wanted me to take her right there on the blanket out at the lake, and I did."

Celeste's mouth went dry. When she opened it to speak, nothing came out.

"I was twenty years old. Been away at that CCC camp for two years, and when I came home, she made sure we ran into each other. I asked her to go for a ride, and we ended up at the lake. She was my first, but I knew I wasn't hers. She..."

"Don't say anymore," Celeste said, backing away from him. "Please, Kent, don't tell me anymore."

"You wanted to know." He hit the porch pillar with his fist. "Now you do."

"I had to know," she murmured, thinking that if she didn't get inside and sit down, she was going to fall down. "I had to know. Don't you understand?"

"So now what?"

"I don't know." She stumbled toward the screen door and yanked it open. "I don't know."

After a few minutes, he followed her inside, where she had curled herself into a tight knot on the couch. "I'm sorry, Velvet," he said. "I didn't mean to hurt you."

"What did you mean to do?"

"I don't know. I was just so...so mad at you."

"Why? Because I wouldn't go to bed with you?" She hid her face against the back of the settee, shocked at her own blunt words.

"I guess so."

"Why would you expect me to...to do that?"

"I shouldn't have. I don't know what got into me."

"But you did." She lifted her face. In the lamplight, his eyes glowed, but not with happiness.

"I was wrong. Wrong about Claudia, wrong about you." He sat down in the chair across from her. "I'm leaving first thing in the morning, Velvet. I don't want to remember you like this."

She sat up. "I'll drive you back to the field."

"No, I'll go downtown and ride back with the fellows at the Canteen when it closes." He rose and stepped toward her, then stopped. "I do love you, Velvet."

She nodded. "I know you do. And for what it's worth, I love you, too."

"I wish I could believe that."

"You can."

"But I'm not still your prince. More like a toad."

She didn't smile. "I don't believe in fairytales anymore."

"Because of me?"

"You said I needed to grow up."

"I've said a lot of things I wish I could take back, but I guess that much was right. I had to grow up overnight when I was fourteen, but you had your sister. You still do."

"There's nothing wrong with that."

"She still calls you 'baby girl,' and that's how you think of yourself—as her baby girl. You haven't had to grow up, because she's always been there to take care of things for you."

Anger flared in Celeste. "I've worked since I was twelve years old and put up with Daddy on top of that."

"You think that makes you a woman?"

She watched the rage building in him again. She'd seen it before, more than once, and retreated from it. Now she felt trapped, even threatened—though not physically.

"I thought it did. Not letting you get all over me makes me responsible, not immature."

"I don't want...you're not a one-night stand,

Velvet. Not by a long shot. We could've gotten married."

"So we could sleep together for a few nights?"

"You know it's more than that."

She dropped her head to hide her face until she got control of her emotions. "I want to know that, Kent. I want to believe you really love me."

"I've said so plenty of times."

"I know."

"But that's not enough, is it? Why? Can you tell me that?"

"I wish I knew."

"You said we needed to talk so we could get to know each other, and we've done that. If you don't know me by now, you never will."

"I know you're a good person, Kent."

"Look, I've been honest with you about what I did. Maybe I should've come clean right off the bat, but I didn't. I'm not perfect. Neither are you."

"I never said I was."

"No, but you wanted to live in a perfect world. That's what you were doing when you stayed in this house in your own room, even though your father didn't care anything about you."

She straightened her shoulders in a show of what she hoped was confidence. "He did once." *And I can't tell you why he didn't love me after Mamma died. You've been honest with me, but I can't be honest with you, not now, not ever. You don't care about a little boy who might really be yours, and you wouldn't care about somebody who doesn't even know who her own father is.*

"Maybe and maybe not. But you held on to the idea that it was all going to come out happily-ever-after in the end, so you stayed."

"You don't know what I did or why." *Why are we fighting? Is this what we're going to remember about our last night together?*

"Well, maybe I don't. I don't know why I gave in to Claudia, other than the obvious. I never did anything like that before. Mother made my life miserable, so maybe I was getting back at her. But that's no good reason for what I did. No excuse."

"If you knew it was wrong, why did you want the same thing from me?"

He stared at her.

"You said I wasn't like Claudia, but you wanted me to be, at least in that way, didn't you?"

He blew out his breath. "I guess I did. I'm sorry."

"So if I'd given in to you, I'd have been just like her, and then you wouldn't have wanted to marry me either."

"That's not true. I love you. I didn't love her."

"Oh, Kent, we're just going around in circles."

"I guess we are. I better go." He stood up. "I'm sorry, Velvet."

"Me, too."

"Will you be all right?"

She shrugged. "Sure."

"I could ask Veda to come over when she gets through at the Canteen tonight."

"I don't need a babysitter."

"That's not what I…oh, never mind."

"You better go, or you'll miss your ride."

"I love you, Velvet."

She nodded but didn't take the hand he held out to her. When he walked out the front door, she slipped into the hall and watched through the screen until the dusk swallowed him up.

****

Celeste didn't fall asleep until dawn. When she woke it was after noon, and when she went downstairs she found a piece of paper stuck in the screen door. "You can write to me at this address if you want to. Please forgive me." In the bottom corner, he'd sketched a small toad wearing a crown.

Chapter Twenty-One

Several times, Celeste tried to find a way to tell Coralee about Kent, but she always held back at the last minute. *I know she'd understand, but she might tell me to forget him, and I don't want to do that. I'm not sure I could anyway. Why can't I just accept that he did what he did and go on? Maybe if the little boy wasn't in the picture...but he is. He's there just like I was when Daddy took Mamma back.*

The girls at the store sympathized with her over Kent's departure. Most of them had someone in service, too—husband, brother, boyfriend, neighbor, acquaintance. She accepted their kind words with appropriate replies, feeling doubly dishonest that she let them keep believing she was heartbroken because he was gone.

But my heart's not broken. I'm just plain relieved that I don't have to see him and try to act like everything is the same when it's not.

When Kent didn't write, she supposed he was waiting for her to make the first move. She tried, without success. The wastebasket beside the desk in the parlor filled up with the crumpled sheets of stationery, letters begun and never finished.

What is there to say? I told him I still loved him, and I do. At least, I think I do. I think I've grown up a lot, too, but that doesn't mean I have to toss out all my principles like Mamma did.

****

She did hear from Kent's brother Neil, who wrote to apologize for their mother's inhospitable behavior and for the scene created by Mrs. Peters.

I guess Kent and I just accept Mother for who and what she is. She's not a bad person. She just likes to be the boss. Things might have been different if Dad hadn't died, but then she started bossing us the way she did him, and we just let her because he did. I don't know what went on between Kent and Claudia or if Jonny could be his or not. (I hope I'm not embarrassing you—we're both adults—or supposed to be.) If he is, Kent owes him something. The poor kid's better off without his mother, as awful as that sounds. She was just plain no good, and maybe it wasn't all her fault. But you're a swell girl, Celeste, and Kent loves you. I hope things work out for both of you.

Kay and I are getting married at Christmas. I got a job teaching history in the high school here, but it doesn't start until September. With both our paychecks, we'll have enough to rent a small apartment—if we can find one these days.

Take care of yourself, Celeste, and keep in touch.

She wrote back, just a quick note wishing Kay and him well. He probably didn't need to know how Kent had left on a sour note, one she wasn't sure could ever be replayed in tune.

****

Mrs. Lowe kept up with the servicemen who passed through the Canteen and always announced, just before they opened every Saturday night, the names of those who had been wounded or killed. "I know it's a somber note," she said, "but I want you young ladies to understand how important it is to be good to these boys while they're here."

Once she said to Celeste, "I hold my breath when I get a list, afraid I'll see Kent's name on it. I pray for him and all the others."

Celeste hugged her. "Thank you, Mrs. Lowe. You'll get a star in your crown for all this."

"All I want is for this war to be over, and our boys to come home safely. As many of them as possible."

****

Veda's brother came home wounded from the Pacific. "He won't go back," she confided to Celeste over lunch one Friday. "He won't ever be the same." She told Mrs. Lowe she couldn't come to the Canteen for a while and started taking the bus home to Winters every weekend.

Just before Thanksgiving, Celeste ran into Pete Frame on her way to the bank. He asked her to have a cup of coffee and proceeded to do what he called spilling his guts. "I'm not cut out for the military," he said, watching for her reaction. "I don't want to kill anybody, not even a Jap or a Nazi."

"I don't guess anybody does."

"Some of the guys don't have any trouble. When we trained with the bayonets, they hit those straw dummies like they were enjoying it."

"I already know you didn't."

"I dream about it, Cece. What's going to happen to me when I do it for real?"

"You'll be all right, Pete. I know you will."

He rubbed his eyes. "I guess so. One of the older sergeants who helped train us told us that he didn't think he could do it either, but when he got to France in 1918, he did. He said when it comes down to you or him, you'll do what you have to do."

"It's just too bad it has to be done at all."

"Yeah. I'm not a coward."

"I know that."

"I can't tell my folks all this," he said. "But I've got to get it off my chest somehow. You always were a good listener."

"When do you have to go back?"

"Never, I wish, but I've only got thirty days. What about you? You have a steady fellow overseas somewhere?"

"I met someone—a bombardier," she said after a minute, "but we don't really keep in touch."

"Why not?"

"It's a long story."

"So it's not serious."

"I thought for a while it might be." She shrugged. "What about you?"

He grinned and pulled out his wallet. "Her name's Alice. I met her during basic training." He handed her a black-and-white photograph of a young woman whose smile looked ready to erupt into laughter.

"She's really pretty," Celeste said, studying the girl's face. "Are you engaged?"

"She said yes, but I couldn't afford a ring."

"A ring's not important."

"We've talked about getting married before I go overseas, but we decided to wait."

"Why?"

"What if I don't get back? She lives at home and works in an ammunition plant. She'll be better off if we don't get married. I can't stand the idea of her being left with a…baby." His voice dropped to a whisper.

"How does she feel about that?"

"She says a few days are better than none at all."

"Then maybe you should grab whatever time you have." The words slipped out before Celeste realized what she was saying.

"You really think so?"

"You're coming home safe and sound, Pete. But I think you should do whatever the two of you feel is right, whether it's getting married now or waiting until after the war."

"I'd like for you to meet Alice."

"I'll look forward to that. After the war and all, when you bring her home."

"Sure, I'll do that, and we'll get together and talk about old times. Maybe by then you and your bombardier fellow will be back in touch."

"It's hard to get to know somebody during a war. Nothing's certain anymore, not even tomorrow."

"You're right about that. I was just lucky with Alice, I guess. In a way, she reminds me a lot of you."

"I hope she likes all the things you do, the things I didn't like."

He laughed. "She's a real outdoors type."

"Pete, can I ask you something? I don't mean to embarrass you, but we were always good friends."

"We still are, Cece. I've thought about you a lot. Ask me whatever you want to."

"The soldier I met…well, actually, I met him before the war, just briefly, but he ended up back here at Concho Field, and I'm helping at the Canteen, so…"

"So you ran into him again, and bells rang." He grinned.

"I thought so. We're alike in all the ways that you and I weren't, but you and I never argued."

"We didn't have anything to argue about. We had a good time. We both knew we weren't going the same direction after high school, and I wasn't trying to get you in the back seat of my car and…" He stopped. "Now I'm embarrassing you, I bet. Things get talked about in the barracks, and a guy sort of loses his inhibitions."

She felt the color creeping into her face and looked away.

"That's it, isn't it? He tried something."

She nodded.

He leaned across the table and folded her hands into his. "Well, it happens, kiddo. That doesn't make him a rotten apple."

"What's wrong with me, Pete? I'm almost twenty-two."

"There's nothing wrong with you. You're a good girl, always were, always will be. But there's a double standard out there. A guy can, and a girl can't. Understand?"

She nodded.

"Don't write him off for one mistake."

"But you..."

"Listen, I'm as human as your bombardier, and I'm not going to tell you I haven't thought about...things. Some guys do more than think. Maybe it's all one and the same."

"Not really."

He squeezed her hands and released them. "Alice said something once, that in a war people just seem to be grabbing today because tomorrow might not come. You just said the same thing, that maybe Alice and I should grab whatever time we have. I'll admit I'd like to, and maybe, when I get back out to Virginia, I'll change my mind and marry her before I ship out."

"You'll know what's right to do."

"And so will you. Give the guy a break, especially if you really care about him."

****

They said goodbye on the corner where Pete caught a bus to his parents' house. It was too late to go to the bank or to Cox-Rushing-Greer to pay on her layaway, so Celeste walked back to the alley behind Woolworth and got into her car. She parked in the small garage behind the house and walked around to get the mail. *I told Pete that nothing was certain, but habits are hard to break. Daddy used to park and then walk around the house for the mail every afternoon, and now I'm doing it.*

When she climbed the steps, the sight of the telegram stuck in the screen door sent her reeling backward against the porch rail. Before the war, telegrams had brought good news as well as bad. Ben had sent her one as a keepsake when Barbara was born. Now, those yellow envelopes were harbingers of doom, like vultures circling the decaying carcasses of people's hearts and hopes and dreams.

With shaking fingers, numb with fear, Celeste tore open the telegram and unfolded it.

KENT MIA OVER GERMANY. STOP. MAY BE POW. STOP. WILL KEEP YOU POSTED. STOP. LOVE, NEIL

Celeste sat by the phone for a long time, re-reading the telegram and smoothing it in her lap as if removing the creases would take away what it said. Finally, she called Coralee.

"Oh, baby girl, I'm so sorry. We'll just keep praying he's okay."

"He's not okay, Sister. Neither am I." Then she told Coralee everything.

"I'm coming tomorrow. We'll make sense of everything."

"No, don't do that.. I'm all right. I tried to write him, but I couldn't. It's been almost six months. Now I can't write him at all."

"Well, it wasn't your fault."

"Wasn't it? I was judge and jury and found him guilty."

"He wasn't honest with you."

"It wouldn't have made any difference. For that matter, I wasn't honest with him."

"Are you saying you couldn't accept what he'd done because of what Mamma did?"

"I'm not sure. Daddy loved me for a while—or pretended to—because he wanted Mamma back.

Then when she died, he punished me for what she did."

"And so you punished Kent."

"Something like that, I guess."

"Men aren't saints, Cece. Women aren't either. No one is."

"I know. I wish I could take back everything, but I can't. Maybe now I'll never get the chance."

"Are you sure you don't want me to come stay with you, at least for the weekend?"

"I'm sure, but thanks. Kent said I hadn't grown up. At first, I didn't think he was right, but now I think maybe he was, just a little. So now I've got to do it. Grow up. On my own."

When she turned on the radio later before sitting down at the desk, the strains of "I'll Be Seeing You" filled the room and tore at her heart. Celeste bit back her tears and picked up the pen.

Dear Kent,

Here's the letter I should have written six months ago. I tried to write, really I did, but I couldn't say what I felt inside. I've thought about you every day, not that it matters now, but maybe you can feel me thinking about you this minute, wherever you are. I've never stopped loving you, and I don't think I ever will. I was mad at you about Claudia and the boy. I was mad at my father for not loving me after Mamma died. He didn't love me because I wasn't really his, you see. But that's a story for another time.

I guess I've thrown away my chance— our chance to have a life together—but I have to tell you I'm sorry, even if you'll never know it. I'm truly sorry for judging you, for expecting you to be perfect when nobody is. Princes only exist in fairy tales, and they're pretty one-sided characters. Maybe, in the long run, toads are more interesting. At least they're more real.

Well, I guess that's all. I'm glad I met you, no matter what.

With all my love,
Velvet

She sealed the letter in an envelope with Kent's name on the front and put it in one of the small cubicles in the desk, then pulled down the roll top in a gesture of finality.

Chapter Twenty-Two

Celeste called Mrs. Lowe, told her about Kent, and asked to be excused from the Canteen on Saturday. When the woman burst into tears, guilt gnawed at Celeste until she felt actual pain. *I'm living a lie,* she thought as she hung up. *My whole life has been a lie. Maybe that's how I'll live forever. Maybe it's what I deserve.*

Mr. Thomas tried to send her home from work on Saturday morning, but she refused. "I'm better off here, keeping busy." *What would he think of me if he knew I hadn't written to Kent the whole time he's been gone? What would he think if he knew Kent probably despises me...if he's even alive to do that?*

Opening the parlor drapes on Sunday morning, she caught a glimpse of a car pulling away from the curb in front of the house. Moving farther to the right, so the porch column didn't block her view, she noticed a small boy standing on the frost-covered lawn and looking around in bewilderment. He wore short pants and a torn sweater, and clutched a brown paper grocery bag. Though still wearing her robe and slippers, Celeste rushed from the house.

A slightly older version of the boy in the sailor suit lifted wide blue eyes toward her. "Grammy said to give you this," he said, holding out a piece of paper.

"I'll read it in the house," Celeste said, reaching for his chapped, icy hand.

Inside, she unfolded the paper and realized it was a birth certificate. On the back, scrawled in pencil, were the words, "You took her place, now you can take her brat."

"She said I belonged to you now." The soft words, resigned, unquestioning, hurt Celeste's heart. At least August Riley hadn't dumped her on the street somewhere.

"Are you hungry?"

He nodded.

"Let's go in the kitchen and have some breakfast. It's warm in there."

She noticed how he edged toward the space heater she'd lighted as soon as she got up that morning. His skin, an unhealthy gray—whether from grime or something else—looked ready to flake off his thin arms and legs.

When he swallowed two bowls of oatmeal before she got halfway through one, Celeste steeled herself to see it come back up. "Do you want something else?"

He looked around.

"More milk? Toast?"

He nodded.

She made cinnamon toast, a favorite from her own childhood, and refilled his glass of milk. He made short work of everything she set in front of him. "How old are you, Jonny?"

"Six."

She checked the information against the birth certificate. He'd turned six on the last day of August.

"Do you go to school?"

He shook his head.

"To church?"

He shook his head again.

"What's in the bag?"

"My stuff."

"May I see?"

He shrugged.

She took out a pitiful assortment of underwear and socks, three short-sleeved shirts, a second pair of short pants, and a pair of faded pajamas. *At least I had what I needed, even if I worked to earn the money for most of it. He's just a baby and can't help himself.*

He leaned his elbows on the table. "What's your name?"

"Celeste," she said. "Cece."

"Okay."

They regarded each other for a long moment. She tried to see Kent in his face, but he was all Claudia, including his blonde hair and blue eyes.

"What else did your grammy tell you?"

"Nothing."

"Just that you belonged to me now?"

"Yep. Do I?"

"I guess you do."

"For always?"

"For now, anyway. We'll see what happens."

****

She left him splashing in the bathtub while she called Coralee, who she knew would be getting Barbara dressed for Sunday School. When Coralee repeated the story to Big Ben, he got on the phone immediately. "I'm going to call my lawyer there in San Angelo. Adam Colley. He'll come out and help you make heads or tails of this."

"What will happen to the little boy?"

"Colley will see that he goes somewhere, a children's home, probably."

"No!" The explosion from Celeste's lips surprised even her.

"What?"

"I'm sorry," Celeste said, "but he's already been thrown away twice."

"You aren't thinking about keeping him, are you? You can't."

"Maybe...he might be all I have left of Kent."

Big Ben blew out his breath in a tired whoosh.

"Coralee told us about all that. But keeping the boy out of guilt, Celeste..."

"It's not guilt. At least I don't think it is. It's just that we're sort of alike. Both of us came up short."

"I guess you could look at it that way, but you're a young single woman. No judge is going to give you custody of a little boy who's not even remotely related to you."

"He might be Kent's."

"And you're not married to Kent. He's not even available to claim paternity and give permission for you to be the boy's guardian."

"His name's on the birth certificate. I could tell them he left him with me when he went overseas. Nobody has to know different."

"For starters, how are you going to get him a ration card so you can feed him? How are you going to put him in school? Get him taken care of if he gets sick?"

"I don't know, but there's got to be a way. Please, Big Ben. Please tell your lawyer that I want to keep him."

****

By the time Adam Colley came back from Brownwood at the end of the week with notarized papers, signed by Claudia Peters' mother, giving Celeste guardianship of Jonny, Celeste had settled into her new role—though she wasn't sure exactly how to describe just what that role was.

"You're just his guardian," the lawyer stressed to Celeste when he brought the papers she needed. "The grandmother could take him back."

"She threw him away. Dumped him on the street like a sack of garbage."

"I'm not saying she would, but that sort of person, well, you never know. She could come after you for money."

Celeste laughed. "She wouldn't get much."

"Adopting him would give you more leverage, but without his father's say-so, you can't do that. Even if he did, you're single. Adoptions are granted to married couples."

"I told you Kent doesn't think he's Jonny's father."

"Didn't he admit to the possibility?"

Celeste felt her face grow hot. She looked away from the older man and nodded.

"The name on the birth certificate is pretty damning, even if it's not factual. I wonder why the mother didn't take him to court for child support?"

"She wanted him to marry her. I guess she didn't want to antagonize him."

"Miss Riley...Celeste...I have a daughter your age, and speaking to you as both an attorney and a father, I've got to say you've gotten yourself into a mess."

"I can't throw him away."

"He's not really yours to do anything with. It wouldn't be throwing him away to turn him over to child welfare. They'd find him a home."

"An orphanage."

"If that's all they can manage. I'll admit people want infants, not six-year-old boys."

Celeste shook her head. "If he's Kent's, and I'm going to believe he is, he's all Kent left behind."

"Well, do it your way. If you run into any problems, you know how to get in touch with me."

****

Jonny took up residence in August Riley's room. It needed work and an investment of some money to become a little boy's room, so Celeste fiddled with her budget to see what she could manage. When Coralee suggested selling the large bedroom suite and using the money to get a smaller set for Jonny, Celeste wondered why she hadn't thought of it herself. With some advice from Mrs. Aikman,

Celeste got a fair price from a secondhand store on North Oakes. She even let Jonny weigh in on a single bed and a chest of drawers. Mrs. Aikman's son-in-law, home on leave, helped put up new wallpaper.

Pearl ran up a bedspread in a cowboy print and sent matching drapes and a quilt. Awed by his new riches, Jonny spent a lot of time in his room playing with the set of plastic cowboys and Indians Celeste bought with her discount at Woolworth and the toy cars she found at the same secondhand shop where she'd sold the furniture.

Her first priority had been to get him some decent clothes so he could go to school. Celeste took the guardianship papers to San Jacinto, the elementary school she'd attended just down the street, and enrolled him. The principal, his own patriotism enhanced when he'd been deemed too old to enlist, listened with obvious sympathy to Celeste's smooth explanation of doing a favor for a friend overseas, and promised to take good care of Jonny. "I'm counting on that," she said as she left his office. "I really am."

She walked Jonny to his classroom and handed him his new school bag, bulging with supplies. He'd slept with it the night before. "Remember to wait for Mrs. Aikman," she told him. "She'll be here to walk you home."

He looked up at her with eyes that had become more alive with every passing day. "I remember, Cece."

"And be good."

He nodded. "I'll be good."

She ruffled his carefully-combed hair, then smoothed it down again. "Okay, pal. I'll see you."

"I'll see you," he echoed.

By the time she got out the front door, she was in tears without understanding why.

****

After considering it from every angle, she confided the entire complicated situation to Veda. "I knew something was wrong right after Kent left," she said. "I'm so sorry, Cece. What can I do to help?"

"Just be my friend—and Jonny's, too."

"Always."

"If Kent comes home…"

Veda grasped Celeste's hands. "We're going to believe that he will."

"If he does, there's Jonny."

"I don't know why it's so hard for a man to admit his mistakes and go on, but it is."

"Maybe it's because we expect them to be perfect."

Veda laughed. "A prince, not a toad?"

"Right."

"Well, they're not. When Kent comes home, he'll have to make a decision, that's all. I hope he's man enough to make the right one for all of you."

Celeste didn't want to tell Mr. Thomas the whole story, but there didn't seem any way to get around it and still make the case for having Claudia's child in her home. He listened without commenting. When she finished, he said, "I commend you, Miss Riley."

"It's the right thing to do."

"For the boy, yes. For you, I wonder. You're a young woman with your entire life ahead of you. You have no guarantee that if…that when Kent Goddard comes home, he'll accept the child. I believe you said he's denied him thus far."

"It's hard for him."

"To own up to what he did? Oh, yes, it's very hard, I'd think. I'm not condemning him. Young people make mistakes, and we know Miss Peters was, well, persuasive."

"She's dead, and Kent may be dead, too, but Jonny's here, and he deserves a home."

"I agree, and I think you've done an unselfish thing to take him in. But as you know, I have daughters of my own. I have to consider what you're doing from the standpoint of a father who wants a happy life for his children."

Celeste took the daybook out of the safe and sat down at her desk. "Thank you, Mr. Thomas. You've been very good to me, and I—"

"If ever Mary and I can help, you know we're here."

"Thank you."

The next week he raised her salary by two dollars a week. "It's not much," he said, "but it's all I can do for now."

"I didn't expect more money. I just told you because I felt like I owed you the truth."

"I know that, Miss Riley, but you can use the extra money. Take it and use it for Jonny, at least for now."

****

At Thanksgiving, she and Jonny, who by now looked more like a child instead of a waif, took the bus to Sterling City to save gas coupons. She felt relieved, though not surprised, when the whole family welcomed him like he'd been part of them forever. Barbara, by virtue of being two years older, took Jonny under her wing. On the ride home, he announced that he liked everybody and thought Pearl was a lot nicer than his grammy.

"Maybe she did the best she could," Celeste observed.

"She didn't like me. She said I was a bas..."

Celeste clamped her hand over his mouth. "That's not a word nice little boys say."

"Am I a nice little boy?"

"Yes, you are."

"Okay."

****

When everything looked settled, she wrote to Neil.

I took him to my doctor for a check-up. He's underweight and a little anemic, but otherwise he's okay. The doctor gave him a tonic, and I'm working with him every night to help him catch up in school. His teacher says he's smart and works hard. He likes school and is making friends. My neighbor, Mrs. Aikman, walks to the school to meet him every afternoon. It's just a few blocks, but I don't feel comfortable letting him walk all the way by himself just yet. He stays with her until I get home right after four. I just told her I was taking care of him for a friend overseas. These days, everybody wants to do something "for the boys," so she's agreeable and doesn't ask questions.

On Saturdays, when I only have to work half a day, he stays here and listens to the radio or plays with his toys. (I'm not sure he ever had any before. He puts them in a box in the closet every night as if he's afraid they'll disappear!) He knows he can go to Mrs. Aikman if he needs anything. I think he must have spent a lot of time by himself, because he doesn't seem to need people around all the time, and he doesn't get into trouble when he's alone.

I know the big question in your mind is why I'm doing this. Maybe I shouldn't tell you Kent told me, on his last night, that Jonny could be his, even though he still insisted he wasn't. But his name is on the birth certificate Mrs. Peters sent along with Jonny, and the lawyer, who helped me take care of the paperwork, said that makes it official from a legal standpoint. When Kent comes home—and I'm going to believe he will—we'll just have to work things out from there.

Meanwhile, Jonny's happy and taken care of, and every child has a right to all that and more.

Neil wrote back saying he wasn't going to tell his mother about Jonny "for obvious reasons." He and Kay were getting married on Christmas Eve after church services. He thanked Celeste for what she was doing and said he'd be in touch as soon as they heard more about Kent. Celeste was sure she read *Thank goodness she dumped the boy on you and not me* between the terse lines.

Celeste and Jonny went back to Sterling City for Christmas. Watching his face light up on Christmas Eve over a new robe and slippers, then over a toy truck and a stocking full of fruit, nuts, and candy from Santa Claus the next morning, Celeste put away her last doubt about the wisdom of taking responsibility for the little boy. "He's mine now," she told Pearl while she helped get Christmas dinner on the table. "Sometimes it seems like I've always had him."

Pearl patted her arm. "Love is what makes a family, Celeste. Being a parent isn't easy, but it's worth every ounce of effort."

"I still wonder if I can do everything I need to do, especially when he gets older."

"All you can do is try. And who knows? Maybe Kent will step in to help."

"I don't think about that, Pearl. I know Coralee told you he left with things pretty strained between us."

"If the two of you really love each other…"

"Maybe we just thought we did. People don't always think sensibly during a war, do they?"

"You were sensible not to rush into a hasty

marriage."

"And not so sensible to take Jonny."

"I wouldn't say that at all. It seems to me that things are working out very well for the two of you."

Celeste stepped back and surveyed the place settings, adjusting a stray spoon beside the sugar bowl. "Well, for good or ill, he's mine, Pearl, and I'm going to take care of him the best I can."

****

It snowed on New Year's Eve. The next morning she helped Jonny build a snowman in the front yard. The phone was ringing when they came inside. "I'll get it," Jonny yelled, barreling toward the hall.

Celeste grabbed him by the collar of his coat. "Uh-huh, hotshot. You go get out of those wet clothes, and put them on a chair in front of the gas heater in the kitchen."

"Aw, Cece!"

"Go." She picked up the phone.

"He's alive," Neil yelled. "Kent's alive!"

"He's…oh, Neil! Oh, thank You, God!" She began to tremble.

"He bailed out just over the border in Holland, and the Dutch resistance hid him from the Germans. I don't know all the details, but he's on his way back to England now. At least, I think he is. The letter was pretty vague, but we're supposed to get another one."

She slid to the floor and cradled the phone against her. "Are they sure it's him?"

"I hope so. I've never given up hope that he's coming home."

"Coming home," Celeste murmured.

"Celeste, are you going to write him about Jonny?"

"I'll have to."

"Mother knows about him now. I think she ran into Mrs. Peters somewhere, and the woman threw it in her face. Then she got it out of me that I knew and…oh, well. Same song, second verse. Or maybe the needle's just stuck."

"It was the best thing that could've happened for Jonny."

"Do you really think…I mean, you've had him a while now…is there anything about him that reminds you of Kent?"

"Not really. He looks like his mother."

"But you think he's Kent's son."

"I don't know what I think, Neil, but I guess I've kind of wished it. Wished for something left of Kent if the worst happened."

"Do you need any help? Money, I mean. Kay and I can send you a little every month."

"We're all right."

"Will you let me know if you need anything?"

"Yes, thanks, Neil. That's kind of you."

"Kent's my brother, and if Jonny might be part of him, well…"

"I understand."

"My brother's a good man, Celeste. One mistake doesn't condemn him forever."

"I was the one who condemned him, and now it's too late."

"Are you sure? I know Kent loves you. He wrote to me about the fight you had the night before he left. It tore him up."

"I thought I knew him, but I realize now I hadn't looked deep enough. I didn't know myself, either. Jonny's made a big difference."

"Maybe Kent'll get sent home now. Like I said, we're supposed to get another letter soon. This one just had the basic information, just what I told you. But I'll let you know as soon as another one comes."

"Thank you, Neil. You're a good brother. A good friend."

Neil didn't answer her right away. "I said a few

things to him that I regret, too, Celeste. He deserved more from me after all the years he put me first." He took a breath and blew it out. "You take care of yourself. Everything will work out."

Chapter Twenty-Three

With Jonny tucked in for the night, Celeste sat down at the desk and took out a box of stationery. *No time like the present. At least he's alive. Whatever happens between us doesn't really matter as long as he's alive.* Words flowed from her pen with amazing ease, but when she re-read the letter, she knew Kent would struggle to understand what she'd said.

Dear Kent,

Neil just called to tell me that you're alive and well and on your way back to England. Neither of us ever gave up hope. Maybe you'll be coming home soon. There are some things I need to tell you first, so here goes.

Mrs. Peters quite literally dumped Jonny on my doorstep one cold Sunday morning about three months ago. He wasn't dressed for the weather, and he was hungry. It took me about five minutes to decide I was going to keep him, not so much for you, Kent, as for me. Jonny and I have something important in common—both of us were thrown away. You see, my mother left the man I called Daddy, and he took her back— and me with her. That's why he had no use for me after she died. I didn't tell you before, because I thought you'd be shocked. And, I was ashamed, even though it wasn't my fault.

Big Ben's lawyer drove to Brownwood and got Mrs. Peters to sign papers giving me guardianship. Whether you're his father or not doesn't matter. What matters is that a little boy is safe, well-cared for, and happy, and I've found a new way to look at my own situation—and at yours as well.

When you come home, maybe we can start over for ourselves and for Jonny. At the very least, you're legally his father because your name is on his birth certificate. Mr. Colley says you can give up your parental rights to me, if that's what you want to do. Whatever you decide about us, I'll accept. I don't have any right to expect anything from you.

I ran into Pete Frame, the boy I used to date in high school. He met someone in Virginia where he went for training. Her name is Alice, and he says she reminds him of me—except, of course, she's a real outdoors type like he is. We talked a long time, and I told him about you. Not everything, just that I felt like I'd messed things up between us by expecting you to be perfect. He set me straight on a few things, and I appreciated it. That was the same afternoon I came home and found the telegram from Neil saying you were missing in action.

I've had a long time to think about that last night and how it might've been different. Then, of course, there's Jonny, and he's made a big difference in my life. I'm totally responsible for another human being besides myself. Sometimes I think he's six going on forty. He's a good little kid and doing well in school despite his late start.

Anyway, we're getting along just fine, and I can't imagine not having him around.

But I'd like to have you around, too.
Take care of yourself, Kent.
All my love,
Velvet

Celeste marked the first letter she'd written *Read First* before tucking it in with the second.

"I don't have any illusions that we're going to live happily ever after," Celeste told Coralee. "He has every right to wash his hands of me. Of both of us."

"If he does, it's his loss. The important thing is, Jonny's all right, and you've changed almost overnight. I can't call you 'baby girl' now. You're a full-fledged woman."

"Kent had a problem with that nickname. I guess I *was* more like your baby than your sister. Anyway, I've come a long way from thinking that a blue velvet dress can change my life."

"In a way, it did."

"Maybe it did. Anyway, that's in the past."

"Don't give up on the future, Cece. I believe in it for you."

****

When Celeste didn't hear from Kent, she wrote to Neil. "We haven't heard from him either," he wrote back. "Maybe he's not getting our letters. That happens sometimes. But I'll call you when I hear from him."

By spring, Celeste decided that the whole thing was a false alarm, even a terrible mistake. Kent might still be missing somewhere. Or, he might be so badly injured that he couldn't communicate. Whatever the reason for his silence, a hopelessness settled over her, threatening her new-found confidence. She was glad for the diversion created by Jonny's cheerful presence. Sometimes she wondered if she had what it took to keep up with a little boy who seemed to be growing every day.

****

At the end of May, Celeste asked off early to attend Jonny's end-of-school program. Wearing long pants and a crisp white shirt with a bow tie he'd picked out himself, he recited "Twenty Froggies Went to School" without a hitch. Celeste smiled until her face ached.

"Change your clothes and go out and play before supper," she said, opening the mailbox and the door at the same time. Her fingers closed around a single envelope, a letter from Kent.

"I'm hungry, Cece."

"I'll fix supper early." She had to retrieve the letter when it dropped from her trembling fingers. "Go change clothes, and don't forget to hang up your shirt."

"I worked hard today. Don't you think maybe I could have a cookie?"

"One."

"Where are they?" The unmasked triumph in his voice brought a smile to Celeste's face despite her anxiety.

"Behind the box of oatmeal in the pantry. Just one, you understand?"

"Sure." He took off in the direction of the kitchen.

"Uh-uh. After you change clothes."

"Aw, Cece."

"And hang up your shirt."

"Heard you the first time," he muttered, hunching his shoulders and turning toward his bedroom.

Closing the door of her room, she sat down on the bed and ripped one end from the envelope.

Dear Velvet,

I'm sorry I haven't written sooner. All my mail got tied up somewhere while I was hiding from the Krauts, and it only caught up with me last week. I was really happy to get your letters, and I read the first one first like you said. I read it three times, as a matter of fact, and thought, "Well, everything's going to be all right now." Then I opened the second one.

What Mrs. Peters did was ignorant and mean, but that's about what I'd expect from her. And I'd expect you to help the boy out the way you did—but not keep him. I admitted to you that he could be mine, but something inside me says he isn't. Even if he is, I wouldn't want to do more than just make sure he was provided for. Claudia had some nerve giving him my name. I guess she thought it would make me give in and marry her, but she reckoned wrong.

I know none of this is the boy's fault, but in a way, it's not mine either, especially since there's no way to prove he's mine. A blood test would only prove he wasn't, and I don't mind doing that. But even if all it says is that I might be the father, I don't want him.

You said in your letter that the two of you had something in common. I'm glad you finally told me about your father—or rather, the man you thought was your father. Now you know it was him with the problem, not you. It doesn't make any difference to me, Velvet. I love you for yourself, not who or what your parents were or weren't.

I love you, and I want to marry you, but I won't raise Claudia's child. We can find him a good place.

Please write again soon.

I love you, I love you, I love you.

         Kent

The excitement of the day faded as a cold, dead

weight settled in the pit of Celeste's stomach. Kent had the right to feel the way he did, but how could he dismiss her feelings so easily? *I love Jonny. It seems like I've been part of his life forever. I can't throw him away again. I won't. Oh, Kent, if I don't hold Jonny against you, then you shouldn't hold him against me.*

They ate supper on the porch, and Celeste let Jonny stay up later than usual. He'd earned a nickel for sweeping Mrs. Aikman's porch, steps, and walk, and used it to buy a new comic book. Celeste could still see the joy in his eyes when the woman tousled his hair and told him he did a good job, then handed him the nickel. But when she had finally tucked him into bed, she couldn't put off the inevitable.

Sitting down at the desk, she wrote,

Dear Kent,

Knowing that you still love me and are willing to forgive my blind judgment, just as I'm willing to forgive your youthful misstep, makes me very happy. "We'll find him a good place," you say. He's a little boy, not a puppy. Whether he's yours or not, he's mine. I've had him for almost seven months. He's a bright, sensitive child, and even with a bad start, he caught up in a hurry. These days he doesn't look as "old" to me as he used to when he first came.

I love him, and I think he returns all my affection. Don't ask me to explain, because I can't. It just happened, and I'm not sorry. If marrying you means giving him up, I can't do it. You have to know I won't change my mind. Whatever happens, I want permanent custody of him, and according to Mr. Colley, you're the only one who can give it to me. He says a judge is likely to hold my being single against me, so I'll find Jonny a father if that's what it takes to keep him. That's not a threat, Kent. It's just the way it is. Now that I have confidence in my ability to be a parent, surely I can be a good wife to someone.

If you don't write again, I'll understand. I love you and want you to have everything in life that will make you happy. I just wish there was some way to work all this out so that all of us could be happy together.

Velvet

That no more letters came from Kent didn't really surprise her. She was glad to have other things on her mind, like finding someone to watch Jonny five days a week during the summer months. Even though he stayed by himself on Saturday mornings, she didn't like the idea of leaving him at loose ends every day from eight to four. Fortunately, the school principal's fourteen-year-old daughter thought fifty cents a day was a fortune, especially when Jonny practically took care of himself. The extra money going out made Celeste look for more ways to cut corners, but it had to be done.

"We'll manage," she told Coralee when she offered to help. "I don't have rent or utilities, just groceries and what Jonny needs in the way of clothes. He's growing so fast."

In June, when the Allies invaded Europe at Normandy, she wondered if Kent had been on one of the bombers that "softened up" the beaches before the first troops landed. For a day or two, she thought of asking Neil, but as she hadn't heard from him again either, she decided it would be better to let things go.

Churchill said the invasion wasn't the beginning of the end but rather "the end of the beginning." Some people said the war could go on another five years. Mrs. Lowe said so long was unthinkable. "All

Dancing with Velvet

those boys. We can't lose all those boys."

Jonny turned seven in August and started second grade in September with a wild enthusiasm that warmed Celeste's heart. In October, the *Standard Times* carried Pete Frame's picture and the notice of his death somewhere in France. Celeste cried until the newspaper was soggy with her streaming tears.

"Gee, Cece, I don't want you to cry," Jonny crooned as he leaned against her shoulder. "I wish I could go fight those mean old Nazis. I'd fix 'em."

She grabbed him with a terror she knew he could feel. "I hope there won't be any more wars, not for you to fight."

He squirmed. "But I would. I'd bomb those bad guys and blow 'em up clear to the sky."

"No more killing," she said, her tears beginning again. "No more, no more, no more."

****

The next week, Pete's Alice wrote to her, saying that Pete had left Celeste's name and address "just in case."

He said you were the nicest girl he'd ever known, except me, of course, and a good friend. We did get married before he left, just a quick ceremony in front of a judge. We only had three days, but it was enough. As I write this, his son is smiling at me from his buggy. Pete's parents want me to come for a visit. They want to see their grandchild. But I have to go back to work soon. (A friend will take care of Peter James during the day.) So, they're hoping to come out here sometime soon. I hope you and I will meet someday, too. Pete told me about running into you while he was home on leave, and I think something you said gave him the courage to say we'd go on and get married before he went overseas. He was such a good man, and I know his son will be a good man, too.

Celeste tucked the grainy black-and-white snapshot of Peter James Frame, Jr. into the same wooden box Pete had made for her keepsakes. *Oh, sweet Alice, I'm so glad you have Pete's little boy. I know, well almost know, how you feel. If I never see Kent again, whether because of the war or because he wants it that way, I have Jonny, and he's everything. I'll give this box to Pete's son someday for his own special treasures.*

****

Jonny said he wanted to be a clown for Halloween. Celeste asked him why he chose that instead of being a soldier or a sailor like most of the other boys. "It's a bad thing, the war is," he said. "But clowns make people smile."

"I couldn't give him up now," Celeste told Coralee at Thanksgiving. "Not for anything—or anyone. Even Kent. Sometimes...sometimes he reminds me of Kent. Oh, not the way he looks, but the way he talks, his sense of humor, the way he can be so serious and understand things."

"You've had a lot to do with that, Cece."

"But there had to be something there to start with, don't you think?"

"I think he's a sweet kid, and we all love him."

****

Veda talked Celeste into going to the Roof Garden on New Year's Eve. "I'll bet that blue velvet dress has been in mothballs forever."

"I'm not going to wear it."

"Why not?"

"It stood for something that doesn't matter anymore."

"A fairytale romance? There's more than one fish in the sea, Cece."

"It was going to change my life. Make me

someone I wasn't. But it didn't do that, and princes don't exist. That blue velvet dress was a dream that never came true."

"You have Jonny. I'm not sure I could do what you've done."

"A few months ago, I'd have said the same thing. Now it's like we've been together forever."

Mrs. Aikman came over to keep Jonny. "I'll be home early," Celeste promised him. "We'll go out in the yard and light sparklers if you're still awake."

Celeste didn't lack for partners, but she caught herself looking around the dance floor as if expecting to see Kent. After the balloons and streamers dropped, and they sang the obligatory *Auld Lang Syne*, she left Veda at her apartment and drove home.

"He tried, but he couldn't keep his eyes open," Mrs. Aikman said, glancing at the little boy fast asleep on the sofa. "He keeled over while he was writing his New Year's resolutions. I just covered him up and left him there on the settee."

When Mrs. Aikman had gone, Celeste knelt beside the sleeping child and picked up the red Big Chief tablet. Across the top of the page he'd written MY NEW YEAR'S RESOLUTIONS FOR 1945. There was only one: *I will be so good my Mom will smile all the time and never cry again.*

Celeste laid her face against the blanket and wept silent tears for a world of Kents and Petes and Alices—and finally, for herself.

Chapter Twenty-Four

After Christmas, everyone began to talk about a quick end to the war. President Roosevelt's death in April came as a shock to the country, overshadowing everything else. Then, early in May, just before Jonny finished second grade, Germany did indeed surrender. Celeste took him downtown, to watch people celebrate in the streets, and then to church, where many of the members had gathered spontaneously to give thanks and pray for the end of the fighting in the Pacific, too.

"JimBob's daddy will come home now," Jonny said the next morning as he carried their plates to the table. "He asked me if my daddy was coming home."

"What did you tell him?"

"I said I didn't have a daddy."

"I see."

"But I do, don't I? Everybody has a mom and a dad." Celeste caught a flicker of hope in his blue eyes that fastened on her.

"Yes, they do."

"But you're my mom now, and you're not married."

Celeste slipped her napkin from its ring and spread it in her lap, buying time to form a reply.

Jonny spread his napkin the way she'd taught him. "Not having a dad around is what that word you told me not to say means, doesn't it?"

Celeste didn't look at him. "You're only a little boy, Jonny. You can't understand everything yet."

"I'm almost eight."

Going on forty. "Yes, your birthday is coming up at the end of the summer."

"You don't like for me to talk about my dad, do you?" He took a big gulp of milk.

"Please wipe your mouth," she murmured automatically. She didn't miss the small sigh that seemed to fill the entire room.

"You didn't forget about the school picnic on Friday, did you?"

"No, I'll be there. Mr. Thomas already said I could take the afternoon off and make it up on Saturday."

"And you didn't forget the cupcakes?"

"We'll make them tomorrow night."

"Blue frosting."

"Why blue?"

"I don't know. I just like it."

"Okay, blue frosting."

In front of the school, just before he got out of the car, he turned to Celeste. "I don't care if my dad doesn't like me, as long as you're my mom." Then he grabbed the school bag with his lunch and tablet and ran off, letting the door slam behind him.

****

"What am I going to tell him, Sister?" Celeste asked when she called the ranch after Jonny went to bed that night. "He's let things go for now, but someday he'll want answers."

"Would you like for Ben to talk to him? Sometimes a man can talk to a little boy better."

"I'll think about it."

"You haven't heard from Kent, I guess."

"No, and I'm not going to."

"Maybe you will."

"No."

"I don't know what to tell you, sweetie."

"There's nothing to tell. Kent isn't going to accept Jonny. In a way, that's not accepting me either."

"Are you sure?"

"I think so. Besides, Jonny and I are a package deal."

****

Celeste checked on Jonny before she went to bed. He slept soundly, one arm thrown back over his head, and the other clutching the airplane Veda's brother sent back the last time she went home. *He knows he's safe. He knows I'll be here in the morning when he wakes up. That's more than he ever had before.* She straightened the covers over his legs, which had grown longer and rounder in the past year.

You and me, kiddo, both of us rejects like the merchandise Mr. Thomas sends back when he finds a flaw. But it's okay. We haven't done too badly on our own. We've muddled through, and it gets better all the time. Maybe someday somebody will want us, and you'll have a dad. But I wish...oh, how I wish it would be Kent.

****

Neil finally wrote to say that Kent was being sent home on leave, then reassigned for the duration of the war.

I'm going to try to talk to him about you and Jonny, but I don't know how he'll take it, was his closing line.

"I hope he isn't reassigned here," Celeste said to Veda over lunch at Concho Drug one Friday. "It would be uncomfortable, to say the least."

"For you or him?"

"For all of us."

"He ought to take a blood test and prove once and for all whether he is or isn't the father."

"A blood test would only prove he isn't. Anyway, he said it didn't matter, that he wasn't going to raise Jonny no matter what."

"But he'll let you raise him."

"Sure, alone."

"Do you still love Kent?"

"That's the funny thing, Veda. In a way, I love him more than ever. Not like I was in love with him before, of course, but because he's flawed like I am. That makes him more real. I want something—someone—real."

"Everybody has flaws."

"I told you about Mamma."

"You're not still thinking about what she did, are you? Look, Cece, she made her choices, just like Kent. If you weren't here, what would've happened to Jonny? We're all here for a reason. How we got here doesn't matter."

Celeste shrugged.

"You're set on keeping Jonny, I guess."

Celeste's eyes widened. "Veda I've had him going on two years. How could I give him up?"

"You couldn't. I was just baiting you to make you think."

"I've thought about it every way there is to think. His grandmother doesn't want him, and Kent's mother sure isn't going to take him. Neil thinks I'm doing a good thing, but he's just glad he and Kay don't have to make the decision about raising him or putting him in an orphanage. Anyway, Jonny wouldn't want to go with any of them. This is his home. I'm his mom."

"Then someone else will come along and want both of you."

"You think so?"

"I do, Cece. Kent doesn't know what he's given up."

****

Celeste and Jonny were playing marbles on the porch on Saturday afternoon when she heard the phone ringing. "Oh, Celeste, thank goodness." Mrs.

Lowe's voice bordered on panic-stricken. "Can you help me out at the Canteen tonight? I'm going to be short four girls."

"Four! Why?"

"Two of them have brothers coming home this weekend, one is sick, and the other one eloped. Eloped! Can you believe it?"

"If Mrs. Aikman can watch Jonny, I'll come. Let me check and call you back."

"Please come, even if you have to bring the boy. He's such a nice, polite little fellow, and nobody will care if he sits in the kitchen and stuffs himself with doughnuts."

Celeste laughed. "He would, too, and then he'd be a nice, sick little fellow. I'll call you back in a few minutes."

****

Jonny sat on the foot of Celeste's bed watching her brush her hair. "Aw, heck, I don't know why you have to go out tonight. We were having a good game."

"We can't play marbles all night, pal."

"But we could listen to the radio. You could watch me draw war maps."

"Why do you draw war maps?"

"All the guys do."

"Oh. Well, we can do that Sunday after church."

"I guess."

"Mrs. Aikman will play checkers with you."

"She always lets me win."

"Tell her you know that she does and not to do it. But say it nicely."

"Okay."

Celeste rose from her dressing table. "I made tuna fish sandwiches for your supper. They're in the refrigerator with some raw carrots and an apple. And you can have chocolate ice cream for dessert. Two scoops, no more."

"I guess maybe you hid the cookies again."

"I have to hide them." She tickled him, and he rolled over on his back, giggling. "You're such a cookie snatcher."

"Aw, Mom, Granny Pearl says I'm a growing boy."

"You're a cookie snatcher." She reached for him again, but he rolled away. "I left two out on the cabinet. After supper, mind you, and not the minute I walk out the door."

"Okay."

"Take a good bath. Tomorrow's Sunday."

"Okay."

"I'll tell Mrs. Aikman to check the corners."

"Aw, Mom."

Celeste kissed his cheek. "See you later, hotshot."

****

Mrs. Lowe greeted Celeste with open arms. "You don't know how much I appreciate this, Celeste."

"I'm glad I could come, Mrs. Lowe. I've missed helping out, but you understand I couldn't leave Jonny every Saturday night."

"Of course, I understand." She stepped back a little. "Celeste, I don't mean to be nosy, but you told me you were keeping him for someone who was overseas. When the war is over, won't he be leaving you?"

"He'll probably stay with me," Celeste said.

"I see. One of *those* things. Well, he certainly seems to love you."

Celeste lifted her eyebrows and tried to look neutral.

"It's a wonderful thing, dear, and Jonny's a sweet little boy, but won't it be difficult for you when Kent comes home?"

Celeste kept smiling. "Oh, I don't think so, Mrs. Lowe. I've told him all about Jonny. Things will work out." She slipped out of her coat. "I'll go see what I can help with in the kitchen."

****

"Where did all these people come from?" Celeste asked Marilyn as she forked doughnuts onto a platter for the fourth time.

"It's been busier this last year. I'm not sure why. Here, take these cookies out with the doughnuts."

Celeste balanced the platters on her arm and reached for a pitcher of fruit punch. "I hope it's over soon."

"Don't we all?"

The din of conversation rising over the music from the phonograph assaulted her ears as she emerged into the main room of the Canteen. *The noise in here is awful. I'm too used to being home where it's quiet.* She skirted a couple dancing on the fringes of the floor and slid the plates into an empty space on the table.

"Hello, Velvet."

She barely righted the pitcher before its contents could drench the tablecloth.

"Kent."

His looked thinner, his face pinched and pale. She noticed the lieutenant's bars on his uniform and a ribbon she didn't recognize on his left pocket.

"How are you?" he asked as she stared, unable to take her eyes from his face.

She swallowed twice before she could speak. "All right."

"I wasn't sure you'd be here."

"I don't come anymore since..." She stopped and started over. "Mrs. Lowe needed me to fill in tonight."

"Is our table still over in the corner?"

"I'm not sure." She tried to see across the packed the dance floor. "Maybe there's one somewhere."

His touch, when he cupped her elbow to guide

her through the crowd, sparked feelings she'd tried to forget. He pulled out a chair for her and sat down across the table. "You look different."

"Older, anyway."

"What are you now? Twenty-three? Twenty-four?"

"Twenty-four next April."

"How's your family?"

"Everyone's doing well. Barbara's growing like a weed. One week she wants to be a movie star, and the next she wants to be a cowgirl."

"I guess you still go to the ranch on holidays."

"Yes."

"Still work at Woolworth?"

She nodded.

"How do you manage with…"

"I worked things out."

"Your hair is different."

"I cut it a little. Easier to take care of."

He glanced away, then back. "I've been reassigned to Concho Field."

She digested the information she wished she hadn't heard. "I'm glad you're not going back."

"Had two planes shot out from under me. Luckily, the second one made it to the Channel before the last engine quit. We got wet, but we all got out in one piece."

"Oh, Kent, how awful for you."

He shrugged. "I'm alive. Lost a lot of buddies, though."

"Pete Frame is dead," she said, choking on the words she'd never actually voiced. "My high school date. We ran into each other when he was home on leave, before he went overseas. He married a girl in Virginia." She hesitated. "He never saw his son."

"Too bad."

"Yes, it is. She wrote to me. Alice. His wife."

"The English girls came to the base for dances

sometimes. They were nice, but they weren't you."

She didn't reply.

"I looked at your picture every chance I got. The one you had made in that blue velvet dress. Do you still have it?"

"Yes, but I don't wear it."

"Not in style?"

"Right. Out of date."

"You have your eye on something newer?"

"Not exactly. The dress stood for something then, a new direction in my life, a change I wanted to make."

"You've made a lot of changes, I guess."

"I've had to."

"Yeah." He looked around again. "Want to dance?"

"Maybe we shouldn't."

"I need to hold you, Velvet. All I've thought about for the last few months, since I knew I was coming home, was holding you in my arms. Sometimes I'd go to bed at night and actually feel you."

"Kent, I meant what I said in the letter you never answered, so I decided you didn't think there was any middle ground for us."

"I didn't know what to say to you. I still don't. I love you and want to marry you. Do you still love me, or is there someone else? You said you were going to be looking."

The accusatory note in his voice irritated her. "There's no one else, Kent. I'm not sure there ever could be."

"Why not?"

"You know what they say about a girl's first love." She tried to smile.

"I guess not, but let's don't talk about it. Dance with me." He stood up and held out his hand.

****

He held her in a way that the chaperones told the girls wasn't appropriate, but no one tapped her on the shoulder. She guessed Mrs. Lowe recognized Kent and explained the situation to the others. When she came to their table later and told Kent how glad she was to see him, she seemed more emotional than usual. Using the fact that the woman lingered beside Kent's chair, Celeste made an excuse to go back into the kitchen.

"You look like you've seen a ghost," Marilyn said, looking up from the bread she was slicing for sandwiches.

"Kent's here."

"Oh, Cece. And you didn't know he was coming?"

"He's been assigned to Concho Field."

"That's wonderful! Now the two of you can get married. When you're ready, that is, and I guess you are, after all this time."

Celeste reminded herself that Marilyn didn't know the story and tried to close her ears. "I'll help you with those sandwiches," she said, going to wash her hands at the sink.

Mrs. Lowe caught her when she came out of the kitchen. "Did you know that ribbon on his pocket is for the Silver Star?"

"No, I didn't. He didn't mention it."

"He didn't say anything to me, either, but I knew what it was when I saw it. Valor in action. That's what it's for." She patted Celeste. "You're a lucky girl."

She saw Kent dancing with another girl, but she noticed he went back to "their" table alone. She brought more cookies from the kitchen before she joined him again. "Sorry. Mrs. Lowe is working short-handed tonight."

"She told me. It's okay. Can you sit down again for a few minutes?"

Celeste nodded.

"I love you, Velvet. Just holding you in my arms again makes me want to never let you go."

"Kent..."

He held up his hand to silence her. "I've thought about it a lot. Why do people fall in love? Do you know?"

She shook her head.

"I think I loved you the minute I looked up and saw you leaning out the window at Woolworth after you dropped the apple on my head. And then when I saw you on the sidewalk outside Cox-Rushing-Greer, with your nose pressed against the window, wanting that dress so bad you could taste it... But I know for sure I loved you from the minute I saw you in it at the Roof Garden."

"I used to dream about a blue velvet curtain and a faceless man wanting to take me behind it. That night, he had your face."

"Really?"

"Really."

"You never told me that before."

"It was the silly sort of thing a girl does. It wasn't important."

"You still look like yourself, but you're not the same."

"I guess I've grown up. You said I needed to."

"I needed to grow up, too. I thought I'd done it, but I was wrong."

"What do you mean?"

"I mean, I had an ego this big." He made a box with his hands. "I thought I'd taken over after Dad died. Looked after Neil, put up with Mother running my life. I guess I thought I was entitled to whatever I wanted."

"Claudia." The name hung between them for a few minutes.

"Yeah." He took a couple of deep breaths. "But I wasn't smart enough to make sure nothing came of it."

Her face flamed.

"Sorry. Didn't mean to embarrass you." He smiled. "But I kind of like it that you still blush. It's sweet. That much hasn't changed." His smile faded. "I found out I wasn't as big as I thought I was. When she told me she was…"

"Kent, maybe we should save this conversation for another time."

"Will there be another time?"

"You know where I am."

"But he's there, too. The boy."

"That's right."

He looked away.

"Do you need your car?"

"It's your car. I gave it to you. Besides, I took some of my back pay from when I was MIA and bought another one when I got home. It'll get me back and forth from the field."

"What about after the war? Are you going to college? I hear the government is paying for soldiers to go to school."

"I might. I don't know if I want to sell plumbing supplies all my life, although I'm darned good at it. What about you? Are you going to work at Woolworth forever?"

"It's a good steady job, and I got a raise."

"Dance with me one more time?"

She thought she should say no, but the next thing she knew, she was in his arms, wanting to stay there forever.

Chapter Twenty-Five

Celeste wasn't sure if she was disappointed or relieved when Kent didn't come to church the next morning. After lunch, she read to Jonny from one of his new library books. When he went off to his room to play with the set of cars for which they'd made a garage out of two shoeboxes taped together, she sat down and tried to lose herself in a fashion magazine Veda had loaned her.

Her eyes crawled over the same page three times before she gave up. *I'm glad you made it back safely, Kent, but why did you have to come here? Why couldn't things have just ended like they were? You want me, but you don't want Jonny, and I'm not going to give him up. Whether or not he's part of you, he's part of me now.*

When the phone rang later, she hoped it was Kent—and hoped it wasn't. "Velvet?"

"Hello, Kent."

"I just wanted to tell you how much I enjoyed seeing you last night." His tone was oddly formal.

"I enjoyed seeing you, too."

"Are you busy? I mean, I'm in town, and we could meet somewhere."

"I'm home with Jonny, like I am whenever I'm not working."

"Doesn't that sort of tie you down?"

"You know I wasn't out running around before."

"Right. Well, I just thought maybe we could take a ride and talk."

"I can't."

"You don't have anybody who could watch him

for a couple of hours?"

"Sometimes my neighbor helps out, but she took care of him for me to come to the Canteen last night. I don't want to ask her again so soon."

"Oh."

"You could come over here, Kent. I have to fix supper anyway."

The silence lasted so long that she thought he'd put the phone down and walked away. Finally he said, "You know I can't do that."

"I know you don't want to. I think I understand."

"Do you? I don't. I understood why you were mad at me over Claudia, but I don't understand why you took in her kid."

"I tried to explain it to you."

"That you felt some sort of tie to him because of your father? I don't see it."

"It started out that way, but now he's mine. We're a family. He loves the ranch, and everybody there loves him, and..."

The click on the other end of the line told her Kent had hung up.

****

On July 4, Celeste took Jonny to Santa Fe Park to see the fireworks. The Thomases, already there and set up in a prime spot, waved them over. "Hello there, young man," Mr. Thomas said.

"You remember Mr. Thomas, the man I work for," Celeste said.

Jonny stuck out his hand the way she'd taught him. "Yes, sir."

Mary Thomas smiled at Celeste. "Why don't you two put your quilt down here and join us? We were hoping to have our oldest grandson today, but his mother's a nurse and got called in to work at the last minute. We'll just adopt Jonny for the evening."

Jonny helped spread the quilt and plopped down. "Does somebody shoot the fireworks out of a gun?"

"Not exactly," Mr. Thomas said. "We say they 'shoot off' fireworks, but they have a special way to do that. Have you ever seen them before?"

Jonny shook his head. "Nope. No, sir."

"Then you're in for a treat."

Just as Celeste started to sit down, she caught sight of Kent standing on the edge of the crowd. She lifted her hand to wave, then dropped it, but he stood there looking at her until she wanted to hide her head under the quilt.

Mr. Thomas noticed her agitation and the reason for it. "We'll keep an eye on the boy," he said.

"No, I…"

"Go ahead," he said.

Celeste crossed the grass, not looking at Kent until she stood in front of him.

"Hi, Velvet."

"Do you want to join us?"

He shook his head. "I'm sorry I hung up the other night."

"That was two weeks ago."

"I just didn't know how to keep talking…about things."

"It's all right."

"Can we take a walk?"

"I have to get back."

"Just for a few minutes? Away from the crowd."

Celeste glanced back at the Thomases. Both of them were watching her. Mary Thomas waved, as if she were giving her permission not to come back right away. "All right. For a little while."

Kent took her hand and led her down toward the river that ran under the Beauregard Bridge. As soon as the trees swallowed them up, he caught her in his arms, and his mouth came down on hers. "Velvet…oh, Velvet."

She clung to him without speaking.

"I love you so much. Every day at mail call, I kept telling myself that tomorrow I'd have a letter from you. When I was hiding from the German patrols, being smuggled from farm to farm in hay wagons, all I could think about was staying alive to get back to you. I was going to do whatever it took to make things right with you again." His lips traveled to her throat.

"Kent…"

"I know, I know, the boy. Claudia meant to come between us, and she did, even after she died."

Celeste pushed him away so she could see his face. "Is that what this is all about?"

"If I took a blood test to prove I'm not his father, would you change your mind?"

"A blood test could show you might be his father."

"It won't."

"How can you be sure?"

"I don't know. I just am."

"It wouldn't make any difference. You don't throw away a child like a worn-out toy."

"I said we'd find him a good place."

"Where? With your mother? Back with his grandmother? In an orphanage?"

"I don't know. Somewhere. We'll have our own children, Velvet."

"Oh, Kent." She turned and began to walk back to the celebration.

"Velvet, please…don't go. Stay here with me. We can work things out."

"Not if it means losing Jonny."

"But you don't mind losing me?"

She didn't turn around. "I think I've already lost you, Kent."

****

"Them fireworks was swell," Jonny observed as he put on his pajamas.

"*Those* fireworks *were* swell," Celeste corrected. "Go brush your teeth. It's late."

"Why do I have to have a babysitter in the summer? I'm eight now."

"Not quite. Besides, you like Patty."

"Sure I like her. She lets me ride my bike and takes me to the park and…"

"And being here with you lets her earn some money."

"You could pay me to be good by myself." He glanced up at Celeste from beneath the lock of blonde hair that always seemed to grow out the day after he'd visited the barbershop.

"You *are* good, Jonny, but I don't like to leave you here all day by yourself."

"Maybe next summer when I'm almost nine?"

"We'll see."

"That means no."

"Not necessarily."

"So does that."

"You know me pretty well."

Jonny crawled into bed and pulled up his blue bedspread imprinted with cowboys on galloping horses. "Sure. We're a team, you and me."

"A team?"

"Yep. Like the Bobcats. You know, the football team at the big school."

"The high school."

"They won a lot of games this year."

"Right." Celeste kissed his cheek. "Now go to sleep."

"Okay. Can I have Krispy Flakes for breakfast tomorrow?"

"I guess so."

"Can I ask Patty to make peanut butter and jelly sandwiches for lunch?"

"Yes."

"Can you not hide the cookies?"

"No. Go to sleep."

"'Night, Mom."

Celeste turned off the light. "'Night, Jonny."

When she went to close and lock the front door, Kent stood on the porch. "I need to talk to you, Velvet."

"Kent, it's late, and..."

"Please."

She unlatched the screen. "I'll come out on the porch." She didn't add, *so Jonny won't hear us*, but she knew he understood why she didn't invite him in.

"I'm sorry about tonight," Kent said, folding himself down beside her on the steps.

"I'm sorry about a lot of things, Kent. I wish I could make you understand about Jonny."

"I don't want to talk about him. I just want to know if you still love me."

"You know I do. Maybe more than ever."

"Then tell me how you can love a person and not want to be with them."

"I don't know."

"You said you thought you'd already lost me. What did you mean?"

"I just don't feel like we see things the same way anymore."

"Only one thing."

"Jonny's not a thing, Kent. He's a little boy. He calls me 'Mom.' "

"And you let him?"

"Why not?"

"I can think of a million reasons why not."

"I wish you'd at least meet him."

"No."

"All right."

"You don't know what it's like for a man to be slapped in the face like that."

"No, I'm not a man, so I don't think like one. But

I do know there's a difference in how we look at things."

"When Claudia told me she was...you know...I didn't believe her at first. When he was born, Mrs. Peters called Mother and told her, and she crawled all over me. I told her I wasn't the father, but when I counted back, well, I knew I could be. Claudia even said she was going to the police and tell them I forced her. She didn't, because they knew her. Everybody in town knew her. Nobody was going to believe that I made her do anything she didn't want to." He dropped his head in his hands.

"Then she started talking about us getting married, and I told her a flat no. She left for a while after that. I started working for the plumbing supply company, so I didn't see her around for a long time. When she came back, she got a job waiting tables in a little bar on the edge of town. She even told me once that she took the baby with her and wanted to know what I thought about *my son* being raised in a bar."

He lifted his face and stretched his legs in front of him. "She just kept on and on, wanting me to marry her, trying to get me to fall for her line again. Then she turned up in San Angelo and went after you. She had some nerve going to my CO and..." He brought his fist down on the porch floor between them. "If she'd left well enough alone, if I hadn't driven her back to town..."

"It was an accident, Kent. Bad brakes. Icy patches on the road. You can't keep blaming yourself for that."

"And then her mother dumped the kid on you."

"It was the best thing that could've happened to him."

"It was a life sentence. For both of us."

"I don't look at it that way."

"All my life, I've had to jump when someone

hollered, and ask how high on the way up. I'm damned if I'll raise Claudia's bastard! But that's what you're holding over my head. Accept him or lose you."

"That's what my father had to do."

"And look how it turned out."

"It's not going to be that way for Jonny."

"Then find him a good home and..."

Celeste stood up. "He has a home, Kent. I'm going in now. It's late, and I have to work tomorrow."

Without waiting for him to reply, she turned off the porch light and closed the front door. Then she leaned against it, thinking she was going to cry, before she realized that the pain in her heart was too deep for tears.

Chapter Twenty-Six

Celeste thought Jonny grew overnight that summer. She watched the newspaper for sale ads and scoured the bargain basement at Hemphill-Wells. Her Christmas layaway at Cox-Rushing-Greer was, of necessity, smaller than usual.

The war crawled on until August. There was talk of invading Japan at the cost of a million casualties. Then it ended in a literal flash. "The bomb" was on everyone's lips. Jonny used his marbles to annihilate a small ant bed in the back yard and renamed his model airplane *Enola Gay*. Mrs. Lowe said they'd keep the Canteen going as long as there were boys waiting to go home.

Celeste didn't hear from Kent. Sometimes she felt overwhelming anger that kept her too tense to rest, and some nights she cried herself to sleep. Dreaming of the blue velvet curtain seemed to be a thing of the past.

When Jonny started third grade the first week in September, Celeste told him he could walk home from school by himself, cautioning him about not deviating from his route or talking to strangers. She gave him a keychain with a key for the back door. She thought he swaggered a lot like General MacArthur when he went next door to show it to Mrs. Aikman.

At the end of the second week of school, Celeste came home from work to be greeted by the announcement that "Some soldier guy was here looking for you, Mom. He said to give you this." Celeste told Jonny to set the table and went to her room to read the note he'd handed her.

Dear Velvet,

I'm being discharged next month, and I'd like to see you before I leave. I'll call you tonight at eight-thirty. You'll know it's me, so if you don't want to talk to me, you don't have to answer the phone.

Kent

After supper, trying not to think of the inevitable confrontation with Kent, Celeste called out Jonny's spelling words for the following week. He insisted on staying a week ahead, even though he never minded getting behind in arithmetic. "I can do it in my head," he argued. "I don't see why I have to line up all those numbers and put in the pluses and the take-aways and the lines and the carry-boxes."

Have I heard that somewhere before? I think so, but I can't remember who said it. "When I think of a good reason, I'll tell you."

"Okay."

She read another chapter from *Robin Hood* and sent him to the bathtub. He made a show of dragging his feet, complaining that he didn't see why he had to take a bath on Friday night when he was just going outside to play on Saturday and get dirty all over again. "Go," she said, swatting his backside with the book.

She was listening to him splash and sing "Comin' in on a Wing and a Prayer" when the phone rang.

"Velvet?"

"I'm here."

"Can I see you before I leave?"

"Yes."

"Maybe we could have dinner. I think there might even be a dance at the Roof Garden on Saturday night."

"I'll have to ask Mrs. Aikman if she can watch

Jonny."

"He doesn't look like me."

"No."

"He asked what my name was, and when I told him it was Kent, he said that was his middle name."

"He knows what his name is, Kent, but he doesn't know anything about you."

"That's good."

"I'm not sure it is, but I just answer his questions as he asks them."

"So he's asked about his father?"

"Not really. He tells his friends he doesn't have one. I guess they draw their own conclusions."

"What do people think about you?"

"Nothing. I told the school and anybody else who asked that I have guardianship for a friend who's overseas. My family and Veda know the truth. Besides, if I'd been pregnant nine years ago, it would've caused a local scandal."

"So everybody knows about me."

"Not everybody. Mr. Thomas knows. I couldn't lie to him."

"You'll understand if I say I'd just as soon he didn't."

"I did what I felt was the right thing, Kent. What anybody else thinks doesn't matter."

"You wouldn't have said that a couple of years ago."

"Circumstances have changed, and I've had to change with them."

"Well, look, see if you can get a babysitter. If I don't hear from you, I'll pick you up about six on Saturday. And wear the blue velvet dress."

"It's really a winter dress. I'd melt in it in September."

"Wouldn't want that to happen. I'll see you."

"See you."

****

Before she could talk to Mrs. Aikman, a friend from Jonny's Sunday School class invited him to spend the night. "Ricky's dad's taking us to the Texas to see Johnny Mack Brown, and we're gonna sleep outside in the backyard in a real tent," Jonny informed her for at least the fifth time, while he stuffed his pajamas into his empty school bag.

Celeste took them out, refolded them, and put them back, then added clean underwear and his Sunday pants and shirt. She handed him fifty cents. "This will buy your ticket and some popcorn."

Jonny put the coin in his pocket. "It's gonna be just us guys tonight. His mom's staying home with his sister."

"That's nice."

"Yeah, pretty swell."

She walked him to the curb, where Ricky and his father waited in the car. "Be good," she said, kissing the top of his head. "I'll see you at church tomorrow."

He hopped into the back seat. "Sure, Mom, see ya."

Kent arrived just as the car drove off. "Was that the boy in the car?"

"He's spending the night with a friend."

"So things worked out."

"He's never spent the night away from home before." Celeste picked up her purse. "I'm ready."

While they ate dinner at the Cozy Café on Chadbourne, Kent told her he'd applied for money to go back to school. "I'm pretty old to be starting out, and it'll be six or seven years before I get my law degree."

"But you'll have what you want."

"Not everything."

She dropped her eyes and concentrated on her baked chicken. "You'll meet someone."

"You sound like you don't care."

"Of course, I care, Kent."

"Then why are you being stubborn about things?"

"You're not being stubborn, too?"

"Maybe I am, but you can't expect me to take a kid I don't even know and pretend he's mine when he's not."

"We've been all over this," she interrupted him.

"It seems to me that two people who love each other could work things out."

"Not when the third person involved ends up getting hurt."

"I don't want to see him hurt, Velvet. I'm not a monster."

"I know you're not, but you're not connected with him the way I am, either. You haven't watched him grow and change. He's not the same little boy I found shivering on the sidewalk in front of my house two years ago."

"You've had to make a lot of sacrifices."

"Not really, just figure things out, that's all." She put down her fork. "Where are you going to school?"

"UT in Austin, I guess."

"What does your mother say? Isn't she expecting you to come home?"

"I guess it took the war to make me cut the apron strings, but I'm done with all that. She's all right. Neil checks on her. He's trying to get her to sell that big house and move to a smaller one or to an apartment. She'd be better off, and she'll realize that eventually."

"I'm going to have to make some decisions, too. When I moved back home, it wasn't going to be forever."

"Are you having trouble making ends meet?"

"Not really. The interest on the money Daddy had invested pays the taxes every year, and he had a savings account. Coralee's been sending me money out of that for utilities. But it won't last forever, and it would be a stretch to pay those, too, on top of groceries and clothes for Jonny and me. I can do it if I have to, though. Mr. Thomas would let me fill in downstairs on Saturday afternoons to earn a little extra."

"So what would you do if you didn't live there?"

"I don't know. I'd have to pay rent on an apartment, so it might be six of one and half a dozen of the other."

"What about a better job?"

"I'd be willing to go somewhere else for more money, but with all the servicemen coming home and needing work, I doubt I'd find anything right now." She looked up and smiled. "But things will work out. They always do."

The wind had picked up as they emerged from the restaurant, and no stars were visible. "It's going to storm," Kent said. On cue, lightning split the darkened sky, closely followed by the rumble of thunder.

"The boys were going to sleep outside in a tent. They'll be disappointed."

Kent opened the door of the car. "Let's get to the St. Angelus before it rains and we get soaked."

They'd danced three times when the lights flickered and went out. When they hadn't come back on in a few minutes, a voice from the back of the ballroom broke through the buzz of impatient conversation. "Folks, I'm the night manager. It's getting ready to come a gully washer outside, and the wind's whipping around pretty strong, so we're going to close off the garden area and shut down this floor. We apologize for interrupting your evening, but you're welcome to stay around the lobby until this thing blows over."

Downstairs, as she watched from the windows

facing Beauregard, the force of the storm stirred a growing unease in Celeste. The Harrises would take good care of Jonny, but he'd never been away from her at night.

She wasn't sure what happened first, whether she heard the cracking sound or felt Kent grabbing her, but a sudden sheet of rain drenched them as two windows blew in, scattering glass across the floor.

Kent propelled her toward the back wall, shoving her against it, his body shielding hers. She listened to a cacophony of screams, loud voices, and undecipherable sounds that made her wonder if the building was about to come down around them. Then, suddenly, it was over, but the silence frightened her more than the storm.

"I have to get to Jonny," she said, trying to squirm out from under Kent's sheltering bulk.

"Take it easy, Velvet. Let's see what's going on first."

"You don't understand. This is the first time he's been away at night, and..."

"We'll get to him as soon as we can. I'm sure he's just fine. You trust his friend's parents, don't you?"

In the light from two kerosene lanterns that appeared from nowhere, Celeste took in the battered lobby. Overturned pot plants spilled damp soil onto the soaked carpet, and water puddled on the leather furniture.

"Stay here," Kent said, pushing her back against the wall. Celeste heard glass crunching under his feet as he strode away.

"Okay, people, listen up!" Kent's voice rose above the others. "I need those lanterns over here so we can see the street." She watched the lights move in the direction of the main door. In a few minutes, Kent's voice, authoritative and definitely in charge, broke into the panicked conversation of those around her. "I said, listen up! Any other guys from Concho Field or Goodfellow Air Base in here?"

Glass crunched again as feet moved toward his voice.

"Anybody outrank me—I hope."

Nervous laughter scattered through the crowd as voices called out, "Corporal, Private, Private..."

Kent chuckled. "Okay, looks like you're stuck with a looie. Here's what we're going to do. Over there at the desk—any phone service?"

"Dial tone," came the reply.

"Okay, then call both bases and see if they got hit, and tell them we did. They'll send in crews to help out."

Sirens, whether fire or police Celeste couldn't tell, pierced the night. Kent continued, "Anybody hurt in here, or just wet and scared?"

Celeste heard the words *wet, scared,* and a few other rather risqué expressions. With the darkness obscuring her face, she let herself laugh and felt better.

"Okay, good, we're all in one piece. If you came in a car, move up this way. Slow. Real slow."

A handful of people moved forward. "It doesn't look too bad out there," Kent said. "Some power lines are down across Irving, so stay away from them. Beauregard's clear, as far as I can tell. Nothing fell on the cars, the ones parked on this side, at least, so if that's you, and you want to try to make it home, be my guest."

"Wait a minute, before you go," the night manager called out. "If any of you can't get home or just don't want to try, we've got a lot of empty rooms, and they're on the house tonight. See me at the desk. And don't think I won't know the difference between Mr. and Mrs. and Mr. and Miss!"

Laughter and a few exaggerated groans followed his announcement. "Form a line, form a line. Don't mob the hand that's rocking your cradle tonight."

In a few minutes, Kent came back to where he'd left Celeste. "Two police officers are here. They'll take over now. One of them said they thought it was a small tornado. A couple of the enlisted men are going to get their girls from out of town checked into rooms here. And some guy said then he'd try to get them back to the field. I have to get back, too, but I'll take you to see about the boy first."

"The Harrises live on Nineteenth. You'll run into it down Main Street."

"If I can get there," he said, taking her arm. "You all right?"

"Just a little wet. I'll dry out."

"Come on then."

It took almost an hour, crawling around scattered debris and dancing with other cars at intersections no longer controlled by lights, to reach their destination. Flashing red and blue lights made Kent slow down at the end of the block where the Harrises lived. Taking in the scene, Celeste knew she'd never really understood what terror was—until now.

Chapter Twenty-Seven

Before Kent could turn off the engine, Celeste jumped out of the car and began to run. "Watch the power lines!" she heard him yell. Her high heels made speed difficult, but the flashing lights of the ambulance in front of the Harris house kept her from slowing down.

On the sidewalk, the Harrises huddled together, with Ricky and Rosemary in front of them. Part of the front porch was gone, victim of a pecan tree whose many branches now covered half the lawn. Spotting the family, Celeste realized the small blanket-wrapped body on the stretcher the attendants were carrying around the house must be Jonny.

She heard herself screaming his name before she skidded to a halt by the open doors of the ambulance. "Out of the way, lady. This one isn't going to make it if we don't get going." She caught a glimpse of a small, pale face. His eyes were closed, and blood matted his wet hair.

"Jonny! Jonny!"

Ruby Harris's arms pulled her away as the doors slammed. "We brought the boys in when the wind picked up, but Ricky said Jonny remembered he'd left his plane outside and slipped out to get it."

Celeste stared at her.

"One of the trees in the back fell on the tent. Bill heard it and went outside and found him."

The breath went out of her. She realized Kent had joined them. "They'll take him to Shannon," he said. "Come on."

Ambulances and cars were lined up on Magdalen Street, waiting their turn to access the sloping drive to the emergency room. Celeste jumped out as soon as the car came to a forced stop and ran the rest of the way.

"My little boy," she told the nurse who barred her way in the receiving area. "A tree fell on him!"

"I think he's over there," the nurse said, indicating a curtained area, "but you can't go in."

"He'll be scared if…"

"Just sit down over there. I'll check on him for you. What was the name?"

"Jonny. Jonny Goddard."

"Just sit down, Mrs. Goddard. I'll be back as soon as I can."

"No, I'm not…" Celeste spoke to the departing nurse's back.

A few minutes later, Kent squeezed in beside her on the crowded bench. "A nurse went to see about him, but she hasn't come back."

"They're working alive in here," Kent said, slipping his arm around her. "She'll be back when she can."

Celeste sat in the circle of Kent's arm, her body frozen with fear but her mind racing. *I shouldn't have let him go. Maybe if I hadn't wanted to go out with Kent so much, I'd have said no. Jonny's just a baby, not old enough to go off by himself for the night. No, that's not right. He's nine years old. I can't hold onto Jonny the way Kent says his mother tried to hold on to him.*

"He'll be okay," Kent said, squeezing her hand.

A young doctor, his whites spattered with blood and other things Celeste couldn't and didn't want to identify, came out from behind the curtain. "Goddard?" he called, looking around.

She wrenched free of Kent's arm and crossed the floor.

"Jonny Goddard? You're his mother?"

Celeste nodded.

"Father around?"

Without really meaning to, she glanced back at Kent. The doctor motioned him over. "His skull is fractured, and there's some internal bleeding. I'm sending him upstairs to surgery."

Celeste felt Kent's arms go around her as her knees buckled. "He'll be better tomorrow." The words that even she knew were trite—and untrue—spilled out.

The doctor dropped his eyes, then seemed to force himself to look at her again. "I'm sorry, Mrs. Goddard, I don't think…well, if he makes it through surgery…and then through the night…but I have to be honest with you. I don't think he will." He took a deep breath. "Fourth floor."

****

Kent rocked her in his arms as they waited. In a few minutes, a nurse came in. "He's holding on, but he needs blood, a pretty rare kind that we don't have. Someone's phoning around trying to find it."

"What type?" Kent asked. His voice seemed to come from far away.

"B-negative."

He stood up. "That's me."

****

When he came back, rolling down his shirt sleeve, he reached for his uniform jacket and sat down across from Celeste. "It's going to be enough."

She thought she heard herself say, "Thank you."

"It doesn't change things," he said after a while.

She nodded that she understood.

"I can't…" He rose and went to the window. "I can't, Velvet. You've got to understand."

"You've done enough, maybe saved his life."

"I've got to get back to the field. Do you want me to go by your house and see if there was any damage?"

"I don't care if the whole thing blew away, as long as Jonny's all right."

"I could call the ranch for you."

"The number is…" She closed her eyes, trying to remember four digits as familiar to her as her own name. "It's in the book by the telephone in the hall. There's a spare key under the mat by the back door."

"Okay."

"What time is it?"

"Just after eleven."

"They go to bed early, so don't call and wake them up. It would scare them to death. Six o'clock. That's when they get up."

"I'll take care of it, and I'll try to get back in tomorrow. I'll call the nurses' station, if I can't make it."

"Thank you."

He leaned over and kissed the top of her head. "It'll be okay, Velvet. "

****

A nurse woke her when Jonny was in a room. "You can't stay with him, and you're really not supposed to be in there at this hour, but go take a quick peek, anyway."

"He's going to be all right, isn't he?"

The nurse didn't meet her eyes. "We won't know for a while. It's that room over there, and he's in the second bed."

Behind the curtain, the dim light above the bed bathed Jonny's face, which had no more color than the pillowcase. His head, swathed in bandages, seemed enormous. Celeste touched his hand, then gathered it up, kissing his limp fingers. "Jonny, it's Mom. You're going to be all right. You just had a bad bump on the head, but it'll be better tomorrow, I promise."

A different nurse poked her head around the

curtain. "You need to leave now."

"I can't. He'll be so scared when he wakes up."

"Rules. You can sit in the waiting room."

"Please, he's only a little boy."

"I'm sorry."

Celeste kissed Jonny's pale cheek. "See you in the morning, pal," she whispered.

****

Celeste thought she dozed off and on, but when daylight pierced her consciousness, it took a moment to remember where she was—and why. Her body felt heavy when she rose from the sofa and started for Jonny's room. A nurse, different from the night before, stopped her. "Visiting hours don't start until nine."

"But he's my little boy."

Another nurse passing them snapped, "Let her," and then mumbled something Celeste didn't understand.

The first nurse stepped aside. "Go on then." As Celeste started for the door, she heard her mutter, "Dammit, why does it always have to be the kids?"

At the sink, Celeste wet a washcloth with warm water and bathed Jonny's face. His eyelids didn't even flutter. She could hear him breathing, like it was a huge effort to pull air into his lungs. She moved a chair close to the bed and stroked his hands and arms in silence.

Veda came just before noon. "Kent called me," she said. "He can't leave the base again until tonight. He said to tell you your house was all right. A few limbs in the yard, but nothing major. He went in and got your sister's number and called her from the field. She's on her way."

Celeste nodded.

"What can I do, Cece? Stay here with you? Go home and get you some things?"

"Maybe later."

Veda sat down on the floor by Celeste's chair and reached for her hand. "I'm here, honey."

****

Even Coralee couldn't coax Celeste away from the hospital for longer than it took to bathe and change clothes. Kent showed up at five to take her back to the hospital. "I can stay until midnight," he said. "Then I have to be back."

"You don't have to stay, but thank you."

"I want to."

"All right."

The first bed in Jonny's room was empty. The nurse said the other boy had gone home. Something told Celeste she was lying. Kent brought the extra chair and put it beside Celeste's. A doctor they hadn't seen before came by and read Jonny's chart, then shone a light into his eyes and left without speaking to them. Kent charged after him. Celeste could hear him through the open door.

"We need to know something."

"He's got a fractured skull."

"Besides that."

"Head injuries don't usually have a good outcome."

"Outcome?"

"He might live, but you might wish he hadn't."

"What the hell does that mean?"

"His brain is probably mush. I don't know how else to say it."

Kent came back into the room. "He's wrong," Celeste said. "He's just wrong."

"Velvet, honey, you've got to accept the truth."

"The truth? What is the truth, Kent? That you slept with his mother? That you don't believe...don't *want* to believe he's yours? None of that matters, because he's mine. Jonny's mine, and he's going to get well. He is."

"Velvet, believe me, I'd give anything if this

hadn't happened to him."

"He's just a little boy. He deserves a chance to grow up."

"Yes, he does. If I could change places with him, I would."

"Why? He doesn't matter to you."

"That's not fair, Velvet. The life of any human being matters to me. I saw enough of them get snuffed out during the war. I know what death's all about."

Celeste's agitation boiled over despite her best efforts. "I don't even know why you're here. I've already told you I won't give him up to marry you, and you've made it pretty clear that you only want me and not him. I guess it would be convenient for you if he…"

"Stop it!" He grasped her shoulders and turned her toward him. "Just stop it!"

Tears spilled down her cheeks. "He said we were a team, the two of us."

Kent crushed her against him. "Velvet, Velvet."

"He's such a good little kid. Everybody says so. I keep seeing him standing there on the sidewalk, skinny and dirty and cold, holding onto that paper bag with everything he had in the world. I got him fed and clean and warm, and he just settled right in with me like he'd been there forever. But I can't help him now, and I feel like a murderer."

Kent rocked her in his arms in silence.

****

Mr. Thomas came to the hospital and told her his wife would take care of the books and not to worry about her job. Veda showed up every afternoon when she got off work and drove Celeste home to eat and change clothes. Then Kent somehow managed to be there to take her back to the hospital, where he stayed with her as long as he could.

"You're going to be sick, Cece," Coralee said on

the fourth day. "You need at least one night in your own bed."

"I can't leave him up there alone in the dark, Sister."

"The nurses take care of him."

"I think they've given up on him. They do what they have to, but no more."

Celeste rummaged in the bookshelf.

"What are you looking for?"

"The Thomases gave him a book at Christmas, about cowboys in America. I thought I'd read to him."

"Cece…"

"What would you do if it was Barbara up there, Sister? Just let her lie there?"

"No, of course not. I'll find you a paper bag for the books."

****

Kent dozed on the sofa in the waiting room, while Celeste read aloud for hours on end. "He can't hear you," a nurse told her.

"How do you know?"

"He's…"

Celeste turned the page and began to read again. On the sixth day, she'd fallen asleep with her head on the edge of Jonny's bed when she heard him say, "You didn't finish about Jesse James, Mom."

Chapter Twenty-Eight

The nurse said the doctor took his time coming because he didn't really believe Jonny was awake and talking. When he finally strolled in, the look on his face, combined with the joy in her heart, made Celeste laugh aloud.

The third time the doctor held up his fingers in front of Jonny's face and asked him, "How many?" Jonny answered weakly, but with unconcealed impatience. "I already told you three times. Can I have a cookie?"

"Not for a few days," the doctor said. "Just liquids until your gut starts working again."

"What's a gut?"

"Your tummy, Jonny," Celeste said. "You haven't had anything to eat for a long time."

"I have, too. I had popcorn at the picture show last night."

"That was a few nights ago. You got hurt in Ricky's backyard."

Jonny frowned. "I did?"

"But you're fine now. You're just fine."

"So when can I have some cookies, Mom?"

****

Veda convinced Celeste to go home for the night. "I'll stay with Jonny."

"You have to work tomorrow."

"So, I'll sleep in on Sunday. God will understand, don't you think? Go on, Cece. Anyway, Kent's waiting for you downstairs. He got a pass when Coralee called to tell him about Jonny."

"Is Kent that soldier who came by the house?"

Jonny asked. "He's got the same name as mine."

Veda shoved Celeste toward the door. "Go on. We'll be fine."

"It's like nothing ever happened," Celeste said as soon as she saw Kent.

"I'm really glad, Velvet."

"The doctor couldn't believe it. I'm not sure I can either."

"I saw a few bad head injuries come back during the war, but I didn't want to give you false hope."

"I never gave up hope, Kent. I couldn't. I didn't give up on you, and I couldn't give up on Jonny."

****

"That soldier came to see me last night," Jonny told Celeste when she arrived the next morning. "The one with the same name as mine."

Celeste glanced at Veda, who nodded. "He came. And I'm going." She waved at Jonny. "See ya, kiddo."

"He brought me a new airplane. Aunt Veda said mine got broke in the storm you told me about yesterday."

Celeste picked up the scale model of a B-17. "He worked in one of these during the war."

"Yeah, he told me. He dropped bombs on people, but he didn't like to, only he had to. They were the bad guys."

"Right."

"He said there's a couple of real B-17s out at the field, and maybe he'll take me to see them."

"Really?"

"Yeah, he said if you said it was okay."

"We'll see."

"Aw, gee, that means no."

"Not always. Did you get any breakfast?"

He made a face. "Yeah, just some stuff that tasted kind of like chicken, but there wasn't any, just water. I looked hard, too."

"It's called broth."

"I want something real, like a banana or some ice cream."

"Soon, I promise."

"When can I get this thing off my head? It's heavy. When can I go home? I bet Miss Bates is gonna be mad at me for missing school."

"Coralee called the school and explained that you got hurt."

"And I won't get a gold star for being at the head of the spelling line."

"You get a gold star for being a chatterbox," Celeste said. "Here, I brought your comic books."

****

Kent came at five and motioned Celeste into the hall. "I've got a twenty-four-hour pass. If you want to go home again tonight, I'll stay with the boy."

"It was nice of you to bring him the plane. Veda's brother gave him the other one. It was his favorite toy." She turned around. "I'll be back in a few minutes, Jonny, okay?"

He grunted and turned the page of the comic book on the bed tray.

Kent and Celeste walked to the waiting room. "He's hungry, and he wants to go back to school," she said. "That's a good sign."

"What does the doctor say?"

"Not much. I think he's mad because he was wrong."

Kent laughed. "You think?"

"That's what the nurse says."

"You're going to have to go back to work, aren't you?"

"Next week. And Coralee has to go home, but Mrs. Aikman will come over and stay with Jonny when he gets out."

"He's a smart kid, isn't he?"

"He didn't even know his letters when I got him. He should've been in school already."

"Velvet, how are you going to pay the hospital bill?"

"I don't know and don't care. All that matters is that Jonny's all right."

"I can help."

"It's not your responsibility, Kent, but thank you."

He uncrossed his legs, then crossed them again. "I've been thinking about it. Maybe it is."

"I wish I could believe that."

Kent stood up and walked to the window. "I'm not saying I could raise him, Velvet, or be the dad he wants. But I can help out with what he needs."

"You're going to school as soon as you're discharged. You'll need every penny."

"The plumbing supply company manager offered me my old job back. I could work a while until the bills are paid."

Celeste caught her breath. "Oh, Kent."

"I mean it, Velvet. The blood type didn't really prove anything, but maybe I owe the boy something, whether he's mine or not."

"I'll talk to the business office tomorrow and see what they say. I'm sure I can pay it out."

"The bank your father worked for would let you borrow if you had to."

"I don't want to do that if I can help it."

"I can't say I blame you. Listen, let me take you out for something to eat, and then home. I'll come back up here and stay the night."

"You'd really do that?"

"For you, Velvet."

She sighed. "I'd rather you'd do it for Jonny, but...I'm sorry. Thank you, Kent. That's very generous of you."

The next morning when she finally got up, Celeste found Kent sitting in the kitchen with Coralee. "The kid kicked me out last night about nine. Said he was big enough to stay by himself. I think he was irritated when I ran out of answers for all his questions. Anyway, I made sure he knew where the cord was if he had to call a nurse and came over here to bunk on your couch."

"You were already out like a light when he showed up, Cece," Coralee said. "By the way, Ben's coming for me around noon."

"I'm glad. You need to go home, Sister. You shouldn't have stayed away from your family so long."

"You're my family, too, sweetie. I wanted to be here with you."

After breakfast, Kent drove Celeste to the hospital. "He's a smart kid, you know."

"You've said that before."

"He wanted to know all about the B-17—the crew, how high it flew, how we dropped our bombs on the targets. Then he wanted to know about the ship I went over on. I had to tell him I didn't inspect it from bow to stern. He said he'd have looked at everything so he'd know how it worked."

"He would have, too."

Jonny pointed to his head as soon as they walked in. "Look, Mom. The doctor took off part of my head this morning."

Celeste inspected the diminished bandage. "I like that."

"And I got some real food this morning, too. Well, not really real, but better than that chicken stuff."

Kent still stood by the door. "I'll be back later," he said to Celeste.

Jonny frowned "I wanted to ask you some more questions."

"I'll be back," Kent said, not looking at him.

****

At four, Kent returned and asked Celeste to

walk down the hall with him. "I've got to get back to the field by five."

"Thank you for what you've done. Jonny told me all about your conversation last night. And he doesn't just have some more questions—he has about a million of them."

"Okay, well..." He looked around and saw the waiting room was deserted. "I love you, Velvet," he said, pulling her against him.

She lifted her willing lips for his kiss.

"I'm not sure I can stand leaving here next month without you."

"I'll miss you."

"Enough to..." He kissed her again. "Never mind. I know the answer to that. I'll call you, Velvet. Take care of yourself." Letting her go, almost abruptly, he walked out of the waiting room. She followed him into the hall and watched until he stepped onto the elevator.

Chapter Twenty-Nine

"He shouldn't be here," the doctor told Celeste when she arrived at the hospital after work on Monday. "I wouldn't have given him a snowball's chance in hell, but I'm going to let you take him home today. Keep him quiet for another week. Then he can go back to school if he doesn't go outside at recess. Take him in to see your family doctor for a check-up in two weeks."

Exhausted from the excitement of coming home, Jonny fell asleep on the sofa immediately after supper. Celeste was washing dishes when Kent telephoned. "I called the hospital. The nurse said you'd left."

"We came home after I got off work," she said. "Jonny can go back to school in another week—with restrictions."

"That's terrific, Velvet. I'm happy for both of you."

"I talked to the business office. The bill isn't so bad. I set up a payment plan that won't ruin me."

"I'm going to help you, Velvet. I've got two more checks coming from Uncle Sam. The other thing I called to tell you was that I got the GI money for school. I can start in January."

"I'm happy for you, Kent."

"But I meant what I said about going back to work for the plumbing supply."

"I know you did, but I've got things worked out. Really. We won't starve or freeze this winter."

"Coralee won't let that happen."

"Big Ben offered me the money for the bill, and I

guess he wouldn't miss it, not really, but I don't want to take it unless I have to."

"No. Listen, I can get another pass this weekend. Maybe we could spend some time together after the boy is in bed."

"I think he'd like to see you, too."

"That's not a good idea, Velvet."

"All right."

"I'll go to the Canteen for a while and then come by."

"Eight, eight-thirty will be fine."

"I'll see you then."

****

Celeste didn't tell Jonny that Kent was coming. She could tell he still tired easily when he didn't protest going to bed before his usual time. At seven-thirty, she cleared his covers of comic books and spread the sheet over him. Leaving a small lamp burning so she could check on him in the night, she closed the door to his room and went out on the porch to wait for Kent.

****

They sat in the swing Ben had put up when he came for Coralee. "He said it would let Jonny get out of the house," Celeste explained. "Jonny loves the one at the ranch."

"It's real nice." Kent reached for her hand. "Nice for big boys and girls, too."

She laid her head on his shoulder, naturally, as if it belonged there. "He's so excited about going back to school Monday, but I'm thinking of keeping him home another week. Mrs. Aikman doesn't mind being here."

"Let him go, Velvet. You can't hold onto him forever, like my mother tried to do with Neil and me." He stroked her hair.

"Is that what she tried to do?"

"I thought so at the time. Maybe I still do.

Sometimes I think that's one of the reasons why I got messed up with Claudia."

"You said that before, in another way. You were tired of being told what to do and when to do it."

"I'm not making any excuses for myself, understand. I was just plain wrong. As wrong as a guy can be, and now my chickens have come home to roost just like Mother said they would."

"You've done well for yourself, and now you're going to school and be a lawyer just like you always wanted to."

"Yeah, I guess. You've done good, too, Velvet. You're not the same girl who dropped the apple on my head nearly five years ago."

"I don't even remember her."

"She was sweet and innocent, and that blue velvet dress was going to change her life."

"Yes, it was. In a way, it did."

"I'm not the same person either, you know. Not the same guy who tried to make it with you on the sofa in the employees' lounge that night. The one who took it as a personal affront that you wouldn't sleep with him the night before he shipped out. That showed up my real immaturity."

"A lot has happened since then."

"A lot of water under the bridge. A lifetime. If I met you now...as who I am now...well, things might've been different." Kent put his lips against her hair.

"How?"

"I'm not sure. Just different."

As the conversation dwindled, Celeste let herself drift into the secure warmth of Kent's presence. The back-and-forth motion of the swing lulled her into a contented state between waking and sleeping. The moment was interrupted without warning as the sound of Jonny's voice brought her upright. His wide eyes mirrored near-panic.

"I woke up, and nobody was there."

She scooted over and made room for him between herself and Kent. "Did you have a bad dream?" she asked, smoothing his tousled hair.

"I don't remember. I woke up, and all the lights were on, but nobody was there. And I cried."

"You cried tonight?"

He shook his head. "No, when it happened. You know, in the other place. I looked and looked and couldn't find anybody, and I hid under the table in the kitchen and cried. I was scared." He squirmed. "But I'm too big to be scared now."

Kent got up and leaned on the porch railing. "You're never too big to be scared."

"Really?" The incredulity in the little voice made Celeste smile.

Kent turned around. "Let me tell you something, pal. I started being scared every time that plane took off, and I didn't stop until we were back on the ground."

"Really? You were scared?"

"I lived and breathed scared. But that's not a bad thing, see. Sometimes being scared helps you be more careful about things. It made me do my job the best I could so we could get the h-, so we could get out of there and go home."

"Dropping the bombs."

"Right." Kent sat down again. "Did you get left by yourself a lot?"

"I guess."

"You said you didn't mind being by yourself on Saturday mornings," Celeste said.

"That was different. You're here when I wake up, and we eat breakfast, and then Mrs. Aikman comes over sometimes, and I know you'll be home…" He ran out of breath and leaned against Celeste. "It's different, that's all. And I don't need a babysitter next summer, either."

"We'll see."

"That means no."

Celeste laughed. "I'm such a mean Mom."

Jonny lifted his face to hers. "No, you're not. You're the nicest Mom in the whole world."

Kent half rose, then sat down again. Jonny snuggled against Celeste. In a few minutes, he was asleep.

"I'll carry him back to bed," Kent said. "He's too big for you."

When he came back, he took Celeste in his arms again. "He had a rotten time of it, didn't he?"

"He doesn't say much, and I don't ask him about it. Sometimes he lets something slip, like he did tonight."

"But it's all behind him now."

"Not really. I don't think he'll ever forget how things were before he came here. I haven't forgotten how Daddy treated me, but I don't think about it much anymore."

"I guess you're right. I won't ever forget the war, either, and I didn't have it anywhere near as bad as the guys on the ground."

"You didn't get a Silver Star for nothing."

"I'll tell you about it someday, but it doesn't matter much right now. The decoration, I mean. It's over. I was lucky enough to get home and get on with life."

"Have you? Gotten on with your life, I mean."

"I guess so."

"It takes a little while to readjust, Kent, but you will. You'll do everything you want to do."

He stroked her cheek. "Sure. Sure, I will if you think so."

****

The next morning, Celeste insisted on walking Jonny down the narrow, winding stairs to his Sunday School class. "You don't need another bump on the head," she said when he complained that he wasn't a baby. But she settled on waiting for him at the top of the stairs before church. In the middle of the first hymn, Kent slid into the pew beside them. Jonny moved a little closer to Celeste, but she noticed he also gave Kent a look of pure adoration.

****

To her surprise, Kent accepted her invitation to lunch. Jonny practically fell over his feet when Kent said he could ride home with him. "I got permission to let the boy crawl around in one of the B-17s out at the field," Kent told her while he set the table for lunch. "You can come, too."

"He'll like that, but watch him, Kent. He doesn't need to fall or…"

"I'll be right on his tail every second. I told my CO about him getting hurt. He's bending the rules, even though the planes are due to be scrapped."

"That's too bad."

"I'll be glad to see them go. All of them."

****

He brought Jonny back just before supper. "You shoulda seen 'em, Mom! They were so big. Kent showed me where the bomb thing was. The Nor…Nor…"

"Norden," Kent said. "They've all been removed, but I explained how they worked, more or less."

"And I got to sit in the pilot's seat and fly and shoot the guns out the sides and go down in the big glass ball that has a gun and turns around."

"Ball turret," Kent supplied.

"Ball turret. Are you going to eat supper with us?"

"I have to go back."

Jonny's face fell. "Oh."

"I'll see you next weekend, maybe."

"Okay." He stuck out his hand. "Thanks a lot, Kent."

They shook hands. "You're welcome, Jonny."

"That's the first time you've called him something besides 'the boy,' " Celeste observed when she walked out with him.

"I guess so."

"Did you tell him to call you Kent?"

"I sure didn't tell him to call me Lt. Goddard. He'd put two and two together."

"And come up with five."

"I don't know, Velvet. He had a good time this afternoon. That's all he's thinking about right now."

"I can tell. It was nice of you, Kent. Thank you."

"I do have to get back. I've got a bunch leaving tomorrow for the discharge center at Ft. Riley."

"The class you just finished?"

"Yeah, but Uncle Sam doesn't need bombardiers now."

"I'm glad."

On the front porch, he kissed her twice. "See you soon."

"Soon."

"I love you, Velvet."

She nodded. "I love you, too."

Chapter Thirty

"I got my orders," Kent said, when he called on the fifteenth of October. "I leave next week."

"Oh, Kent, so soon?"

"I'll be at the discharge center until my papers are processed, and then I'm officially a civilian again."

"So then you'll go home."

"Just for a visit, and a short one at that. Mother's already hounding me about taking that job with the plumbing supply company and living at home."

"She doesn't want you to go to school?"

"Not if it means moving out of town. But that's the way it has to be. Listen, I'm going to bring you some money this weekend."

"You've still got two months before your school funding kicks in. You have to live."

"I'll be okay. I've got something in the works. I'll tell you about it this weekend."

"I can get a babysitter for Saturday night."

"It would be nice to go to the Canteen one last time. I hear it's closing down in December."

"November, actually. Mrs. Lowe and the others decided the time has come. It's harder to get volunteers now. Everybody wants to get back to normal and forget about the war."

"I don't blame them. Okay, then, we'll go dancing."

"I'll have to go as a volunteer, but Mrs. Lowe will be okay with that. I'll call her tomorrow."

Kent showed up for supper on Saturday night

with flowers for Celeste and a puzzle for Jonny. "You won't get this finished in a month of Sundays," he said.

"Bet I will. Look, Mom, it's a plane."

"A B-24, not a 17. They're bigger."

"You can use the dining room table," Celeste told Jonny. "Fold up the cloth and put it on the sideboard."

"Thanks, Kent," he called over his shoulder as he ran off.

Kent kissed the back of Celeste's neck. "I miss seeing you in the blue velvet dress."

"I was going to wear it, until the warm weather came back this week."

"Warm weather or the part of a past that you don't want to bring back?"

"Maybe both. You can set the table."

"I thought that was Jonny's job."

"You brought him a new toy, remember?"

Kent laughed. "He sure liked it. Maybe he'll grow up and be a pilot. Have a career in the military."

"I hope not."

"I meant in the peacetime army, Velvet."

"Maybe that would be all right."

"I decided not to stay in the reserves. I don't want to get called up again before I finish school."

"Do you think you would?"

"Can't tell."

He slid an envelope from his pocket and laid it on the cabinet. "Here's the money I promised you. Use it however you want to. On the hospital bill or for something you need."

"Kent, I'm doing all right."

"I want you to have it. There's a hundred dollars there."

"A hundred dollars!"

He opened the cabinet and took out three plates.

"Just take it, Velvet. I owe you a lot more."

"You don't owe me anything."

"Sure, I do. I owe Jonny, anyway."

"You've spent a lot of time with him. That's all he wants."

"He's a good kid."

After Mrs. Aikman walked over to stay with Jonny, Celeste and Kent left for the Canteen. "I told you I had some things in the works," Kent said as he parked. "I'm going home for a visit—can't get out of that. Anyway, I want to spend some time with my brother. Then I'm coming back here until I start school in Austin after Christmas."

"Here? How?"

"Well, I took that job with the plumbing supply company but only on a temporary basis. They want to set up a warehouse here because of the location. San Angelo's sort of a good hub for a wheel covering this area. Anyway, they've rented a place down on Oakes Street, near those railroad storage places, and I'm going to set things up and hire a staff."

"That's wonderful, Kent."

"It's a pretty sweet deal, all right. I was at the right place at the right time."

"What about a place to live?"

He grinned. "Mrs. Clay was more than happy to rent me your old room."

"That's too much of a coincidence."

He held up his hand as if to swear. "It's true. It'll come empty just a few days before I need it."

"I'm so glad." She felt his arms slip around her.

"Me, too." His lips caressed hers, gently at first, then harder. "I love you so much."

And I love you, too, more than I have words to say. Lately it's been almost like we were a real family...a family like we could be if...but I know I can't count on anything. Just tonight. Maybe tomorrow. But after that... She pressed closer in his arms.

"You okay, Velvet?"

"Yes."

"You're trembling."

"Am I?"

"What's wrong?"

"Nothing's wrong, Kent. Everything's right." *Tonight, anyway. I won't even think about tomorrow and the day after that and...*

She gave herself up to his lips on hers, his hands stroking her hair and neck, and the security of his warm bulk against her.

****

The Canteen was practically empty that night, so Celeste had plenty of free time to spend dancing with Kent. "We've had a good long run," Mrs. Lowe told them, pausing at their table. "I think we helped."

"I know you did," Kent said.

She patted him. "What's next for the two of you?"

"Kent's going to school," Celeste said before he could reply. "He's going to be a lawyer."

"Are you and Jonny going along?"

It was Celeste's turn to search for words.

"I'll be back here working a temporary job until after Christmas," Kent said, not looking at Celeste. "And you don't uproot a kid in the middle of the school year."

"That's true, you don't. Well, I'm sure the two of you will work it out." She moved away.

Kent stood up. "Let's dance, Velvet."

****

After church the next day, Kent took Celeste and Jonny to lunch at Watson's Cafe. "Miss Ruby's homemade pies have meringue a foot tall," he told Jonny.

"Do not. You're pulling my leg."

"Just a little."

"A foot is as tall as a ruler."

"I think you've grown a foot lately."

"You think so? Really?"

"At least."

Jonny squirmed in the old-fashioned ice cream parlor chair. "I hope I'm gonna be big like you."

Celeste felt Kent withdraw momentarily, but then he was back.

"Who knows, pal? You've got a few years to go."

After lunch, they started down the sidewalk, past the high school gym and on toward the junior college. "I went to school here, and so will you," Celeste told Jonny.

He darted up the steps and tugged at one of the locked gym doors. "I bet I play basketball in there."

"Could be," Kent said.

Jonny hit the second step and jumped the rest of the way to the sidewalk. Kent reached to steady him. "Take it easy, pal. You don't want to crack your noggin again."

Celeste watched Kent fold the child's hand into his. *Oh, Kent, he loves you. I love you. Will you miss us the way we're going to miss you?*

****

After Kent left for the field, Celeste went to tuck Jonny into bed. "I had a good time today," he said, relinquishing his comic books without the usual protest.

"I did, too, Jonny."

"Miss Ruby's pie really did have meringue a foot tall."

"Maybe not quite."

"It was fun taking a walk, too. It was like we…" His voice trailed off.

Celeste knew she shouldn't ask, but she did anyway. "Like we what?"

Jonny scooted down in the bed and turned his

face away from her. "Like we were a real family," he mumbled. "You know, a mom and a dad and…" His voice trailed off.

Celeste rested her hand on his hair. "I guess it was like that."

"I wish Kent wasn't leaving."

"I do, too, but he'll come back to visit."

"It'll be just you and me again, won't it?"

"You said we were a team."

"Yeah." His yawn was mostly contrived. "'Night, Mom."

Celeste leaned over and kissed his forehead. "'Night, Jonny."

In the hall, she leaned against the door and pressed her fists into her eyes.

****

Kent came by the store on Monday. "I'm leaving for Brownwood a little early," he said. "I'll park my car there and catch a bus up to Ft. Riley."

"Why don't the two of you take a little break in the employee lounge," Mr. Thomas suggested.

"Sounds good to me," Kent said. "Thanks."

"And lock the door," the man called after them.

Downstairs Kent cradled Celeste in his arms. "I'll miss you."

"I'll miss you."

"I'll call when I can."

"All right."

He took her face in his hands and kissed her. "I love you, Velvet. It's been good for us lately."

"I think so, too."

"I know we still have some things to work out."

"Yes."

"I'm not going to tell you I can be part of Jonny's life, the way he needs a man in his life. Not unless I'm sure I can do it. That would be worse than nothing."

"Yes."

"Sometimes I think he's kind of attached himself to me, and other times he seems to be holding me at arm's length."

"I think he senses things might be changing for all of us, and he isn't sure that's what he wants."

"You've done a good job, Velvet. A great job, as a matter of fact."

"I wasn't sure I could be a good mother. I hardly remember mine. But Coralee filled in with me, and I've seen her with Barbara. Pearl's a wonderful example, too."

"I think you had it in you, and when the chips were down, you pulled it out."

"Maybe I did."

He kissed her again. "I'm going to say something I probably shouldn't, but you probably know it already. I still want you, Velvet. Want you more than I ever did. But I've been faithful to you. A little late, maybe, but faithful all the same."

"You didn't even know me when…"

"Yeah, I know, but I always knew you'd be there. I remember Dad telling me how important it was to believe there was one right girl for every boy. I guess he thought Mother was the right one for him. They seemed happy enough, even if she did call the shots. For what it's worth, I wish I'd waited for that one girl—for you."

He kissed her once more, then held her away from him. "Gotta go, Velvet. But I'll be seeing you." He touched the tip of her nose with one finger. "Count on it."

****

Kent called to let Celeste know he was back in Brownwood, a civilian again, and had a few loose ends to tie up before he could get to San Angelo. When she told Jonny, the news unleashed a torrent of questions she knew he'd been holding in. "Are you going to marry him, Mom? Is he going to live here?

Can I stay, too?"

Celeste took a deep breath. "Jonny, you're always going to stay here. This is your home. We're a family. A team, remember?"

"But if you get married, maybe you'll want babies."

"I hope I'll have them, if and when I get married. You'd like a brother or sister, wouldn't you?"

He scowled. "Maybe."

"Well, it's not going to happen tomorrow."

"But are you going to marry Kent?"

She took another deep breath, then another. "We've talked about it, but we have some things to work out first. He's got to go to school and be a lawyer, like he's always wanted."

"He said that would take a long time. I asked him. He said six or seven years. You'll be old then."

She laughed. "Not really, but you'll be almost grown up."

"If you and him got married, would he be my dad? I wouldn't mind having a dad, not if he was nice to me like Kent."

"You and he," Celeste corrected.

"Okay."

"Being a dad is a big responsibility."

"I'd be a lot of trouble, I guess, huh?"

"I don't mean that. You're not any trouble at all. But it's different with us. We've been together a while and worked things out. Like you said, we're a team."

"Yeah, we're a team, Mom."

Chapter Thirty-One

Celeste didn't repeat the conversation to Kent when he called a few days later to say he was driving to San Angelo the next morning. "I can pick Jonny up from school, if that's all right."

"He'd like that. The bell rings at three-twenty."

"Then I will. See you soon, Velvet."

"Soon."

****

Over supper, Jonny leveled a barrage of questions at Kent, this time about the new warehouse and what was in the other buildings on Oakes Street. "He doesn't quit, does he?" Kent asked when Celeste came back from putting Jonny to bed.

"He's curious."

"He's just plain smart. Really smart."

"He likes school."

"I did, too. Not math, though. The rules drove me crazy, when I could do it all in my head."

Celeste chewed her lip. "You told me that before. And Jonny said it, too, about pluses and minuses and boxes and carries."

"You're kidding."

"No, that's what he said."

"You said you'd paid off the hospital bill," Kent said, changing the subject.

"All done, thanks to the money you gave me."

"I'm glad it helped." He patted the couch. "Come over here, and turn out the lights on your way."

"What if Jonny gets up and wanders in here?"

"If he's like most nine-year-old boys, he'll say 'Oh, yuk,' and run for cover."

"I guess I don't know much about boys." Celeste curled herself beside Kent.

"You forgot one of the lamps," he said.

"No, I didn't. That's for insurance."

Kent nuzzled her ear. "I remember the afternoon I saw your face after your father knocked you around. For days after that, all I could think of was how to keep you safe."

"You found a way—the room with Mrs. Clay."

"I'll be honest—I was glad he died. It meant he couldn't ever hurt you again."

"I wasn't glad. More like relieved that it was over…and a little sad that things wouldn't ever be right between the two of us."

He laced their fingers together. "I'll only be here until Christmas. That doesn't give us much time to work things out."

"You keep talking about working things out, Kent. I don't really have anything to work out. I mean, this is my life, here with Jonny. I want you in my life, too, but only if you really want to be here."

"My dad was great, and I always thought I'd be like him."

"But you're not sure."

Kent didn't say anything for a few minutes. When he spoke, his voice sounded like it was coming from somewhere far away. "I had a friend in school. Well, not a friend, exactly, but we were in the same class. His stepfather beat the crap out of him on a regular basis. The police would go out and haul the guy in. He'd spend the night in jail, and then Benny's mother would go bail him out and take him home again. The child welfare people even went out one time, but the guy ran them off with a shotgun, and they never went back."

"What does that have to do with you?"

"That afternoon I saw you, after your father beat you up, Benny flashed through my mind, and I swear, I might've killed your father if you hadn't pulled me off of him."

"I don't believe you could've done something like that."

"Maybe not, but you were scared enough then I was going to. Anyway, Benny's stepfather finally killed him, and then he got put away for good. Some of the neighbors ran the mother off, too."

"She should've protected her son."

"At the time, I thought that, too, but maybe she couldn't."

"You were making a point."

"Just that I wonder if I'd ever hurt Jonny. Not beat him, you understand, but there are other ways to do damage to a kid. He'd know if I didn't really accept him...love him...especially if we had kids of our own, and I want that, Velvet."

"I want a baby, too," Celeste murmured. "Your baby, Kent. Someday."

"I did what I did to Claudia..."

"You weren't responsible for her death."

"I might've put her in the position of feeling desperate about having to raise a child alone."

"Do you think she was desperate or just determined to get you one way or the other?"

"I don't know. Does it matter?"

"I think it does."

"I don't want to see her every time I look at Jonny."

"Do you?"

"Sometimes. I resent the hell out of her, Velvet. At the same time, I'm ashamed of what I did."

"Being sorry for doing something you shouldn't have is a good thing, but one mistake doesn't have to ruin your life."

"If I could believe that, I wouldn't be worried about what I might do to Jonny."

"At least you've gotten this far thinking about

it."

He began to kiss her. "Let's just stop talking about it. About anything."

She folded her arms around his neck. "That's a good idea."

****

Kent came for supper every night, often bringing groceries with him to help keep the pantry stocked. Afterward, he helped Jonny with his homework. Celeste thought maybe Jonny's need for help was more a ploy on his part to get Kent's attention. She liked Kent's attention, too, after Johnny went to bed.

Kent described his job like it was a favorite hunting dog. "You really like what you're doing, don't you?" Celeste asked one night while she mended a pair of pants for Jonny and sewed some buttons on one of Kent's shirts.

"I know the business inside and out. It's a good feeling."

"Being a lawyer will be a good feeling, too."

He got up and walked to the window, then back. "I've been thinking about that, Velvet."

"You've changed your mind?"

"I don't know if wanting to be a lawyer was just a dream I had to get me away from home, or if I really wanted to be one. Seven years would be a lot of time to waste on something I didn't really want once I got it."

"Like the blue velvet dress."

"What?"

"I really wanted that dress. It was going to change my life, and I worked hard to earn the money to get it. Then, when you didn't show up for the next dance at the Roof Garden, I hung up the dress in the back of my closet and realized I hadn't wanted the dress so much as I'd wanted what it represented."

"Freedom from your father?"

"More like freedom from myself. I was in such a

rut. I dreamed of a handsome prince who was going to carry me away to his castle, where we'd live happily ever after. What I decided I got was fifty dollars down the drain."

"So maybe I wanted to be a lawyer because I saw it as a way of setting myself free from a life I was unhappy with."

"I can't answer that for you, Kent. You have to decide. But whatever decision you make, I want you to be happy."

****

Celeste knew the question was inevitable; still, when it came, she felt unprepared. "Mom, what is Kent's whole name?"

Taking refuge behind the open refrigerator door, she said, "Here, pour the milk."

Jonny did and handed it back to her.

"What is Kent's whole name?"

"He'll be here in a little bit. Why don't you ask him?"

"Okay. But it said Goddard on his uniform. Like me."

"I see."

"Yeah."

He's so reasonable. I don't know what I'd do if he weren't.

"Is Kent going to the ranch with us when we go for Thanksgiving?"

"He'll go home to be with his family in Brownwood."

"I thought we were sort of like family."

"He has a mother and a brother, you know that."

"I wonder if he knows my grammy."

Celeste forced herself to breathe. *How do you explain to a nine-year-old boy that he's not even supposed to be here?* "Go turn on the lamps in the living room. It's getting dark. Do you have homework?"

"Spelling words."

"We'll get on them right after supper."

She meant to warn Kent, when he came in through the kitchen door with a bag of groceries, but Jonny heard him and came running. "Hi, Kent."

"Hi, yourself. How many licks did you get in school today?"

"Aw, I never get licks."

Kent set the paper bag on the cabinet. "I got a few."

"You didn't neither."

"Did, too. I brought a snake to school when I was in the fourth grade. Or maybe it was the fifth. Whatever, I slipped it in the teacher's desk, and when she opened the drawer, she hollered so loud the principal came running. I got three good licks with his wooden paddle. More when I got home."

"What kind of snake? I saw a green garden snake in the backyard."

Celeste bent down to get eye-to-eye with him. "Don't you even think about doing something like that."

"Bet it was funny," Jonny said, going off into a fit of giggles.

Celeste smacked Kent's arm. "Thanks for giving him ideas."

Kent laughed. "He's not going to take a snake to school, Velvet. Relax."

"I wouldn't be too sure about that."

She held her breath through the hash made from Sunday's leftover roast, waiting for Jonny to spring his questions on Kent. When it didn't happen by the time she served chocolate pudding for dessert, she relaxed a little. More to get them out of the kitchen and away from her hearing in case Jonny remembered what he wanted to know, she sent them to the parlor and told Jonny to get his spelling book so Kent could call out the words.

While she washed, rinsed, and dried the dishes in slow motion, she wondered if she could find other chores to keep her in the kitchen. *You're being ridiculous. You've got to face it sooner or later. So does Kent. He's a grown man, and if he can't answer Jonny's questions honestly…but how? What can he say that Jonny will understand?* Finally, with no excuse to stay, she ventured out.

Jonny looked up as she came in. "His whole name is just like mine," he said, as if he'd only posed the question to her seconds ago. "Jonathan Kent Goddard."

"I see."

"I bet you knew that." Celeste tried to discern a note of accusation in his tone, but she couldn't.

"I guess I did." She glanced at Kent's face, composed, without expression.

"And he knows my grammy. He knew my first mom, too."

"I see."

Her knees too weak to hold her any longer, she sank down on the couch.

"Yeah, he knew her a long time ago before I was born."

Celeste's eyes pleaded with Kent to say something, but he sat in stony silence.

"He said she said he was my dad." Jonny fiddled with the loosened cover on his speller. "That's why I have the same name."

"Right."

"He said it's okay if I have his same name." Jonny's eyes darted around the room, into the corners, back to his speller, and up to the ceiling. "He said it was okay," he repeated like he was reassuring himself.

"Do you know all your spelling words?" Celeste asked in an attempt to stop the endless one-sided discourse.

"Yep." Jonny got up. "I'm gonna go take a bath now."

"Without being told?" Celeste asked, trying to sound humorous and failing.

"Yep."

Celeste thought his shoulders drooped a little as he left. "What did you tell him?" she asked, turning on Kent.

"As much of the truth as I thought he could handle, but not as much as I know myself. I answered his questions, all right? Just like you said you do. No more than he wanted to know, and no less."

Celeste closed her eyes. "I'm not criticizing you, Kent. He was asking me about it before you came. I didn't have a chance to warn you."

"That wouldn't have made it any easier." Kent leaned forward in the chair, elbows on his knees. "He also wanted to know if we were going to get married. I said he'd have to ask you, and he said he already did."

"He asked me if he'd have to leave if we got married, and I had a baby."

"Poor kid."

"I told him we were a family, the two of us."

"You may be the only one who could make something like that happen."

"Anybody…"

"No, not anybody, Velvet. You're special. You took a little boy nobody ever cared for before and made him a pretty savvy kid who knows where he belongs."

"He told me once that his grandmother called him a…a bastard." Her voice dropped to a whisper. "And he knew what it meant."

Kent winced. "Velvet, if I tried to be his father and failed, it would be the worst thing I ever did."

"Are you sure you'd fail?"

He didn't answer her question, saying instead, "In my case, maybe, just maybe, you took a little boy pretending to be a man and made a real man out of him. But as for trying to be Jonny's father and failing, the problem is, I'm not sure I wouldn't."

Chapter Thirty-Two

Jonny never brought up the subject again, not with Celeste, nor with Kent who kept coming for dinner every night and picking them up for church on Sundays. On a Saturday early in December, Kent suggested he and Jonny spend the morning downtown while Celeste worked. "He said we're gonna see Santa, but I told him I know Santa isn't real," Jonny whispered on the way to the car.

"Remember I told you that Santa Claus is the spirit of Christmas—the giving part."

"Right, like the wise men gave all that stuff to the baby Jesus."

"Yes."

Kent and Jonny were waiting in front of the store when Celeste got off at noon. "We've been Christmas shopping," Jonny announced, "but I'm not gonna tell you what we got."

"I'll tie your ears to your toes if you do," Kent said.

Jonny grabbed his ears and grinned.

They went across the street for lunch. "Remember we ate here the second time I ever saw you?" Kent asked.

"I couldn't believe I let you pick me up."

"I didn't pick you up. I picked you out."

"You couldn't have. I was the only girl staring in the window of Cox-Rushing-Greer."

"She was looking at a dress," Kent said to Jonny. "A beautiful blue velvet dress she wanted more than anything in the world."

"Did she get it?"

"She got it. We went dancing."

"Why do grownups like to dance?"

Kent winked. "You'll know in a few years." He turned back to Celeste. "Actually, we went by the St. Angelus and found out there's a dance tonight. And it's cold enough to wear the velvet dress."

"Mrs. Aikman is out of town."

Kent shook his head. "I ran into your friend Veda while Jonny and I were waiting for you. She said she'd be more than happy to come over tonight."

"But she always goes to the dances at the Roof Garden."

"Not this one."

"She was just being nice."

"She said she'd come."

****

"I haven't worn this dress in years," Celeste said as Kent opened the door of the car. "I'm surprised it still fits."

"It looks a little loose to me."

"Not really."

"Too loose is better than being too tight, isn't it?" He closed the door and went around to the other side. "You're gorgeous, Velvet. More beautiful than ever, and that's going some."

They didn't talk in the elevator that whisked them to the top floor. Kent paid their admission fee but didn't move to help her with her coat. "Leave it on and come outside with me."

"It's cold out there."

"Just for a few minutes. I've got a couple of things to tell you."

Unease began to nibble at her stomach. "All right." She stepped through the French doors onto the tile of the outdoor pavilion.

When she shivered, not altogether with the cold, Kent put his arm around her shoulders and moved her close to him.

"First of all, I've thought about college and law school and decided it isn't what I want."

"Oh, Kent, why? Are you sure? You have the money, and everything's all set up."

"I'm sure. It's like you said—it was something that was going to change my life, only now my life doesn't need changing. I have what I want, Velvet." He reached for her hand. "I talked to Mr. Bozeman, and he said he'd rather have me manage the warehouse than anybody else. I'd actually sent him a couple of guys to talk to last week, but he didn't hire either one of them."

He brought her fingers to his lips and kissed them.

"Look, I can always take some business classes at the junior college here, if I decide I need them, but I know the plumbing business inside out. I like it, too. Mr. Bozeman said since I was staying on, he wanted to open a wholesale store in the front and sell to contractors. There's lots of building going on since the war."

"But what if you look back and wish you hadn't given up this chance at school?"

"Did you look back, Velvet? When you took Jonny, you said you knew it was what you wanted. So did you look back?"

"No, and I never will."

"I won't either. It feels right, doing what I know, what I enjoy. Not going off to tilt with windmills. I've done my share of fighting, in Europe and at home, too. I'm tired of it. I made it through the war alive, which is more than a lot of guys did. It's time to live. Really live."

He slipped a jeweler's box from his pocket. "Will you marry me, Velvet? I'll be the best husband I know how to be. The best father, too. All I can do is try, but I think now... I think I just might succeed."

He opened the box and took out a ring. The

small, perfect diamond gleamed in the reflected light from the ballroom. "It's not big, but it's a good one." He slipped it on her finger. "And, by the way, Jonny helped me pick it out."

Epilogue

"This one?" Kent Goddard held up the tie his wife had laid out with his shirt, socks, and suit.

"That's the one."

"I don't like it."

"You bought it when you bought the suit. Wear it."

He shook his head and draped the tie around his neck and began to knot it. "I don't remember picking this out."

"You picked it out, Kent."

He caught sight of her in the mirror as she slipped on the black silk dress bought for the occasion. "Zip me, please," she said, joining him in front of the mirror.

"I like this dress."

"It cost enough."

"I told you I didn't care what it cost." He put his lips against the back of her neck as he brought the zipper to the top. "We don't celebrate our golden anniversary every day."

"No, it's one of those once-in-a-lifetime occasions," she said, rummaging in her jewelry box.

"Smart-aleck."

"There it is."

"What?"

"My other earring." She held it up.

"Those were Coralee's, weren't they?"

"Actually, they belonged to our mother." She sighed. "I wish Coralee were here today. I really miss her."

He slipped his arms around her. "I do, too,

honey."

"But Barbara and her bunch will be there."

"And our bunch and half the town," Kent said, reaching for his jacket. "I guess this tie's all right."

Celeste straightened it slightly. "It's fine."

****

"You look beautiful, Mother," Gina said as Celeste and Kent walked into the fellowship hall of the new church, built in the fifties.

"How about me?" her father asked.

She kissed his cheek. "You're still the handsomest man in San Angelo, Daddy."

"Where's Emily?" Celeste asked, glancing around for her oldest granddaughter.

"She'll be along."

Colonel Jon Goddard (USAF Ret.) came out of the kitchen. "Just doing some reconnaissance on the refreshments," he said, embracing both his parents.

"You'll be doing KP if you messed anything up," his sister retorted.

"Listen, pipsqueak, I've put up with you since you were a howling infant, so don't get smart with me at this late date." He leaned over and kissed the top of his sister's head.

"Don't call me pipsqueak." Gina drew herself up to her full five feet and craned her neck to look at her brother.

Celeste rolled her eyes. "Don't start, either of you."

"So Emily will be along, and I assume the rest of the progeny will be also," Kent said.

"They're all around here somewhere." Jon glanced around the room. "My boys are in the corner with whatever that thing is they play games on morning, noon, and night. Karen'll kill them if she finds out they brought it."

"Tell her to wait until after the party," Kent advised.

"The twins are fussing with the table that has the guestbook," Gina said. "I'd better go tell them to leave things alone."

Celeste nodded toward the small stage at one end of the room. "They even hired a piano player."

"Does that mean we get to dance?"

"Maybe until people start coming in." Celeste put her hand through his arm. "Let's get out of the way."

Kent waved to the young man at the piano. "Are you one of Gina's students?"

The musician nodded. "Yes, sir."

"I guess you're too young to know 'Stardust.' "

"No, sir, I know it." He started to play. "That's why Mrs. Bonner hired me for this afternoon. I know all the old songs."

"Are you saying I'm old?"

Celeste tugged on Kent's arm when she saw the young man's face redden. "I thought we were going to dance."

Kent winked at the pianist and held out his arms to Celeste.

****

Celeste spotted Emily first. "What..." She turned to Gina. "What is she doing in that dress?"

"Daddy knows about it. It was his idea."

"Why?"

"He just said it was the reason the two of you met."

"Not entirely. He's never let me forget I dropped that apple on his head."

"I know, but Daddy said he was sure glad you bought that dress."

"I am, too."

"He said you were going to give it away, but he convinced you to keep it for Emily."

"She looks better in it than I ever did."

"I doubt that."

Emily approached her grandmother with a question in her eyes. "Grandpa left the back door open so I could go in and get this dress," she said. "That's why I'm late."

"You're beautiful, Emily." Celeste hugged her.

"Were you wearing it when you met Grandpa?"

"No, I was looking at it."

Emily frowned. "But he said..."

"It's a long story," Celeste said. "One of these days I'll tell it to you."

"There's my beautiful girl," Kent said, approaching them with arms outstretched.

"Maybe you should've told Mimi," Emily whispered.

"She's beautiful, isn't she, honey?"

Celeste nodded. "Yes, she is, but she better be careful if she doesn't want it to fall off her. I'm betting the seams aren't too sturdy after all these years."

A look of horror passed over Emily's face. "I'd be mortified!"

"Just be careful." Celeste ran her hand over one shoulder and down one sleeve. "And don't bring it back, okay?" She glanced behind her granddaughter. "Isn't that your steady over there?"

"Don't encourage her," Gina said as the girl ran off. "Ron doesn't want her going steady."

"I wouldn't worry about it yet," Kent said. "How many boyfriends did you go through before you met Ron?"

Gina rolled her eyes. "Oh, Daddy, go mingle."

****

"It was a nice party," Kent observed as he unlocked the front door. "A really nice party."

"I just want to get these pantyhose off."

He chuckled. "Need any help?"

"Not a chance."

"You're no fun."

"I've been known to be."

He reached for her, but she swatted him away. "You can help warm up some leftovers if you're still hungry."

"We could've stopped for a hamburger."

"We need to finish the meatloaf." Celeste headed down the hall to their bedroom. "Put it on a bun if you want a hamburger."

****

They carried their plates to the porch and sat in the swing. It wasn't full dark, but the locusts were already whirring, and a few fireflies darted in and out among the irises.

"When we got married, did you think about our golden anniversary?"

Celeste tucked her feet under her. "No. Did you?"

"No, but I knew it would be forever, however long forever lasted."

"Just about everything's gone now—the old church, the St. Angelus and the Roof Garden, Woolworth. Cox-Rushing-Greer's been closed for years. There's no bargain basement at Hemphill-Wells anymore. I don't know how people live without a bargain basement."

"But we're still here, right in the same house we started in."

"Buying Coralee's half made good sense. We've owned it for…how long have we owned it?"

"Forty years, maybe. It didn't take long to pay off."

"It was the right thing to do, even if we had to add on when Gina came along."

"It's a nice house. Homey. You made it home, Velvet."

"You earned the money for it. You ended up owning the whole plumbing business and gave all of us everything."

"I had some good luck. Mainly, I made the right decision about not going to law school."

"Do you ever think about how things might've been different if you'd gone to school instead of staying here?"

"Never. Jonny didn't need to be uprooted, and living here was a lot better than some cramped student apartment. Besides, he went to law school and had a nice career in the Air Force, too."

"Do you think he regrets turning down that chance for the DNA testing a few years ago?"

Kent shook his head. "You heard what he said when we mentioned it—that it was a little late, we were stuck with each other, and we were so much alike it was downright spooky."

Celeste laughed. "He's right. Besides, I don't think he really wanted to know. Your name is on his birth certificate, and I legally adopted him. He's always known where he belonged."

Kent drained his glass and set it aside. "Whether he's got my genes or not, he's my son. Sometimes I look at him and wonder how I got so lucky."

"Gina said the other day if she could've hand-picked an older brother, she'd have chosen him. Even with an almost twelve-year age difference, they've been close."

"She sure didn't come as easy as Jonny, did she?"

"Well, she got here. A little later than we planned, but worth the wait."

"Worth the wait but not everything you went through." Kent pulled her against him as if shielding her from the memories of four miscarriages and a fifth pregnancy that risked her life.

"I still wish your mother had accepted Jonny."

"She never even accepted us, Velvet. I was supposed to be the good son. Stay home and take care of her and all that."

"Well, both kids have had Neil and Kay and their children. And my family, and even Big Ben and Pearl until Gina finished high school. They didn't lack for family to love them."

"Even marrying late, the way he did, Jonny ended up with a real fine family of his own."

"Those two tours in Viet Nam nearly did us both in. I could've done without those."

"He came home in one piece. We can't ask for more."

"It's been a good life, hasn't it?"

"The best."

"You're the best, Kent. The best husband and father and grandfather."

"I've tried."

"And succeeded beyond your wildest dreams."

"We had to work through a lot of things, but I think that just made us appreciate each other more." Kent lifted her hand to his lips. "I appreciate you more everyday, Velvet. Every morning I wake up next to you and think about how things could've turned out so much different and how glad I am they didn't."

"I'm glad, too." She traced the outline of his jaw with the tip of one finger. "Emily says we're still honeymooning, and that it's downright embarrassing."

"What does she know at fifteen?"

"She's sixteen. And she's right, you know. We're still honeymooning."

****

The mantel clock chimed ten-thirty before they went in. A single lamp burned in the living room. Kent went over to the entertainment center and pushed a CD into the player. The strains of "I'll Be Seeing You" filled the room.

"Dance with me, Velvet."

"Didn't we do enough dancing at the party?"

He took her hands and moved her toward him. "You were the prettiest girl at the Roof Garden that night."

"You were the man of my dreams. My handsome prince."

"Well, I turned into a toad for a while, I guess, but it all ended up okay." He rested his cheek against her hair. "I went back to the hotel that night and dreamed about dancing with the girl in the blue velvet dress. And fifty years later, I'm still dancing with her." He held her closer. "Dancing with Velvet. All my life. Forever."

A word about the author...

Judy Nickles has been spinning tales since she could hold a #2 pencil. A retired teacher who lives in Arkansas, a state rich in scenic byways and historical lore, she loves to travel and always manages to find a novel idea along the way.

Many of her characters are drawn from family stories culled from years of genealogical research in seven states. She hopes to pass on to her grandchildren her fascination with the past and the drive to bring it to life in the written word.

Thank you for purchasing
this Wild Rose Press publication.
For other wonderful stories of romance,
please visit our on-line bookstore at
www.thewildrosepress.com.

For questions or more information
contact us at
info@thewildrosepress.com.

The Wild Rose Press, Inc.
www.TheWildRosePress.com

To visit with authors of The Wild Rose Press
join our yahoo loop at
http://groups.yahoo.com/group/thewildrosepress/

CPSIA information can be obtained at www.ICGtesting.com
Printed in the USA
BVOW012354090712

294605BV00006B/5/P

9 781612 171999